REVEALED

BY P. C. CAST AND KRISTIN CAST

Marked

Betrayed

Chosen

Untamed

Hunted

Awakened

Destined

Hidden

Revealed

Redeemed

Tempted

Burned

The Fledgling Handbook

Dragon's Oath

Lendia's Curse

Neferet's Curse

Kalona's Fall

REVEALED

A House of Night Novel

P. C. CAST and KRISTIN CAST

ST. MARTIN'S GRIFFIN
NEW YORK

REVEALED. Copyright © 2013 by P. C. Cast and Kristin Cast. All rights reserved. Printed in the United States of America. For information, address St. Martin's Press, 175 Fifth Avenue, New York, N.Y. 10010.

www.stmartins.com

The Library of Congress has cataloged the hardcover edition as follows:

Cast, P. C.
    Revealed : a House of Night novel / P. C. Cast and Kristin Cast. — 1st ed.
        p. cm.
    ISBN 978-0-312-59443-5 (hardcover)
    ISBN 978-1-250-03849-4 (e-book)
  1. Redbird, Zoey (Fictitious character)—Fiction.   2. Vampires—Fiction.
3. Fantasy fiction.   4. Occult fiction.   I. Cast, Kristin.   II. Title.
    PS3603.A869R48 2013
    813'.6—dc23

                                                                2013026665

ISBN 978-1-250-06140-9 (trade paperback)

St. Martin's Griffin books may be purchased for educational, business, or promotional use. For information on bulk purchases, please contact the Macmillan Corporate and Premium Sales Department at 1-800-221-7945, extension 5442, or write to specialmarkets@macmillan.com.

10 9 8 7 6

For all our readers who have asked us intriguing questions about Neferet's past. Hope you enjoy the answers!

ACKNOWLEDGMENTS

We thank and appreciate our family at SMP. We heart our publisher!

Thank you, again, to our hometown friends for their enthusiasm, good humor, and support—especially Chera Kimiko, Karen Keith, and Kevin Marx. T-Town is The Best. You guys make us smile!

Thank you, Dusty, for the brainstorming help and pointing me in the right direction when I'm stuck. I love you!

And speaking of brainstorming help—CZ, you are a pearl of great price!

As always, we love and appreciate our amazing agent, Meredith Bernstein, without whom the House of Night wouldn't exist.

REVEALED

PROLOGUE

Zoey

"Wow, Z, this is a seriously awesome turnout. There are more humans here than fleas on an old dog!" Stevie Rae shielded her eyes with her hand as she looked around at the newly lit-up campus. Dallas was a total jerk, but we all admitted that the twinkling lights he'd wrapped around the trunks and limbs of the old oaks gave the entire campus a magickal, fairy-like glow.

"That is one of your more disgusting bumpkin analogies," Aphrodite said. "Though it's accurate. Especially since there are a bunch of city politicians here. Total parasites."

"Try to be nice," I said. "Or at least try to be quiet."

"Does that mean your daddy, the mayor, is here?" Stevie Rae's already gawking eyes got even wider.

"I suppose it does. I caught a glimpse of Cruella De Vil, a.k.a. She Who Bore Me, not long ago." Aphrodite paused and her brows went up. "We should probably keep an eye on the Street Cats kittens. I saw some cute little black and white ones with especially fluffy fur."

Stevie Rae sucked air. "Ohmygood*ness,* your mamma wouldn't *really* make a kitten fur coat, would she?"

"Faster than you can say Bubba's drinkin' and drivin' again," Aphrodite mimicked Stevie Rae's Okie twang.

"Stevie Rae—she's kidding. Tell her the truth," I nudged Aphrodite.

"Fine. She doesn't skin kittens. Or puppies. Just baby seals and democrats."

Stevie Rae's brow furrowed.

"See, everything is fine. Plus, Damien's at the Street Cats booth, and you know he'd never let one little kitten whisker be hurt—let alone a whole coat," I assured my BFF, refusing to let Aphrodite mess up our good mood. "Actually, everything is more than fine. Check out what we managed to pull off in a little over a week." I sighed in relief at the success of our event and let my gaze wander around the packed school grounds. Stevie Rae, Shaylin, Shaunee, Aphrodite, and I were manning the bake sale booth (while Stevie Rae's mom and a bunch of her PTA friends moved through the crowd with samples of the chocolate chip cookies we were selling, like, zillions of). From our position near Nyx's statue, we had a great view of the whole campus. I could see a long line at Grandma's lavender booth. That made me smile. Not far from Grandma, Thanatos had set up a job application area, and there were a bunch of humans filling out paperwork there.

In the center of the grounds there were two huge silver and white tents draped with more of Dallas's twinkling lights. In one tent Stark and Darius and the Sons of Erebus Warriors were demonstrating weaponry. I watched as Stark was showing a young boy how to hold a bow. Stark's gaze lifted from the kid and met mine. We shared a quick, intimate smile before he went back to helping the boy.

Missing from the Warrior tent were Kalona and Aurox. For obvious reasons, Thanatos had decided the Tulsa community wasn't ready to meet either of them.

I agreed with her.

I wasn't ready for . . .

I mentally shook myself. No, I wasn't going to think about the Aurox/Heath situation now.

Instead I turned my attention to the second of the big tents. Lenobia was there, keeping a sharp eye on the people who clustered like buzzing bees around Mujaji and the big Percheron mare, Bonnie. Travis was with her. Travis was always with her, which made my heart feel good. It was awesome to see Lenobia in love. The Horse Mistress was like a bright, shining beacon of joy, and with all the Darkness I'd seen lately, that was rain in my desert.

"Oh, for shit's sake, where did I put my wine? Has anyone seen my Queenies cup? As the bumpkin reminded me, my parents are here somewhere, and I'm going to need fortification by the time they circle around and find me." Aphrodite was muttering and pawing through the boxes of unsold cookies, searching for the big purple plastic cup I'd seen her drinking from earlier.

"You have wine in that Queenies to go cup?" Stevie Rae was shaking her head at Aphrodite.

"And you've been drinkin' it through a straw?" Shaunee joined Stevie Rae in a head shake. "Isn't that nasty?"

"Desperate times call for desperate measures," Aphrodite quipped. "There are too many nuns lurking around to drink openly without hearing a boring lecture." Aphrodite cut her eyes to the right of us where Street Cats had set up a half-moon display of cages filled with adoptable cats and bins of catnip-filled toys for sale. The Street Cats had their own miniature version of the silver and white tents, and I could see Damien sitting inside busily handling the cash register, but except for him, running every aspect of the feline area were the habit-wearing Benedictine nuns who had made Street Cats their own.

One of the nuns looked my way and I waved and grinned at the Abbess. Sister Mary Angela waved back before returning to the conversation she was having with a family who were obviously falling in love with a cute white cat that looked like a giant cottonball.

"Aphrodite, the nuns are cool," I reminded her.

"And they look too busy to pay any attention to you," Stevie Rae said.

"Imagine that—you may not be the center of everyone's attention," Shaylin said with mock surprise.

Stevie Rae covered her giggle with a cough. Before Aphrodite could say something hateful, Grandma limped up to us. Other than the limp and being pale, Grandma looked healthy and happy. It had only been a little over a week since Neferet had kidnapped and tried to kill her, but she'd recovered with amazing quickness. Thanatos had told us that was because she was in unusually good shape for a woman of her age.

I knew it was because of something else—something we both shared—a special bond with a goddess who believed in giving her children free choice, along with gifting them with special abilities. Grandma was beloved of the Great Mother, and drew her strength directly from our magickal Oklahoma earth.

"*U-we-tsi-a-ge-ya*, it seems I need help at the lavender booth. I simply cannot believe how busy we are." Grandma had barely spoken when a nun hurried up. "Zoey, Sister Mary Angela could use your help filling out cat adoption forms."

"I'll help you, Grandma Redbird," Shaylin said. "I love the smell of lavender."

"Oh, honey, that would be so sweet of you. First, could you run to my car and get into the trunk. There is another box of lavender soaps and sachets tucked back there. Looks like I'm going to sell out completely," Grandma said happily.

"Sure thing." Shaylin caught the keys Grandma tossed to her and hurried toward the main exit of the school grounds which led to the parking lot, as well as the tree-lined road that joined Utica Street.

"And I'll call my momma. She said just let her know if we get too busy over here. She and the PTA moms will be back here in a sec," said Stevie Rae.

"Grandma, do you mind if I give Street Cats a hand? I've been dying to check out their new litter of kittens."

"Go on, *u-we-tsi-a-ge-ya*. I think Sister Mary Angela has been missing your company."

"Thanks, Grandma." I smiled at her. Then I turned to Stevie Rae. "Okay, if your mom's group is coming back, I'm gonna go help the nuns."

"Yeah, no problem." Stevie Rae, shielding her eyes and peering through the crowd, added, "I see her now, and she's got Mrs. Rowland and Mrs. Wilson with her."

"Don't worry. We can handle this," Shaunee said.

"'Kay," I said, grinning at both of them. "I'll be back as soon as I can." I left the cookie booth and noticed Aphrodite, clutching her big purple Queenies cup, was right on my heels. "I thought you didn't want a lecture from the nuns."

"Better than a lecture from PTA moms." She shuddered. "Plus, I like cats more than people."

I shrugged. "Okay, whatever."

We'd only gotten partway to the Street Cats tent when Aphrodite slowed way down. "Seriously. Effing. Pathetic." She was muttering around her straw, narrowing her eyes, and glaring. I followed her gaze and joined her frown.

"Yeah, no matter how many times I see them together, I still don't get it." Aphrodite and I had stopped to watch Shaunee's ex-Twin BFF, Erin, hang all over Dallas. "I really thought she was better than that."

"Apparently not," Aphrodite said.

"Eeew," I said, looking away from their way too public display of locked lips.

"I'm telling you, there's not enough booze in Tulsa to make watching those two suck face okay." She made a gagging sound, which changed to a snort and a laugh. "Check out the wimple, twelve o'clock."

Sure enough, there was a nun I vaguely recognized as Sister Emily (one of the more uptight of the nuns) descending on the too-busy-with-their-tongues-to-notice couple. "She looks serious," I said.

"You know, a nun may very well be the direct opposite of an aphrodisiac. This should be entertaining. Let's watch."

"Zoey! Over here!" I looked from the train wreck about to happen to see Sister Mary Angela waving me over to her.

"Come on," I hooked my arm through Aphrodite's and started to pull her to the Street Cats tent. "You haven't been good enough to watch."

Before Aphrodite could argue, we were at the Street Cats booth, facing a beaming Sister Mary Angela. "Oh, good, Zoey *and* Aphrodite. I need the both of you." The nun made a gracious gesture to the young family standing beside one of the kitten cages. "This is the Cronley family. They have decided to adopt both of the calico kittens. It's so lovely that the two of them have found their forever homes together—they are unusually close, even for littermates."

"That's great," I said. "I'll start on their paperwork."

"I'll help you. Two cats—two sets of paperwork," Aphrodite said.

"We came with a note from our veterinarian," the mom said. "I just knew we'd find our kitten tonight."

"Even though we didn't expect to find two of them," her husband added. He squeezed his wife's shoulder and smiled down at her with obvious affection.

"Well, we didn't expect the twins, either," his wife said, glancing over at the two girls who were still looking in the kitten cage and giggling at the fluffy calicos that would be joining their family.

"That surprise turned out great, which is why I think the two kittens will be perfect as well," said the dad.

Like seeing Lenobia and Travis together—this family made my heart feel good.

I had started to move to the makeshift desk with Aphrodite when one of the little girls asked, "Hey mommy, what are those black things?"

Something in the child's voice had me pausing, changing direction, and heading to the kitten cage.

When I got there I instantly knew why. Within the cage the two calico kittens were hissing and batting at several large, black spiders.

"Oh, yuck!" the mom said. "Looks like your school might have a spider problem."

"I know a good exterminator if you need a recommendation," the dad said.

"We're gonna need a shit ton more than a good exterminator," Aphrodite whispered as we stared into the kitten cage.

"Yeah, uh, well, we don't usually have bug issues here," I babbled as disgust shivered up my back.

"Eesh, Daddy! There are lots more of them."

The little blond girl was pointing at the back of the cage. It was so completely covered with spiders that it seemed to be alive with their seething movements.

"Oh, my goodness!" Sister Mary Angela looked pale as she

stared at the spiders that appeared to be multiplying. "Those things weren't there moments ago."

"Sister, why don't you take this nice family into the tent and get their paperwork started," I said quickly, meeting the nun's sharp gaze with my own steady one. "And send Damien out here to me. I can use his help to take care of this silly spider problem."

"Yes, yes, of course." The nun didn't hesitate.

"Get Shaunee, Shaylin, and Stevie Rae," I told Aphrodite, keeping my voice low.

"You're going to cast a circle in front of all of these humans?" Aphrodite whispered at me.

"Would you rather have her do that, or have Neferet start *eating* all these humans?" Suddenly Stark was there, beside me. I could feel his strength and his concern. "It is Neferet, isn't it?"

"It's spiders. Lots of spiders." I pointed at the cages.

"Sounds like Neferet to me," Damien said quietly as he joined us.

"I'll get the rest of the circle." Aphrodite dropped her cup and started jogging back to the bakery tent.

"What's the plan?" Stark asked, his eyes not leaving the ever-growing nest of spiders.

"We protect what is ours," I said. Then I pulled my cell phone out of my pocket and tapped the name THANATOS. She answered on the first ring.

"Something has changed here. I can feel the approach of death." The High Priestess didn't raise her voice, but I could hear the tension thrumming through it.

"Spiders are materializing in the Street Cats booth. Lots of them. I've called my circle to me."

"Neferet." She spoke the name solemnly, confirming my gut reaction. "Invoke the protection of the elements. Whatever the Tsi Sgili is materializing, we know it isn't natural—so use nature to expel it."

"Will do," I said.

"I'll begin the raffle—call the attention of the humans to the Warrior tent. They'll be safest there. Zoey, be as discreet as you can be. It only serves Neferet's purposes if today ends in panic and chaos."

"Got it." I hung up.

"Are we circling?" Damien asked.

"Yep. We're using our elements to get rid of this bug problem." I didn't hesitate, nor did I wait for the rest of my circle. While Stark looked on protectively, I took Damien's hand. He and I faced the kittens' cages.

"Air, please come to me," Damien said.

I felt the response of his element instantly. "Focus it," I told him.

He nodded. "Air, blow this Darkness away."

The wind, that had been almost teasingly lifting Damien's hair, rushed from him, swirling around the nest of spiders and making them writhe angrily.

"*Ladies and gentlemen, fledglings, and vampyres, this is Thanatos, High Priestess of Tulsa's House of Night, and your hostess this evening. I ask that everyone please make their way to the center of the campus and the silver and white Warrior tent, our raffle is beginning and you must be present to win.*"

Thanatos's voice over the loudspeaker sounded so normal, so principal-like, that it made the skittering nest of spiders seem even more abhorrent.

"Oh, no, you don't need to worry about the details." Sister Mary Angela was herding the young couple and their twin girls from the booth. "My assistants will have the kittens all ready for you to pick up after the raffle."

"Why are the kids holding hands like that?" I heard one of the little girls ask.

"Oh, I'm sure they're just praying," Sister Mary Angela said smoothly. Then, over her shoulder, she told the half dozen or so nuns who had been running the booth, "Sisters, be sure the young people have the privacy they need for their prayers."

"Of course, Sister," the women murmured. Without question or hesitation, they spread out, creating a semi-circle around their tent, the cat cages, and the rest of the campus, effectively forming a nun curtain between possible gawkers and us.

Then Shaunee and Stevie Rae were sprinting up with Aphrodite, bursting through the nun barrier, and skidding to a halt, eyes bugging wide at the seething mass of insects.

"Ah, shit!" Shaunee said.

"Ohmygood*ness*!" Stevie Rae pressed her hand over her mouth in distaste.

"Neferet seriously makes my ass hurt," Aphrodite said, grimacing at the spiders.

"We need to get all the elements here and have them kick these spiders off campus," I said. "But we can't make a scene."

"Yeah, 'cause Neferet would want to F everything up by causing a big ol' scary scene and freaking out the humans," Shaunee said. "No worries, Z. I'll keep it on the back burner." She walked purposefully over to Damien, who held his hand out to her. She took it and, staring at the mass of dark legs and pulsing bodies, "Fire, come to me." The air around us warmed. The beautiful black girl smiled and continued, "Heat 'em up, but don't make 'em fry."

Fire did exactly as she asked. There was no smoke or flames or fireworks, but the air around us got really warm and the mass of spiders twitched in obvious discomfort.

I looked around, just then noticing that Shaylin hadn't joined us. "Where's water? We need Shaylin for the circle."

"She's not back from the parking lot," Stevie Rae said. "I called her phone, but she's not answering."

"Probably can't hear it," Damien said. "There's a lot going on out there."

"Okay, no problem. I'll stand in for water," Aphrodite said. "It won't be as strong, but at least it'll be a complete circle."

Aphrodite started to move to take Shaunee's hand when Erin stepped through the nun barrier.

"I knew a circle was going on! I could feel it," Erin said, then she curled her lip at Aphrodite. "*You're* going to call water? Ha! You're a piss poor substitute for me—the real deal."

"You're a real something, that's for sure," Aphrodite told her. "But a *deal* isn't it."

"I told you not to have anything to do with these pussies," Dallas said, sneering at a nun who tried to keep him outside their barrier.

"I know what you said, baby." Erin sent him a flirty smile. "But you know I gotta do what I gotta do. And I'm not cool with water being left out of a circle."

Dallas shrugged. "Whatever. Seems like a waste of time to me. Plus, why the hell are your idiot ex-friends circling during the open house?" His mean, sharp gaze narrowed, as if he just realized what the nun barrier meant. "Hey, what's going on in here?"

"We don't have time for this," I snapped. "Stark, get rid of Dallas, and be sure he stays shut up until the open house is over."

"Gladly!" Smiling, Stark picked Dallas up by the back of his shirt and pulled him away from us and from the center of campus. Dallas was struggling and cussing, but he was little more than a buzzing mosquito to Stark's strength. I turned to Erin. "No matter what else has happened, you're water and your element is welcome in our circle, but we don't need any negative energy here—this is too important." I nodded to the spiders. Erin's gaze followed mine and she gasped.

"What the hell is that?"

I opened my mouth to evade her question, but my gut stopped me. I met Erin's blue eyes. "I think it's what's left of Neferet. I know it's evil and it doesn't belong at our school. Will you help us kick it out?"

"Spiders are disgusting," she began, but her voice faltered as she glanced at Shaunee. She lifted her chin and cleared her throat. "Disgusting things should go." Resolutely, she walked to Shaunee and paused. "This is my school, too."

I thought Erin's voice sounded weird and kinda raspy. I hoped that meant that her emotions were unfreezing and that, maybe, she was coming back around to being the kid we used to know.

Shaunee held out her hand. Erin took it. "I'm glad you're here," I heard Shaunee whisper.

Erin said nothing.

"Be discreet," I told her.

Erin nodded tightly. "Water, come to me." I could smell the sea and spring rains. "Make them wet," she continued.

Water beaded the cages and a puddle began to form under them. A fist-sized clump of spiders lost their hold on the metal and splashed into the waiting wetness.

"Stevie Rae." I held my hand out to her. She took mine, then Erin's, completing the circle.

"Earth, come to me," she said. The scents and sounds of a meadow surrounded us. "Don't let this pollute our campus."

Ever so slightly, the earth beneath us trembled. More spiders tumbled from the cages and fell into the pooling water, making it churn.

Finally, it was my turn. "Spirit, come to me. Support the elements in expelling this Darkness that does not belong at our school."

There was a whooshing sound and all of the spiders dropped

from the cages, falling into the waiting pool of water. The water quivered and began to change form, elongating—expanding.

I focused, feeling the indwelling of spirit, the element for which I had the greatest affinity, and in my mind I pictured the pool of spiders being thrown out of our campus, like someone had emptied a pot of disgusting toilet water. Keeping that image in mind, I commanded: "Now get out!"

"Out!" Damien echoed.

"Go!" Shaunee said.

"Leave!" Erin said.

"Bye-bye *now*!" Stevie Rae said.

Then, just like in my imagination, the pool of spiders lifted up, like they were going to be hurled from the earth. But in the space of a single breath the dark image reformed again into a familiar silhouette—curvaceous, beautiful, deadly. Neferet! Her features weren't fully formed, but I recognized her and the malicious energy she radiated.

"No!" I shouted. "Spirit! Strengthen each of the elements with the power of our love and loyalty! Air! Fire! Water! Earth! I call on thee, so mote it be!"

There was a terrible shriek, and the Neferet apparition rushed forward. It surged from our circle, breaking over Erin like a black tide. With the sound of a thousand skittering spiders, the specter fled through the main entrance of the school and then disappeared completely.

"Holy shit. That was seriously gross," Aphrodite said.

I was going to agree with Aphrodite when I heard the first, terrible cough.

I felt the circle break before I saw her fall to her knees. She looked up at me and coughed again. Blood sprayed from her lips. "Didn't think it would end like this," she rasped.

"I'm getting Thanatos!" Aphrodite called as she sprinted away.

"No! This can't be happening," Shaunee said, dropping to her knees beside the already blood-soaked Erin. "Twin! Please. You'll be fine!"

Erin fell into her arms. Damien, Stevie Rae, and I shared a look, and then as one, we joined Shaunee while she held her friend.

"I'm so sorry," Shaunee sobbed. "I didn't mean anything bad that I said to you."

"It's—it's okay, Twin." Erin spoke slowly between wracking coughs as the blood bubbled in her throat and streamed crimson from her eyes and ears and nose. "It was my fault. I—I forgot how to feel."

"We're here with you," I said, touching Erin's hair. "Spirit, calm her."

"Earth, soothe her," Stevie Rae said.

"Air, envelop her," Damien said.

"Fire, warm her," Shaunee spoke through her tears.

Erin smiled and touched Shaunee's face. "It already has warmed me. I—I don't feel cold and alone anymore. Don't feel anything except tired . . ."

"Just rest," Shaunee said. "I'll stay with you while you sleep."

"We all will," I said, wiping tears from my face with the back of my sleeve.

Erin smiled one more time at Shaunee, and then she closed her eyes and died in her Twin's arms.

CHAPTER ONE

Neferet

The reflection from the past that had suddenly manifested in Zoey Redbird's mystical mirror had been a terrible reminder of the death of Neferet's innocence. It had been so unexpected for Neferet to see herself again as a broken, beaten girl that the memory had shattered her, leaving her vulnerable to the mutinous attack from the creature that had been her vessel. Aurox had overcome her, gored her, and hurled her from the penthouse balcony. When she had hit the pavement below, Neferet, former High Priestess of Nyx, had, indeed, died. As her mortal heart had ceased beating, the spirit within her, the immortal energy that had made her Queen Tsi Sgili, had taken over, dissolving her broken shell of a body and living . . . *living.*

The mass of Darkness and spirit nested together, going to ground, waiting, waiting, surviving, while the Tsi Sgili's consciousness struggled to continue to exist.

The violated girl in the mirror had resurrected a memory that Neferet believed had long ago been dead . . . buried . . . forgotten. That past had risen with a force that she had been utterly unprepared to battle.

Alive again, the past had killed Neferet.

Neferet remembered. She had once been a daughter. She had

once been Emily Wheiler. She had once been a vulnerable, desperate child, and the human male who should have been her most vigilant protector had molested, abused, and violated her.

The instant Emily's reflection had flashed within the magickal mirror, all the decades of power and strength that Neferet had fashioned into a barrier she had used to repress that violation, that murdered innocence, evaporated.

Gone was the mighty vampyre High Priestess. Only Emily remained, staring at the ruin of her young life. It was Emily who Aurox gored and hurled onto the lonely pavement at the base of the Mayo Hotel. It was Emily who took Neferet with her in death.

But it was the spirit of Queen Tsi Sgili that survived.

True, her body had been broken, her mind shattered, but the energy that was Neferet's immortality lived, though her consciousness hovered on the edge of dissolution. The comforting threads of Darkness welcomed and strengthened her, allowing her to first borrow the likeness of insects, then of shadows, then of mist. The spirit of the Tsi Sgili drank the night and vomited the day—sinking into the sewer system of downtown Tulsa and moving slowly, but inexorably in one direction—what remained of Neferet had a never resting compulsion to seek the familiar—to find that which would make her whole again.

The Tsi Sgili was aware when she crossed the boundary between the city and the place she knew best. The place that, even disembodied, her spirit recognized because it had drawn her to it for so many years. She entered the House of Night in the form of fog, thick and gray. She drifted from shadow to shadow, absorbing the familiar.

When she reached the temple at the heart of the school, the specter recoiled, though smoke and shadow, energy and darkness, cannot feel pain, just as they cannot feel pleasure. The malevolent energy of the Tsi Sgili recoiled in reflex, much like the severed leg of a frog twitches in response to a hot skillet.

It was that inadvertent twitch that changed her course, causing her to drift close enough to the place of power that she *did* feel. The Tsi Sgili could not recognize pain or pleasure, but what remained of Neferet knew power. She would always know power.

In sticky drops of oily wetness, she sank into the hole in the earth. She absorbed the energy buried around her, and through it she drew to her the ghostly residue of what was happening above her.

The Tsi Sgili might have remained like that—formless, faceless, simply existing—had death not chosen that moment to approach.

Like wind that blows clouds to shroud the sun, death's approach was invisible, but the Tsi Sgili felt the brush of it before the fledgling began to cough.

Death was even more familiar to the specter than was the school or the place of power. Death drew her up from the pit in the ground. In a rush of excitement the Tsi Sgili's spirit manifested in the first form that had come to her near the beginnings of her power—that of the ever-questing, ever-curious, ever-resilient eight-legged insect.

The black spiders, moving as one, materialized to seek out and to feed from death.

Ironically, it was the fledglings' circle that opened the energy conduit which enabled Neferet to gain enough consciousness so that she was able to focus and borrow the ancient power of death and, ultimately, to find herself once more.

I am she who was Emily Wheiler, and then Neferet, and then Tsi Sgili—queen, goddess, immortal being!

Until that moment, finding the familiar had been her focus.

As death descended upon the fledgling, the Tsi Sgili's spirit fed from it, gathering energy so that finally her memories coalesced from fragments of past and present to one true *knowing*.

The shock of that knowing caused raw energy to surge through her spirit, fragmenting the threads of Darkness and fueling the refashioning of her body. She had been almost fully formed when the elements had expelled her. Exploding from the circle, Neferet fled.

She made it only as far as the iron gate that served as barrier between the human street and the vampyre school grounds. There, her body solidified, and she had burned through all of her siphoned power until she'd been left gasping, weak as a newborn, barely clinging to consciousness. Neferet crumpled against the wall that was boundary to the House of Night.

She must feed!

Hunger was all she knew until she heard his raised voice, spiteful and sarcastic, quipping, "Yes, dear. Of course you're right. You're always right. I don't want to stay for the ridiculous raffle either—I'm absolutely not interested in the five hundred dollars worth of tickets I bought on a chance to win that 1966 T-Bird the vampyres are giving away. No, no problem! And, as you said *so many times,* we should have called a driver and taken a limo. So, so sorry you're inconvenienced by waiting for *me* to walk all the way to where we parked, get our car, and drive it back to pick you up while you sit on a bench and rest yourself. Oh, and I'm so, so glad you were able to allow those two City Council assholes to stare at your boobs while you whispered to them and spread your crazy gossip about Neferet. Ha! Ha! Ha!" His sarcastic laughter drifted to her through the night. "If you actually paid attention to anyone but yourself you would know that Neferet can take care of herself. Penthouse vandals no one so much as got a peek at? Not hardly. That mess looked like the result of a female temper tantrum. I feel sorry for whoever caused Neferet's temper to explode, but I don't feel sorry for Neferet."

Neferet forced herself to sit up, listening with all her being. The human had said her name. It must be a sign that he was a gift from the gods.

The Lexus not ten feet from where she crouched lit up as he touched the key fob and muttered, "Damned woman. All she does is gossip and manipulate, manipulate and gossip. I should have listened to my father and never married her. All I've gotten from my twenty-five years with her is high blood pressure, GERD, and an ungrateful daughter. I could've been the first single mayor Tulsa's had in fifty years and had my pick of the young daughters of old oil money if I hadn't already been chained to her . . ."

His grumbling trailed off into unintelligible background noise when her supersensitive hearing honed in to his heartbeat.

She sighed gratefully. He did, indeed, sound like dinner. She would not thank the gods of fate who had sent him to her. She would accept their aid as no more than what she deserved—an acknowledgment that they were pleased to have her return to their immortal ranks.

He was opening the door to the sedan when she stood. Neferet put all of her longing and hunger into the one word that was his name: "Charles!"

He paused, straightened, and peered her way, trying to see through the darkness. "Hello? Is someone there?"

Neferet did not need light to see. Her vision moved through the Darkness easily, comfortably. She saw his carefully combed hair, the well-tailored lines of his expensive suit, the sweat on his upper lip, and the pulse in his neck that beat steadily with his life's blood.

She stepped forward and shook back her long auburn hair, exposing the lushness of her naked body. Then, as if it were an afterthought, she raised her hands in an unsuccessful attempt to shield her most private parts from his widening eyes. "Charles!" Neferet repeated his name. This time she added with a sob, "They've hurt me!"

"Neferet?" Obviously confused, Charles took one step toward her before halting. "Is it really you?"

"It is! It is! Oh, Goddess, that it would be you who discovered me out here, naked, wounded, and all alone. It is so terrible! So much more than I can bear!" Neferet wept as she covered her face with her hands, allowing him to get a more thorough look at her body.

"I don't understand. What has happened to you?"

"Charles!" his name shrilled behind them from the school grounds, making them both pause. "What is taking you so long?"

"Dear, I've found—" Charles began to call back to his wife, but Neferet moved quickly toward him. She clutched his hand, cutting off his words. "No! Don't tell her it's me. I couldn't stand for her to know what they've done to me," she whispered desperately.

His gaze was completely focused on Neferet's bare breasts when he cleared his throat and continued, "Frances, dear, be patient. I dropped the car fob, and just now found it. I'll have the car there in another minute or two."

"Of course you dropped it! You're so damn clumsy!" came the venom-filled retort.

"Go to her! Forget that you ever saw me." Neferet whimpered as she scrambled back within the shadows beside the school wall. "I can care for myself."

"What are you talking about? Of course I won't go and leave you out here naked and hurt. Here, put on my coat. Tell me what has happened to you. I know your penthouse was vandalized. Were you kidnapped?" Charles spoke as he moved to her. Taking off his suit jacket, he held it out to her.

Neferet's gaze went to his hands where they gripped the jacket, offering it.

"Your hands are so large." Overwhelmed by images from the past, Neferet found it hard to speak through lips that had gone cold and numb. "Your fingers. So, so thick."

Charles blinked in confusion. "I suppose they are. Neferet, are you in your right mind? You seem very out of sorts. How can I help you?"

"Help me?" Her ravenous mind thrust Neferet forward from Emily's past. "I shall show you the only way you may help me."

Neferet did not waste any more of her energy speaking to him. In a single predatory movement she knocked aside the offered jacket and slammed Charles against the wall. His breath left him in a shocked *oof* and he fell to the grass, gasping for air. She did not allow him time to recover. She pinned him to the ground with her knees and, making her hands into claws, ripped open his throat. As his thick, hot blood sprayed from his jugular, she fastened her lips over the gash and drank deeply. Even as he died, he did not struggle. Completely under her spell, he moaned and tried to lift his arms to more fully embrace her. His breath gurgled, ending his moans, and his legs kicked spasmodically, but Neferet's strength grew as he moved more closely to death. She drank and drank, draining him body and spirit, until Charles LaFont, mayor of Tulsa, was no more than a bloodless, lifeless shell.

Licking her lips, Neferet stood, staring down at what was left of him. Energy surged through her. How she loved the taste of death!

"Charles, goddamn it! Do I have to do *everything* myself?" His wife's voice was coming closer, as if she were moving toward them.

Neferet lifted her bloody hand. "Mist and darkness, I command thee. Shield my body. Now! Cover me!"

Instead of obeying her and hiding Neferet from seeking eyes, the deepest, darkest of the shadows only quivered restlessly. Through the night she felt more than heard their reply: *Your power wanes, reborn Tsi Sgili. Command us now? We shall see . . . we shall see . . .*

Rage was a luxurious emotion Neferet could not afford. She kept her anger close to her, choosing it over Charles LaFont's crumpled suit jacket. Clothed only in blood and rage and fading power, Neferet fled. She had reached the ditch on the opposite side of Utica Street when LaFont's wife began screaming.

Her screams made Neferet smile, and though Darkness did not obey her command and cloak her, the Tsi Sgili ran with the other-worldly litheness of an immortal. As she fled through the opulent midtown neighborhood, Neferet imagined how she must appear to any mortal who might be lucky enough to glance out her window. She was a scarlet wraith, a Banshee from ancient times. Neferet wished she could bring to life the Old Magick curse of the Banshee—that any mortal filled with hubris enough to dare to look upon her would turn to stone.

Stone . . . I wish . . . I do so wish . . .

The death of the mayor did not fuel her far. Too soon Neferet's fleetness faltered. Waves of weakness broke over her body with such intensity that she stumbled over the next curb, gasping for breath.

No houses here. Where am I?

Confused, Neferet looked around, blinking at the brightness of the 1920s style streetlights that dotted the park. Instinctively, she moved away from the lights and deeper into the shrubs and winding paths in the heart of the park.

It was on the small ridge, surrounded by sleeping azalea bushes, that Neferet's breath finally returned to her, allowing her thoughts to clear enough that she recognized her location.

Woodward Park—not far from the House of Night. Neferet looked up, searching for Tulsa's downtown skyline. *The Mayo is too far away. I'll not make it there before dawn.* And even if she could reach her penthouse before the sun lifted from the horizon and sapped her of what remained of her strength, how would she get past the humans that worked at the front desk? Darkness was not obeying her. Uncloaked, she would be a naked, blood-covered vampyre—a thing to loathe and imprison—especially on the night their mayor had been killed by a vampyre.

Perhaps she should have considered her alternatives more carefully before she'd ended LaFont's miserable life.

Neferet felt her first sliver of panic. She had not been this alone and vulnerable since the night her father had killed her innocence.

The Tsi Sgili shuddered, remembering his large, hot hands; his thick fingers; and the stench of his fetid breath.

Neferet sobbed, remembering also the shadows that had comforted her as a young girl, and the Darkness that had soothed her broken innocence. "Have all of you deserted me? Have none of my dark children remained faithful to me?"

As if in answer, the bushes before her whispered with movement, and from within a fox emerged. The creature stared at her with no visible fear. Neferet was awed by the beauty of its amber and red fur, and the intelligence in its brilliant green eyes.

The fox is my answer—my gift—my sacrifice.

Neferet gathered the remnants of her power. Silently and swiftly, she struck, breaking the fox's neck with a single blow. While the light faded from its eyes, Neferet laid the body across her lap and clawed open the dying creature's throat. She lifted the fox so that its blood ran sluggishly down her arms, and her breasts, pooling around her like a warm spring rain.

"If it is a sacrifice you need, then for you doth this creature bleed! This blood only opens the door. Return to me and Tulsa will pay you more . . . more!"

The deepest shadows beneath the azalea bushes stirred. Slowly, almost tentatively, a few threads of Darkness slithered toward Neferet.

The Tsi Sgili blinked tears from her eyes. They hadn't abandoned her! She bit her lip to keep from crying out in gratitude when the first of the tendrils brushed its frigid flesh against her while it sank into the warmth of the fox's blood and began to feed. Others soon joined it, and though there didn't come forth the hundreds, even thousands, of tendrils she had once commanded, Neferet was pleased that there were enough of them who answered her call that it seemed the ground around her had been transformed into a nest of Darkness. She inhaled the night deeply, feeling the power that pulsed through it. If she could just remain with her familiar threads she could feed them, and in turn they would hide her and nurture her until she truly regained her strength, and her purpose.

My purpose? What is my purpose?

Memories flooded her weakened mind with a cacophony of voices and visions: she was a young girl—*your purpose is to be Lady of Wheiler House!* She was a young High Priestess—*your purpose is to follow the Path of the Goddess!* She was a more mature vampyre who had begun to listen to the whispers of Darkness that seemed to drift to her on the wind—*your purpose is to help me break free of my earthly jail and reign at my side!* She was powerful, fed by threads fashioned from night and magick—*your purpose is to amuse me and to be my Consort!*

"Enough!" Neferet cried, burying her face in the soft, musty fur of the sacrificed fox. "I've had enough of others telling me my purpose." Resolutely she stood, drawing the remnants of her pride and power to her. "I killed and you have fed. Now to succor and safety I will be led!"

The tendrils of Darkness rippled, wrapping around her bare legs, gently tugging, compelling her forward. Wordlessly, Neferet followed Darkness to a path that led to a wide stone stairway that meandered down a rocky ridge until she stood on the street level of the empty park, staring into an insignificant, grotto-like area tucked between landscaping and pathways. Rock and shrubs mostly obscured its mouth, which opened to a wide expanse of grass that eventually led to Twenty-first Street. The threads released their hold on her and disappeared into the cleft in the stones. Again, Neferet followed them, climbing to the maw of the grotto. She drew a deep, fortifying breath as she crawled into the utter blackness, and paused in surprise at the musty, wild scent that surrounded her within.

Her threads had led her to the fox's den.

Neferet sank into the earth, welcoming the scent of her prey. She could almost feel the warmth of the animal's body lingering in the nest it had so recently departed. Neferet curled there, with only blood and Darkness covering her, closed her eyes, and finally allowed sleep to claim her.

CHAPTER TWO

Zoey

"Z, there you are! I've been looking all over for you. This is really not a cool time for you to be hiding out here."

Stark's voice startled me and I jumped, rubbing the goose bumps from my bare arms and frowning up at him. "I'm *not* hiding. I'm just out here . . ." My voice trailed off and I glanced around. *What was I doing out here if I wasn't hiding?* Thanatos had rushed Erin's body from the shocked, gawking eyes of the visiting humans to the infirmary. Automatically, my circle had followed her. She'd called orders to the professors and Sons of Erebus Warriors to escort our guests from the school grounds and close down the campus. I think everyone assumed that I had been helping to guide the humans out. I'd meant to help. I'd even started to, but then I overheard what a group of the locals were saying, and I'd needed to get away. It was annoying as hell that a fledging dying in her own blood caused a bunch of PTA moms and politicians to gossip and speculate—and were they whispering about the dead kid, freaked out about the fact that she had barely turned eighteen and was dead? Nope. They'd been talking about Neferet! Whispering about how she'd been fired from the House of Night and then gone public with what they were calling her anti-vampyre opinions, and *then* she'd disappeared after her penthouse had been vandalized.

I'd even heard one of the Tulsa City Council members say that they wouldn't be surprised if vampyres had been sending Neferet a message to get out of town, and that "poor Neferet" could have been a victim of House of Night violence.

That had really pissed me off, but what could I have said to the guy? *We didn't so much vandalize and threaten her as we rescued my grandma from her evil clutches and then we tossed her off the roof of her penthouse.* Yeah, like that would have gone over great.

Hearing them talking about "poor Neferet" had been more than I could take. Hell, my circle and I had just kept "poor Neferet" from materializing in the middle of our open house and eating the locals! "Poor Neferet" might even have been responsible for Erin's body rejecting the Change. It seemed too much of a coincidence to me that Erin had died right after the gross, semi-formed ex–High Priestess had passed through the fledgling's body.

So, instead of screaming at the locals, I'd taken advantage of the chaos caused by a fledgling dying publicly, and slipped away by myself to sit on a bench at the far side of the stables; take a long, deep breath; and think. I exhaled that breath and continued to think. "Stark, I'm not out here hiding." I reasoned through what I was feeling aloud. "I just needed a second to myself to deal with the poo storm that's going to be caused by all of that—" I waved a hand in the direction of the main campus, and finished. "—all of that mess."

He sat beside me on the bench and took my hand in his. "Yeah, I get it. Dealing with death is tough on me, too," Stark said quietly.

"Yeah," I said, and a little sob escaped with the word. Goddess, I was such a hypocrite! "You know what? I'm as bad as those gossiping humans. You were right. I am *hiding* out here feeling pissed and sorry for myself instead of being freaked that one of our circle just died."

"Z, I don't expect you to be perfect. No one does." Stark squeezed my hand. "You know it won't always be like this."

My stomach clenched. "I think that's the problem. I *don't* know that it won't always be like this."

"This is the second time we've beaten Neferet—and she didn't look so good tonight. Seriously—spiders? That's all she's got? She can't keep fighting us forever."

"She's immortal, Stark. She can't be killed, so she *can* keep fighting us forever," I said gloomily. "And she'd changed from spiders to yucky, gooey, black crap that was starting to reform her body. Ugh. She's back."

"Well, at least everyone knows she's turned bad," he countered with.

"Nope, *everyone* doesn't know she's turned bad. Vampyres know it—and the High Council had decided to not do squat to her. Humans, local humans—hell, our own mayor and his council— think that she's practically Glenda the Good Witch of the North. What pissed me off tonight was that I overheard some of the guys in suits and the PTA moms talking about her and wondering if we had something to do with her penthouse being vandalized last week because 'poor Neferet,'" I air quoted, "hasn't been seen since then."

"Really? I can't believe they're saying that."

"Believe it. Neferet's press conference set the stage for her to look like a victim if anything happened to her."

"Doesn't matter. Doesn't change the fact that we had to kick her ass to get your grandma back. We were cloaked that night. No one saw us, so all that talk is just bullshit gossip. It doesn't mean anything."

"Gossip always means something, Stark. In this case I think it means that it's going to take some major bullpoopie hitting the fan for anyone who isn't a vampyre to know how evil Neferet is."

"You're probably right about that, but that's actually good news," Stark said.

"Huh?"

"Neferet has never known how to lay low and let a situation cool down. And she sure as hell has never been able to pull off being a victim. If she can manage to get herself together— literally—and manifest a body that's more than black snot, she's right back where she was before. She's eventually going to realize that the local humans aren't going to bow down and worship her. A bunch of them even feel sorry for her. That is going to piss her off big time and Neferet will mess up. Again. Then she'll be outed with the humans, just like she was with the vamps. That'll leave her no shit pot to stir here, and if she can't stir up some shit, Neferet will find someplace else to haunt. Getting rid of her for good could actually be, as Stevie Rae would say, easy-peasy."

"Stevie Rae!" I felt a flush of guilt. "Crap. I pretty much left her alone to deal with the Erin death mess."

"Thanatos is handling it, and by *it* I mean Shaunee. Stevie Rae and Kramisha are getting the kids together for the bus. Everyone wanted to know where you were, which brought me out here looking for you."

"Sorry. I guess my second to breathe is up. I'm ready to dive back into crazy. Let's go say bye to Grandma before we get on the bus."

"I'm with you, Z." Stark stood, pulled me to my feet, and kissed me softly. "I'm always with you, even if that means I'm with crazy, too."

I was still in his arms, feeling safe, when we heard the screaming start.

"Holy crap, what is that?"

I could feel the tension in Stark's body. "Someone's hysterical."
He took my hand again, and listened for a few seconds before he
began guiding me toward the entrance to the field house. "Come
on. It's coming from around the other side of the school. Stay
close to me. I have a bad feeling about this."

Oh, Goddess! Please, don't let it be another kid dying . . . was all
I could think as we cut through the field house and jogged to the
school's parking lot.

We were coming from a different direction than everyone else,
so no one noticed us at first, and Stark and I got to get a good look
at the creepy scene. In the middle of the parking lot—surrounded
by dazed locals, and a gaggle of Benedictine nuns who were
herding her from her headlong run from the front gates of the
school—was a tall blond woman having an absolute and utter
hysterical meltdown. She was wearing meticulously tailored
black slacks; a light blue, skintight cashmere sweater; and a
thick strand of expensive-looking pearls. Her hair had come
loose from a rich lady updo, and blond wisps were sticking out
from her head like she'd been electrocuted. Even though the
nuns had managed to get her to stop running in circles, she was
shrieking and flailing her arms like a crazy person.

I admit that my first reaction was to feel super relieved that it
was a freaked-out local and not another dying fledgling.

Sister Mary Angela stepped from the crowd and began trying to calm the woman down. "There, there, madam. I know it is
distressing when a young person dies, but we all know death is
never far from every fledgling. They accept it, and so must we."

The screaming woman paused in her hysterics and blinked at

Sister Mary Angela as if she'd just realized where she was. She drew a deep breath and her face twisted, changed, going from terror to anger so quickly it was scary. Later I realized that should have made me recognize her.

"You think I'm crying about a *fledgling*? That's absurd!" the woman hurled the words at the nun.

"I'm sorry. I don't understand wh—"

Aphrodite rushed up, interrupting the nun and looking wide-eyed at the crying woman. "Mom? What's wrong with you?"

"Oh, shit!" Stark spoke under his breath to me. "That's Aphrodite's mom."

I'd dropped his hand and was moving forward before my mind had time to catch up with my actions.

"They've killed him!" her mom shrieked at her.

"Him? Who?"

"Your father! The mayor of Tulsa!"

The crowd gasped along with me. Aphrodite's face went bloodless and white. Before she could speak again, Lenobia rushed up, saying, "Ladies and gentlemen, some of you have already met me. I am Lenobia, Horse Mistress of this House of Night, and on behalf of our High Priestess and our faculty, I am sorry that you were witness to the tragic events of this evening. Let me help you find your vehicles so that you may make your way home in safety."

"It's too late for that!" Aphrodite's mom screamed at Lenobia. "There is nothing *safe* about tonight. None of us will ever be *safe* as long as we coexist with you bloodsuckers!"

When Aphrodite just stood there staring at her mother, I stepped forward, surprised by how calm my voice sounded. "Lenobia, this is Aphrodite's mom. She says her husband has been killed."

"Mrs. LaFont," Lenobia reacted instantly. "There must be some mistake. It was one of our fledglings who met an untimely death tonight."

"The only mistake about it is that more of *you* didn't die tonight." Mrs. LaFont whirled around, pointing an accusing finger toward the school wall where it met the main entrance and the open iron gate. I could just make out what looked like someone lying on the ground. "He is still there. Where he was left dead and drained by a vampyre!" Then she dissolved once more into hysterical sobs, this time clutching brokenly at her daughter.

"I will go." Darius's voice was strong and steady. He touched Aphrodite's shoulder gently before he jogged to the dark shape. Once there, he crouched. He hesitated before he returned to us, standing and taking off his jacket, and draping it over what had to be a body. Then he returned to Aphrodite. She was still holding her sobbing mother. "I am sorry," he told her. "It is your father, and he is dead."

Mrs. LaFont's sobs became a horrible, keening wail. The rest of the crowd had begun to whisper with a restlessness that felt like anger and fear combined. The panic that was building was almost a tangible thing. I knew if someone didn't say or do something quickly, an already awful night could potentially turn dangerous. I raised my voice, glad I still sounded way calmer than I felt.

"Aphrodite, you need to take your mom into the school. Darius, call 911 and tell them that the mayor is dead. Lenobia, Stark, Sister Mary Angela, and the Benedictine nuns, please help these people to their cars. I'll help get Aphrodite and her mom settled and then go find Thanatos. She'll know what to do."

People had actually started to move and do what I'd told them to do when Aphrodite's mom suddenly pulled away from her daughter. "No!" she shrieked, shaking her head and causing the last of her bound hair to fly loose around her shoulders. "I won't go inside that building ever again. *They killed my husband!*"

"Mother," Aphrodite tried to reason with her. "We don't know how Dad died. He had high blood pressure. He might have had a heart attack."

"His throat was ripped open and his blood was sucked from his body. That is not a heart attack. That is a vampyre attack!" her mother shouted at her.

I glanced at Darius for confirmation. He nodded slightly and continued to speak into his phone.

Ah, hell.

"Mrs. LaFont, if it was a vampyre attack I promise you that we will find the killer and bring him or her to justice," Lenobia said solemnly.

"It's just like your ex-High Priestess said—you are violent! That's why she broke with you. We should have listened to her. We should have all listened to her. Poor Neferet was only your first victim . . ." Mrs. LaFont sobbed.

"I'm going to make sure the humans continue to leave. Zoey, get that woman's mouth under control," Lenobia whispered to us as she hurried past Stark and me. Then she raised her voice. "Okay, ladies and gentlemen, again I apologize for the tragedies tonight. Let the good sisters and me help you to your cars. The Tulsa police will be here soon, and the last thing they need is to have their crime scene polluted."

"I better help her," Stark murmured.

"No, you better help *me*." I grabbed his hand. He gave me a question mark look. I lowered my voice and leaned into him. "You heard Lenobia. Her mouth needs to be shut. I need some of your red vampyre mojo," I explained.

His eyes got big, but he nodded and whispered back, "What do you want me to do?"

"Let her cry, but no more screaming or shouting," I said quietly.

He nodded again, and we went to Aphrodite, who was staring helplessly at her sobbing mom.

I met Aphrodite's gaze, willing her to understand the true meaning of my words. "Stark's going to *talk* to your mom. Is that okay with you?"

Aphrodite's eyes flicked to Stark, then to her mom, before coming back to me. "Yeah. Actually, I think that's a really good idea." She took her mom's elbow and, speaking to her quietly, said, "Mom, you're right. We don't need to go inside the school. But there's a pretty courtyard right over there, away from the vampyres. Why don't you and I sit at one of the benches while we wait for the police to get here? Okay?"

"The *human* police! I want the *human* police to find your father's vampyre killer!"

"Like Lenobia said, the human police are on their way. Right now Stark and Zoey are going to come with us while we wait. You know, Stark's not a normal vampyre. He's a Guardian. He's, uh, worked with the police before—the *human* police," Aphrodite fictionalized as she guided her mom away from the crowd and toward the small, dark courtyard just outside the professors' quarters. "So, Mom, I want you to let Stark ask you some questions while we wait for the human policemen to get here."

Stark stepped up, nodded at Aphrodite, and then took her place beside Mrs. LaFont. "Ma'am, I'm really sorry about your husband," he said in a soft, charming voice. Even I could hear the mesmerizing red vampyre magick within it as he continued. "I'm going to make sure you're safe and all I want you to do right now is to go with me to the courtyard and cry quietly there. It would really be helpful if you didn't scream or shout anymore."

Aphrodite and I let out twin sighs of relief when we heard her echo back to him, "I'll go with you to the courtyard and cry quietly there. No screaming or shouting."

"Are you okay?" I asked Aphrodite while we followed Stark and her mom.

She moved her shoulders. "I don't know. They—I mean my parents—they have never liked me. Actually, they've been mean to me for as long as I can remember. Seriously, it was a relief to have them out of my life. But it feels weird and sad to know my dad's body is over there by the wall."

I nodded and linked my arm with hers, wanting to reassure her with touch, even though I knew she wasn't usually a toucher. "I totally understand what you mean. When my mom died it hadn't mattered that she'd been mean to me for years, and picked the step-loser over me. All that mattered was that I'd lost my mom."

"She was hugging me while she cried," Aphrodite said, sounding young and broken. "I can't remember the last time she hugged me."

I couldn't think of anything to say in response to that, so I just stood there with Aphrodite, holding tightly to her, and listening to her mom's sobs while the sound of police sirens got closer and closer.

I was glad to see Detective Marx again, even though the circumstances were what Stark later called a complete and total cat herd. Marx, at least, wasn't a vampyre-hating human. He had nice brown eyes, and I remembered how they lit up when he'd told me about his twin sister and how even after she'd been Marked and gone through the Change, the two of them had still kept in contact. It was nice to know that at least one cop in Tulsa wasn't going to open the doors to a human lynch mob because Stark's red vamp mojo ran out super fast, and Aphrodite's mom was definitely in a pro-lynch mob state of mind.

"Arrest them!" Mrs. LaFont hurled the words at the detective. "Arrest all of them! A vampyre did this, and a vampyre should pay for it."

"Ma'am, whoever is responsible should pay for this crime, which is why I'm going to thoroughly and carefully investigate your husband's murder. I will find who did this. I give you my word on it. But I cannot, and will not, arrest every vampyre at this school."

"Thank you, Detective. As High Priestess here I agree with and appreciate your professionalism, as well as your integrity." I was super relieved to hear Thanatos's authoritative voice. "Please be assured we will cooperate fully with your investigation. We, too, want the mayor's killer to be found and brought to justice, as we do not believe a vampyre to be responsible for this tragedy."

"My husband's throat was ripped out and his blood was sucked from his body! That is a vampyre attack." Mrs. LaFont's eyes slitted at Thanatos. Her voice was filled with venom.

"It certainly looks like a vampyre attack," Thanatos agreed. "Which is the first reason to doubt that a vampyre committed this crime. Why would a vampyre kill the mayor of Tulsa at the House of Night during one of our open houses, and leave his body at our front gate to be discovered by humans as well as vampyres? It makes no sense."

"You prey on humans. *That* makes no sense!"

"Ladies, please, arguing does not help," Detective Marx tried to intercede, but Mrs. LaFont ignored him.

"Do you deny that you are intimately allied with Death?" She snapped the question at Thanatos.

"My Goddess-given affinity is, indeed, an affinity for death. I have a gift that enables me to help the spirits of the dead find their way to the Otherworld."

"Is that what you were doing with my husband? Seducing and trapping him? Helping him find his way to a fictitious vampyre otherworld?" Her voice got louder and louder with each question she hurled at Thanatos.

"Of course not, Mrs. LaFont. I had nothing to do with your husband's death." Thanatos turned to Detective Marx. "You may question any of the people who were at the open house tonight. I was always in view of the public. Even when tragedy struck and one of our fledglings rejected the Change and died, I remained accessible to our faculty and our students."

"A fledgling died here tonight as well?" the detective asked.

Thanatos nodded. "She will be missed."

"Why are you asking her about the fledgling? Everyone knows they could drop dead at any second. That's normal for their kind. My husband was *killed by a vampyre*. That is not normal!"

"If a vampyre did kill my father, I can promise you that vampyre isn't part of this school!" Aphrodite suddenly said. Then, when everyone was staring at her, she bit her lip and looked away uncomfortably.

"Are you saying you know who killed your father?" Aphrodite's mom sounded like she was entering Crazy Town again.

Aphrodite swallowed hard and then surprised me by blurting: "The only vampyre I know who would do something like this is one who would want to set up the House of Night to take the blame." She paused, and I tried to catch her gaze and telegraph a big DON'T SAY IT look, but Aphrodite was staring at her mom, like she could actually make Frances LaFont believe her. "Mom, our old High Priestess, Neferet, has a big grudge against us, all of us. She's mean, Mom. Worse, she's evil. She'd do something like this."

"That's ludicrous, Aphrodite! Neferet was a friend of your father's. He appointed her to be a liaison between vampyres and the city. She wouldn't have killed him!"

"Neferet was just using Dad and the city," Aphrodite insisted. "She's never wanted to make friends with humans. She hates humans. Actually, the only thing she hates more than a human is our House of Night, especially after she was kicked out of here. So it makes perfect sense that she'd kill Tulsa's mayor at the House of Night during our open house. She knows it'll make major problems between humans and vampyres."

"High Priestess?" Marx turned to Thanatos before Mrs. LaFont could chime in. "What do you know about Neferet and her motives?"

"As I said in an interview for Fox News more than a week ago, Neferet has been let go by our House of Night. I believe what Aphrodite is saying does make sense. Neferet was very angry with us."

"Angry enough to kill?" the detective asked.

Thanatos sighed. "I'm afraid she is capable of great violence. That is one of the reasons the High Council stripped her of her position here and her title of High Priestess of Nyx. Despite what she said to the mayor and the City Council members, Neferet was the one who advocated violence against humans, and not us."

"If you knew she was violent, you should have come to us with your concerns," said Marx grimly.

"They didn't come to you because what they're saying is a bunch of lies!" Mrs. LaFont exploded. "Just tonight some of the City Council members, Charles, and I were talking about how odd it is that Neferet's penthouse had been vandalized, and that she then disappeared, all *after* she took a public stand against what has been going on here at the House of Night. Charles himself said he suspected foul play."

Aphrodite looked totally shocked. "Mom, you can't really believe that."

"Of course I do! Neferet had the strength to speak out against vampyre killers. Your father took her side. And now she is missing and your father is dead." She turned her blazing gaze on the detective. "And just exactly what are you going to do about these heinous crimes?"

"Mrs. LaFont, please—" the detective began, but LaFont interrupted him. "No, I've had enough of this. My husband is dead, and I will not sit passively by with his murder and allow blame to be cast onto the blameless. I'm going home. I'm calling my attorney. None of you have heard the last of me." Her spiteful blue eyes found Aphrodite. "And you're coming with me. Let's go. Now."

Mrs. LaFont had walked several steps from us before she realized her daughter wasn't following her. She stopped, turned, and lifted her lip in a sneer that looked so like Aphrodite at her very worst that I know I must have gawked like a tourist. "Aphrodite, I said you're coming home with me. *Now.* And I meant it."

"No," Aphrodite said simply. I thought she sounded really tired, but her voice was steady. "I am home, and this is where I'm staying."

"Your father's killer is one of them!"

"Mom, I already told you, if a vampyre killed Dad, it's not one of these guys."

"Aphrodite, I'm not going to tell you to come with me again."

"Good. That means I won't have to tell you no again. I'm sorry Dad is dead, and that means you're alone. But I haven't lived with you for almost four years. You're really not my family anymore."

"Detective, can I force her to come with me?" Mrs. LaFont asked him.

"Actually, that's a good question." The detective looked from Aphrodite to Thanatos. "I don't see a crescent on her forehead. Is her Mark covered for some reason?"

"No. Aphrodite is an unusual member of the House of Night. She was once Marked, but her crescent disappeared, though the gifts Nyx gave her when she was a fledgling did not disappear, hence the fact that our High Council has named her a Prophetess of Nyx. So, though Aphrodite is not fledgling nor vampyre, she has been Chosen by our Goddess, and will always have a home at the House of Night."

Detective Marx blew out a long breath. "Well, being Marked and Chosen by Nyx means that Aphrodite was emancipated from her human parents. Though the circumstances are odd, I'd say that with the ruling of the Vampyre High Council, her emancipation remains valid. Mrs. LaFont, I believe the answer to your questions is no, I cannot force your daughter to go with you."

"Aphrodite." Mrs. LaFont's voice was frigid. "Will you do as I say and come home with me, or will you choose to remain with your father's murderers?"

"I choose my real family and my real home," Aphrodite said with no hesitation, sliding her hand into Darius's and holding tightly to him as her mother spewed venom at her.

"Then I wish I'd never given birth to you. Don't ever call me your mother again. Don't ever speak to me again. I deny your existence completely. You are as dead to me as is your father." Mrs. LaFont turned her back to her daughter and walked quickly away.

In the silence her mother had left behind, Aphrodite's voice seemed very small when she said, "I'd like to really go home now. I'll be on the bus, waiting for you guys to get done here."

"Bus?" Detective Marx asked.

"Yes," Thanatos spoke wearily. "Some of our students and vampyres have chosen to live together off campus. Dawn is nearing. They really should be returning to their home."

"Is this new off-campus housing because there is a new kind of vampyre?" He glanced at Stark's red tattoos. "A red vampyre?"

"There is, indeed, as Neferet announced in her public interview, a new type of vampyre among us, and some of them are among the fledglings and vampyres who have chosen to live off campus," Thanatos said, her voice growing wary.

"And is what Neferet said about these new vampyres also true?"

"If you mean the part about us being violent and dangerous—no. That's not true," Stark said, meeting the detective's gaze.

The detective hesitated, and then, with terrible finality, he said, "High Priestess, I am going to have to insist none of your fledglings or vampyres be allowed to leave campus until we have investigated tonight's crime more thoroughly and are able to rule out a killer being from your House of Night. If you require one, I'm positive I can wake up a judge and get an injunction ordering your campus to remain closed, but I have to tell you I think it would look better if an official order wasn't necessary."

With no visible hesitation, Thanatos said, "There is no need for an injunction. I will voluntarily comply with your request. Zoey, tell the students to get off the bus. Until further notice, everyone will be living on campus."

CHAPTER THREE

Aphrodite

"I don't know which is worse, the fact that the asshole police aren't letting us go home to the depot tunnels, or the fact that I've actually started thinking of those shitty tunnels as home," Aphrodite muttered as she dug through her purse. "Where the hell is my bottle of Xanax?"

"Let me help you, my beauty." Darius gently took the Red Valentino purse from Aphrodite, unzipped a little side pocket within, and pulled out the pill bottle. "Xanax or wine, not both," he said, holding the bottle just out of her reach.

"My dad is dead," she said flatly.

"I think the point is, Darius doesn't want to see you dead, too," Zoey said, plopping heavily down on the couch next to her in the little infirmary waiting room. "I get what you're feeling, and I know it might seem like a good idea to make yourself totally numb tonight, but there's no way to escape the death of a parent."

"Even a shitty parent?" Aphrodite asked Z.

"Yeah, even one of those," Zoey nodded knowingly. "You're going to have to deal with it sometime. From my experience I'd say that it's better to do that sooner rather than later."

Aphrodite frowned, but put down the bottle of red wine she'd been drinking straight out of. "Fine. I choose Xanax."

"But only one," Darius insisted.

"Again, fine. Just give it to me. Even semi-numb sounds really good right now."

Darius was putting the little blue pill in Aphrodite's palm when Shaunee's voice caused her to look up in surprise. "I don't want to be numb. Not even semi-numb." Shaunee entered the waiting room, followed by Stevie Rae, Rephaim, Damien, and Thanatos. "If I'm numb I might forget what happened tonight, and that means I'll forget the last night of Erin's life. Her life deserves to be remembered. And, Aphrodite, your dad's life deserves to be remembered, too."

Aphrodite popped the pill into her mouth and swallowed it without anything to drink. "When I remember my dad, I'm going to remember a weak man who was bullied by my mom into being a shitty guy. I'm not sure I want to remember that. What are you going to remember about Erin? How you two split one brain for all that time, or how you two split up?"

"Seriously, Aphrodite, I'm real sorry your daddy died tonight, but that's no reason for you to be mean to Shaunee," Stevie Rae said.

"Stevie Rae, we all deal with death our own way," Aphrodite explained, sounding way more patient than she felt. "My way is to just say things right out, and I'm sorry if that makes you uncomfortable, but I'm not being mean. I'm being real. So, which is it, Shaunee?"

"Both," Shaunee said slowly. "I'm going to remember my Twin like she really was, not all good or all bad. Most people aren't all of either." She looked from Aphrodite to Zoey. "How do you remember your mom?"

Zoey's sigh was long and sad. "I try to remember the vision Nyx gave me of her entering the Otherworld. She was at peace then, and that's a good memory."

"Well, I don't have that option with my dad," Aphrodite said. "I'm not sure where he is, but my best guess is it's not Nyx's Otherworld."

"You may be surprised," Thanatos said.

Aphrodite looked at her in obvious shock. "Are you telling me you saw his spirit enter the Otherworld?"

"No, I was not present at his death, and his spirit did not stay to communicate with me, but I can tell you that I sensed a great amount of peace lingering in the earth at the site of his death. I hope it helps you to know that when I sense such a strong presence of peace after a death it is because the spirit that has departed has been freed from a life of turmoil, tragedy, or sadness. I believe your father's spirit was relieved to be free of this life, and he will come around again reborn into happier circumstances."

Aphrodite blinked hard several times, and kept the tears from falling from her eyes. It took a long time for her to collect herself, but her friends waited patiently. When she finally spoke, her voice was shaky. "Th-thank you for telling me that, Thanatos. It does help. I honestly can't remember a time when my dad was ever really happy. I hope—" She paused, cleared her throat, and then continued. "I hope he finds happiness next time around."

"That will be my prayer to Nyx," Thanatos said.

"Mine, too. And mine. Yeah, me, too," echoed the others.

"Are we going to watch Erin's body for the next few days?" Zoey's question seemed to jar the room.

"That won't be necessary," Thanatos said.

"Well, I know this isn't exactly a pleasant subject, but someone needs to say it." Zoey spoke as if she didn't notice, or care, that everyone was staring at her in horror.

Aphrodite hid a surprised smile. *Wow, Z was really starting to sound like a proper bitchy High Priestess.*

"Right here are two vampyres," Z continued as she motioned

toward Stark and Stevie Rae, "who as fledglings rejected the Change and 'died,'" she air quoted. "Just like Erin 'died' tonight," Zoey air quoted again. "And both of them un-died and came back as red fledglings within a couple of days. So, I think we need to—"

"Z, no," Stevie Rae said, looking uncomfortable. "Erin's not coming back."

"Stevie Rae, I said this isn't pleasant, but we have to deal with it," Zoey bulldozed on. "Who is going to watch—"

"No one need watch the dead fledgling," Thanatos cut Zoey off. "She is truly dead."

"Thanatos saw her spirit enter the Otherworld," Shaunee said quietly. "Nyx welcomed her."

"I can promise you that Nyx didn't welcome any of us when we died and then un-died," Stevie Rae added.

"Nope, she didn't," Stark agreed.

"Erin is really dead," Damien said.

"Okay, I just . . . well, I didn't mean to sound cold or anything like that," Zoey explained haltingly. "It's just that I thought we needed to be sure."

"We are sure," Thanatos said.

"I'm with Z about telling it how it is, and I think we need to be sure about something else, too," Aphrodite said. She met Thanatos's wise gaze. "The circle expelled what looked like Neferet's partially reformed body, and when she was kicked out of campus, she passed through Erin, and went out in the exact direction Dad was found. I think we need to find out for sure if Neferet killed both of them—Erin and Dad."

Thanatos's shoulders slumped. "I'm afraid there is no way to be completely certain, but Aphrodite's supposition about who could be responsible for both deaths does makes sense. I felt the presence of death only moments before Zoey called to tell me about the spiders. That death could have been Erin's rejection of the Change beginning, or it could have been Neferet attempting to manifest from the dead." She looked questioningly around the group. "Did any of you notice whether Erin was showing signs of sickness before tonight? Did anyone hear her cough or say she had been unusually tired lately?"

"Why don't you try asking somebody who really knew her and gave a shit about her?" Dallas said from the hallway outside the room where he stood, looking pissed off.

"Dallas, I am glad you have joined us. Come, sit, talk with us. When you are ready to see Erin's body, and to bid her farewell, I will take you within, and tell you of the joyous welcome our Goddess gave your dear friend's spirit as she entered the Otherworld this night," Thanatos said.

"I don't got anything to say to any of you. She was *fine* before that goddamned circle was cast! I didn't want her to do it. I tried to stop her. I would've stopped her if Miss I'm the Boss of Everyone hadn't told her Warrior to get me outta the way. I didn't even know Erin had died until a few minutes ago when I finally busted outta that fucking closet." Dallas's eyes were hostile red slits. "I don't know who you're trying to blame for this massive fuck-up, but I can tell you that I know the truth, and so will everyone else here at the House of Night—Erin is dead because of some shit Zoey Redbird and her friends caused to happen in that circle tonight. She was fine until then, and if I would've been able to stop her, she'd still be fine!"

The lights in the waiting room began to flicker as Dallas's anger became palpable.

"It's past time for you to shut up, Dallas," Stark said, rising to stand between the angry red vampyre and Zoey.

Darius joined him, shoulder to shoulder. "Erin rejected the Change. That didn't have anything to do with Zoey's circle."

"She didn't want you to stop her," Shaunee had started to cry again. "She wanted to be part of our circle again."

"She didn't want shit to do with any of you!" Dallas yelled.

"You will not raise your voice in anger so soon after a young fledgling's untimely death." The strength within Thanatos's voice had the lights steadying and Dallas taking a step back. "If you wish to bid your friend farewell with peace and love and respect, then you are welcome to do so. If you wish to spew anger and sow dissent, then you must leave, Dallas, and take your negative energy with you. It has no place at the bedside of one who has recently joined our Goddess."

"I'll tell Erin good-bye in my own way, and it won't be with the people who caused her death!" Dallas growled the words, and with a sneer he backed several more steps away before turning and running from the infirmary.

"He's gonna be a serious problem," Stark said.

"He's been a serious problem since he found out about Rephaim and me," Stevie Rae said, chewing her lip. "That screwed him up."

"That is not your fault," Rephaim said, taking Stevie Rae's hand.

"Yeah, well, I wish I didn't feel like it was," Stevie Rae murmured, leaning into her boyfriend. "It's just that he used to be so sweet, and now he's not just a douche, he's a dangerous douche." She looked at Thanatos. "I hate to say it, but I have a feeling Erin's death is going to be the excuse he needs to do something stupid like come after us."

"Yeah, and with all of us being stuck together here on campus, Dallas and the asstards who follow him are going to be stirring up as much shit as they can," Aphrodite said.

Stark's intake of breath had the group turning to him. "Shit pot stirring—that's the same thing that Neferet's into. And we know that right before Neferet snatched Grandma Redbird, Dallas was in communication with her."

"Which means if Neferet has managed to pull herself together enough to reform her body, chances are she's going to contact Dallas again as a way to get the inside scoop on what's going on at the House of Night," Zoey finished for Stark.

"With Dallas blaming Erin's death on us, he'll be as happy as a vulture on a meat wagon to do anything he can to mess us up," Stevie Rae said.

Aphrodite grimaced at Stevie Rae's bumpkin analogy, but she had to agree with her logic. "The worst thing that could be done to mess us up would be to figure out a way to prove one of the House of Night vampyres killed my dad."

"I believe your supposition is correct. Neferet killed your father. I also believe her manifestation may have caused Erin's body so much trauma that it rejected the Change—so, quite literally, Neferet could be guilty of the taking of two precious lives tonight," Thanatos said.

"She'll be wanting to shove that guilt onto someone else," Aphrodite said.

"Yep, she'll be wanting to plant evidence to make it look like someone from here did it," Z agreed with her. "Dallas would help her do that. There's no doubt about it."

"That must be prevented," Thanatos said.

"How? This is a school, not a military fortress. It's just not that tough to sneak in and out of here. We all know that—we've all done it. And we have to remember that Neferet knows her way around this school even better than we do," Aphrodite said.

"Then my task is really rather simple. I must devise a way to prevent Neferet from entering our campus," Thanatos said.

"Actually, you need to prevent more than just Neferet. I can see Dallas, or any of his disgusting friends, sneaking in and out and doing whatever batshit crazy thing Neferet has cooked up for them to do. *She* wouldn't actually have to do anything; she likes to delegate. It makes her feel powerful," Aphrodite said.

"Good point," Z agreed.

"I will meditate on this, and until I have an answer I will be quite certain the school grounds are being patrolled diligently. Kalona and Aurox will not allow anyone to enter our campus during daylight hours." Thanatos said. "In the meantime, it is almost dawn. You all need rest."

Aphrodite stood up, and was surprised to feel the room rock slowly around her. Grateful the Xanax was beginning to work, she leaned against Darius's strong arm. "Well, I'd say that I don't want to sound like a bitch, but that would be a lie. I don't care what I sound like. You and the rest of the School Council need to know that Darius is going to be staying with me in my old dorm room." Aphrodite spoke to Thanatos in a firm, no nonsense voice that reminded her a little uncomfortably of her mother. "I know that's against the rules, but so is kidnapping someone's grandma, killing a human for no reason, and causing a fledgling to reject the Change and die—and that's only three of the long list of rules that have been broken by the bad guys recently. So, I'm breaking a rule for the good guys. I don't want to sleep without my Warrior, and I can promise you that Z feels the same way." Aphrodite shot a humorous look at Stevie Rae. "The bumpkin would be insisting that she sleeps with her Bird Boy, but he's going to be a bird and, apparently, she's still refusing to put him in a cage at night—right, Stevie Rae?"

"I'm not talkin' to you when you call Rephaim Bird Boy." She frowned at Aphrodite.

"Yep, just as I thought. Still no cage. Anyway, we've been fighting evil and saving the effing world for months now, and I need my Warrior. I'm not sorry if that makes you uncomfortable. The end."

There was a long pause while Thanatos and Aphrodite locked gazes, and then Thanatos said, "I believe there is precedence for Warriors to share the sleeping quarters of their Priestesses, especially if they believe their Priestesses could be in danger."

"Z is always in danger," Stark said quickly.

"As is my Prophetess," Darius added, sliding a protective arm around her.

Aphrodite smiled. "I guess that settles that."

"Stevie Rae, I know you'll be sleeping alone as soon as the sun rises," Shaunee spoke softly. "And if you wouldn't mind too much, I'd really appreciate it if you stayed with me in the dorm room I used to share with Erin. I—I don't think I can stay there by myself."

"Oh, heck yeah, I'll stay with you!" Stevie Rae said, hugging Shaunee. "But I'm gonna need to leave the window open for Rephaim."

"We can do that," Shaunee said. "No problem."

"Just be sure you tie the blackout drapes into place so that no sun can get in during the day," Zoey reminded her. She glanced at her watch. "How long until sunrise?"

"Twenty-four minutes," Stevie Rae and Rephaim said together.

"Okay, you guys go get settled. Stark, go on up to my old room and do like I told Stevie Rae—be sure the drapes are tied closed. I'll check up on the rest of our group and be sure they're all set, at least for today," Zoey said.

Aphrodite watched her. Z sounded normal, but there was something about her—an edge to her voice—an unusually strained look to her face—dark shadows under her eyes. All that didn't quite add up to everyday Zoey. Everyday Zoey got tired, and even grumpy once in a while, but she always snapped out of it, and did what needed to be done. Aphrodite realized that the more closely she studied Z, the more she saw a girl who was doing what needed to be done, but who was obviously *not* snapping out of it.

"Z, why don't you let Thanatos take care of tucking the kids in tonight. You pulled our circle together and kicked Neferet out of here. Using that kind of power drains you—physically and mentally. We're not screw-ups hiding out and licking our wounds by ourselves anymore. It's a pain in the ass to be stuck here, but there are good points to being stranded at our House of Night. No more calling for cheap pizza to be delivered down the street. Bow Boy, you need to take your girl by the kitchen and grab her something real to eat and drink before the sun turns you into toast," Aphrodite said.

"I don't need you to tell me how to take care of Z," Stark snapped at her.

"Nice. That's how you're going to respond to decent advice? That's real mature," Aphrodite said, shaking her head woozily.

"If Darius wasn't holding on to you, you'd be on your ass," Stark said.

"Would you two *stop bickering*!" Zoey shouted, and then took a deep breath and let it out slowly before she continued. "Aphrodite's right. I'm super tired and I need to eat."

"Rest and restore your energy," Thanatos told Zoey. Then she glanced from Aphrodite to Stark. "And your High Priestess is correct. Your bickering helps no one except those who wish to sow dissention amongst us."

"Sorry," Stark muttered to Aphrodite. "I get touchy when Z gets tired."

"Apology accepted. And I get messed up when one of my parents gets killed," Aphrodite leaned even more heavily against Darius. "Would you please take me to bed, handsome?"

"Gladly," Darius said. He bowed respectfully to Thanatos, Zoey, and Stevie Rae, and then he practically carried Aphrodite from the room.

They were walking under the old oaks that shaded the grounds around the girls' dormitory building when pain knifed through Aphrodite's temples, blinding her. Her body jerked spasmodically, causing her to cry out and fall from Darius's arms, where she crumpled against the earth as the vision violated her.

> With great power come great responsibilities
> Weigh the pleasure of leadership and luxury with the
>   sword Damocles
> When she believes the ancient is the key to all her needs
> Then is when all will tumble down; then is when Light
>   bleeds and bleeds . . .

Aphrodite was truly fucked. Not only was she having the killer of a headache and the blackout that came before one of her visions, she was also hearing poetry.

Goddess, she hated poetry.

Figurative language sucked hairy ball sacs, which was, indeed, personifying figurative language and therefore forcing her to use that which she hated to explain, that which she hated.

She would have laughed at herself, but the pain wouldn't let her.

At the edge of her consciousness Aphrodite was aware that Darius was calling her name and stroking her hair.

He'll keep me safe. Okay, Nyx, I'm ready for whatever you have to show me. Goddess, I'm glad I already took a Xanax. Wonder if this will earn me one more glass of wine when I'm back and—

Aphrodite's consciousness was ripped from her body, exploding through her eyes with a force that broke blood vessels and caused her head to pulse with pain.

Not that she felt those sensations just then. Aphrodite's spirit was following a slender silver ribbon of light that carried her away . . . away . . .

Aphrodite's spirit dropped down into the vision, and into Zoey's body.

Goddess, she hated experiencing terrible shit that happened to people, especially when those people were her friends. Aphrodite steeled herself and peered out of Zoey's eyes.

Z was sitting in the cafeteria. It seemed like she was alone in there, except for Aurox. She was staring up into Aurox's eyes, and he was calling her Zo and telling her to take a chill pill. Aphrodite felt the flood of Z's emotions as his words awakened something within her. She was so confused and torn between what she wanted, and what she thought she should do, that Zoey's insides felt like a cauldron of boiling emotions. Aphrodite could feel the heat of her emotions expanding from the center of Z's chest, almost like they were actually burning her. She was wondering what the hell that was about, but then Z, along with Aphrodite, was tasting Aurox's blood. So, pretty much everything else went out of her mind.

Drinking the big blond Bull Boy's blood wasn't nearly as disgusting as Aphrodite would have thought—not that she'd thought about drinking the kid's blood. Ever. Maybe part of the not-too-disgustingness of it was brought on by the fact that Z was definitely into the blood stuff. Huh. Z really did have a thing for Aurox. That was something she needed to remember. Along with the weird burning.

Then the scene changed and Stark was there, as per typically, spoiling all her (and Z's) fun. He was acting like a possessive douche, so he and Zoey were fighting, which was annoying.

It was not white-hot-anger-making, though. But that's what Aphrodite felt within Z. The girl was incredibly pissed.

That scene shifted into another, where the only thing that was the same was Z's frustration level. Aphrodite couldn't tell where she was. It wasn't bright, sparking daylight, but it definitely wasn't night, either, because the sky was bothering her eyes, so Zoey was keeping her gaze down, until some crappily dressed guys started messing with her. Zoey stood up to them, which Aphrodite totally agreed with, but then her anger level went way into the danger zone. Aphrodite watched helplessly as Z raised her hands and let loose all of the frustration and anger and confusion that had filled her. Aphrodite barely got a glimpse of the faces of the two guys, but the terror in their looks would forever be branded into her memory as they were hurled against a stone wall and blood exploded everywhere.

Change of scene again, and this time Aphrodite wasn't looking through Zoey's eyes. She was viewing her from a distance. Z had returned to the House of Night. Her anger had changed, and now she looked upset, scared, and confused. But that's not the only change Aphrodite saw. She could *see* that Zoey carried something with her. Part of it was terrible. It looked like fleas or some kind of flesh-eating lice were clinging to Zoey, crawling under her skin. Yet as Aphrodite stared, completely grossed out, the crawling things shook and shifted, looking like glitter, or maybe even a beautiful cloak that was covering Zoey. And then Aphrodite blinked and the things changed back to horrible, crawling, nesting insects.

Aphrodite had no fucking idea what the things were, but it was pretty obvious that they were *not* coming from Zoey. They weren't element based. Aphrodite's mind raced. What had been pissing Z off so badly was normal stuff—boy frustration and people acting stupid in general. What was abnormal was Z's reaction. *Could that be because it wasn't really Zoey's reaction—it was frustration and anger flowing into her, being absorbed by her, being used by her, and Zoey didn't realize it? And then why the hell did the things change, and look beautiful? Aphrodite didn't know what was going on, but she did know the end result was Zoey being angry and powerful and completely out of control.*

That terrified Aphrodite.

The next scene followed so quickly that Aphrodite felt vertigo-ish dizziness.

From Z's perspective Aphrodite watched herself being led, handcuffed, into a prison cell. Right before the iron door slammed, shutting her into the claustrophobic solitary confinement cell, Zoey's shoulders slumped. The anger that had filled her so powerfully and completely had been snuffed out. Utterly devastated, and filled with self-loathing, Zoey watched the iron door shut as if it sealed her tomb. Then the young High Priestess, and Aphrodite's best friend, went to the corner of the cell, slid down the wall, hugged her knees to her chest, and began rocking back and forth, back and forth. Three words repeated over and over through Zoey's mind: *I deserve this. I deserve this. I deserve this. I deserve this . . .*

Zoey had no hope left.

And then Aphrodite was yanked from Z's point of view again and found herself hovering over the center of a great cathedral. Nauseated, she looked down to see that the parishioners were dead. All of them. Each of their throats were slashed and their bodies had been sucked dry of blood.

A triumphant voice repeated three words over and over through Aphrodite's mind: *I deserve this. I deserve this. I deserve this. I deserve this . . .*

> *With great power come great responsibilities*
> *Weigh the pleasure of leadership and luxury with the*
> *   sword Damocles*
> *When she believes the ancient is the key to all her needs*

Then is when all will tumble down; then is when Light
  bleeds and bleeds . . .

The piece of poetry repeated through Aphrodite's mind as the final disturbing scene dissipated and her spirit exploded back into her blind, pain-filled body.

"Darius!" she gasped, choking for air and pressing her hands against her closed, bleeding eyes.

"I'm here! You are safe!" he said. "I'll send for Zoey and—"

"No!" with the last of her strength she told him. "Don't let Z know. Don't let anyone know."

"I will do as you say, my beauty. Rest. I will always keep you safe."

Then Aphrodite allowed herself to pass out.

CHAPTER FOUR

Zoey

"I never thought I'd wish school wouldn't have been canceled," I said, while I paced restlessly back and forth across the dorm room floor. "I don't know what the hell Thanatos was thinking. Going to class today would at least give us something to do. And tomorrow is Saturday. We do *not* need a long weekend."

Stark rolled over in bed, looking tousled and only half awake. He smiled his cute, cocky grin at me and did look totally cute and cocky, which wasn't a bad thing. "If you come back to bed I'll give you something to do."

Still, I was too worried to be in the mood, so I batted my eyes innocently and in a clueless voice asked, "You'll give me *and* the entire school something to do? That's ambitious, even for you, Stark."

"You know that's not what I meant! Way to kill a mood, Z."

I paused in my pacing long enough to laugh and give him a quick kiss. "Sorry, I slept crappily. I kept having nightmares about Dallas and his disgusting friends planting pieces of the mayor's bloody clothing in Thanatos's desk, and Lenobia's barn, and even Erik's drama classroom. Then after the cops arrested all of them, Neferet swooped back here and said she'd be happy to do her old job again, *and* bring in a bunch of new teachers. In my dream

Neferet was a big, black leech, and our new teachers were all giant spiders." I shivered. "Eesh, I hate leeches. And spiders."

"Come here." Stark patted the bed beside him.

I sighed, but I sat. When he started kneading my shoulders I felt some of my tension begin to fade. "You always know how to make me feel better."

"Yep, and I always will. Just sit here for a little while and let me work on those knots in your shoulders, and try not to overthink everything for a few minutes."

"I don't overthink. I prepare." I meant to sound tough and High Priestess-like, but there was no way on earth I could sound like that when he was giving me a seriously excellent shoulder rub.

"You overthink. And we are going to have plenty to do today. We're going to go to the cafeteria and eat breakfast with our friends, and then we have to be sure all of our fledglings have rooms—especially our red fledglings. Z, we gotta be careful about where those kids spend the daylight hours. I'm with you in thinking Dallas is up to some shit, and I don't want any of us hurt because he's a mean little asshole."

"He seriously has anger control issues," I said. I tried to pull away from Stark so that I could think better, but he tugged me back down beside him and kept working on my shoulders.

"No, you sit here. We need to talk about stressful stuff, but you gotta learn to relax. The best way I can keep you from stressing totally out is to keep rubbing your shoulders."

"You may have to keep doing that for the next several days."

"That's cool with me," he said, and kissed my neck, making me shiver—this time in pleasure.

"Well, good. That makes me almost look forward to the next several days," I said.

"Glad to hear it. And since I've got you in a receptive mood, I want you to promise me something."

"What?" I instantly began to tense up again.

"Stop it." He kneaded my shoulders harder, causing me to melt under his strong hands. "You know I'd never ask you to promise me anything awful. All I want is for you to keep our circle out of Erin's funeral."

"Why? I figured it would be a nice thing to do—maybe even a way Shaunee can have closure. Shaylin's already shown an affinity for water, so it's not like there would be a big empty space where Erin used to be."

"Yeah, well, that was my first thought, too. But that was canceled out by all the hateful crap Dallas said to us last night."

"You think he'd cause a fight at Erin's funeral? That's low, even for him."

"He wants to fight, that's for sure, but causing one at the funeral would only get him and his friends in big trouble with Thanatos, and I don't think he's ready to be in that much trouble yet. But here's what I was thinking about—you heard him talking about how Erin didn't want anything to do with you or your circle, right?"

"Yeah, right."

"Z, think about it, even when Erin joined the circle it didn't look to me like she was doing it because she was feeling sorry she'd been such a bitch. What I heard her say was that she didn't want Aphrodite standing in for her."

"Yeah, that's what she said," I admitted.

"Did her attitude change after I got Dallas out of there? Did she apologize to you, or Shaunee, for the shitty way she'd been treating you guys?"

"No. When she saw the spiders she agreed with me that they're disgusting and said disgusting things have to go."

"Z, I don't like talking bad about a dead kid, and that's not what I'm meaning to do, but I think it *is* important to remember that Erin had changed sides before she died, even though she knew that Neferet and Dallas had chosen Darkness over Light."

"Yeah, that's true. But it feels wrong to hold that against her now. I mean, Thanatos saw Nyx welcome her to the Otherworld. If the Goddess can forgive her, can't we?"

"I think there's a big difference between forgiving her and making her into something she wasn't just because she's dead. I might be wrong, but it doesn't seem healthy to have our group, especially Shaunee, idolizing her."

"Yeah, I get what you're saying, and my gut's telling me you're right."

"See what I mean about not wanting your circle to make a big show at her funeral?"

"I do. Okay, I'm going to talk to Shaunee and be sure her closure comes from knowing Erin is in the Otherworld and at peace with Nyx. I don't see why Thanatos wouldn't be cool with leading her funeral."

"We need to focus on moving forward—not on looking back," he said.

"Good point. Which reminds me, I better check on Aphrodite and make sure she's okay, too. The mayor was a crappy dad, but he was her dad. She's gonna be messed up by this death."

"Z, Aphrodite was messed up *before* his death."

I smacked his leg. "She can be hateful, but she's still my friend."

"And why she is, is a mystery to me."

"Hey, Aphrodite is one of us, and we're going to need to stand together and be strong for whatever nastiness Neferet is cooking up."

"I know. I was just mostly kidding. Aphrodite's a bitch, but she's our bitch," he said.

I laughed. "Exactly."

"Okay, I think you're noodle-like enough." Stark squeezed my shoulders one last time, and then kissed me on my neck. "I'm starving. Let's go get some breakfast and then deal with whatever crazy the day brings."

"This was the first thing that really made me heart the House of Night," I said happily as I ladled a gihugic pile of spaghetti onto my plate. "Psaghetti! For breakfast! I love our cafeteria."

"When you say psaghetti you sound like you're six years old," Stark said, bumping my shoulder before he asked the cook to give him the *other* breakfast choice, the traditional (and boring) scrambled eggs and bacon.

I went to the drink bar and filled up my glass with brown pop—fully leaded—*with* caffeine—calling back to him, "Not six—nine. That's when I made up the *psaghetti madness* song." I cleared my throat and launched into "Pa-sghe-ti, pa-sghe-ti!" and even did the psaghetti dance on my way to our booth. I was just thinking that maybe the day wouldn't be so bad. After all, it had started with a shoulder rub and psaghetti! But just as Stark was sliding in next to me I heard a deep, masculine voice echoing my *psaghetti madness* song.

I didn't need to look at the cafeteria line to know who was singing. All I needed to do was look at Stark's face. He'd been grinning at my psaghetti celebration, but that happiness had disappeared from his face, leaving instead a tense, serious expression that made him look frustrated *and* pissed.

"How old were you when you met Heath?" Stark asked.

"Nine," I said. It made me feel miserable and helpless, but my gaze wouldn't stay on Stark's face. It was drawn to the guy who was still singing my song while he heaped psaghetti on his plate.

I wondered if it would have helped if Aurox hadn't been so cute. He did a dorky guy version of the dance I'd just done as he headed over to the drink bar.

Nope, I decided, feeling my stomach do the weird butterfly thing it used to do when Heath would walk into a room. Aurox could have looked like a troll and he'd still make my stomach do flip-flops because *he shared Heath's soul.*

"Good morning!" Damien came in with Shaunee, Stevie Rae, and Rephaim, who waved and said hi to Stark and me as they hurried to get in line and fill their plates.

They didn't seem to notice that Stark and I didn't say anything in return.

"Hey there, Aurox. Wanna sit with us?" I heard Damien give him a cheery invite.

"Sure, that would be great," Aurox said.

"Awesome—Z and Stark are already at the table. It's that one over there." Damien pointed at us, which is when his happy-schmappy expression slid away, and was replaced by an *uh-oh* look. "Um, that is if there's enough room and it's okay with Z and Stark, and, um . . ." Damien trailed off uncomfortably, his cheeks getting pink.

"Fuck!" Stark said under his breath so that I was the only one who heard him. Then he sat up a little straighter and called, "Yeah, no problem. We got room for Aurox."

When Aurox sat down directly across from me I focused on shoveling psaghetti into my face.

"So, where'd you learn that song?" Stark shocked the bejezzus out of me by asking Aurox.

"What song?" Aurox answered around a mouthful of noodles.

"Never mind," Stark muttered.

The long, uncomfortable silence wasn't broken until Damien and the rest of our group smooshed into the booth.

"Have y'all seen Aphrodite today?" Stevie Rae asked.

I looked up then to see everyone shaking their heads.

"Or Darius?" she added.

More head shaking.

"Crap," I said. "I need to go check on her. It's not like her to hermit in her room."

"Yeah," Stevie Rae agreed. "She calls breakfast the beginning of the day's fashion parade. You know she actually told me once that she could predict which girls were going to turn into their fat, flabby mammas by how much makeup they wore to breakfast?"

"That girl is super crazy," Shaunee said.

"Is wearing a lot of makeup to breakfast good or bad?" Damien asked.

"I have no clue," Stevie Rae said. "I try to quit listenin' if Aphrodite talks too long. She kinda hurts my ears."

"Is her prediction about the girls part of her prophetic gift?" Aurox asked.

I couldn't help laughing with everyone else. Well, everyone except Stark. Instead of laughing he was stabbing his scrambled eggs like he was trying to kill them.

"No," Stevie Rae answered Aurox. "It's part of her hateful gift, which we're pretty sure wasn't given to her by Nyx."

"Oh, sorry," Aurox said, looking sheepish. "That was probably a stupid thing to ask."

"Hey, no worries, roomie," Damien said, smiling kindly at him. "Aphrodite baffles all of us."

"Roomie?" I heard myself asking. "You guys are sharing a dorm room?"

"Yes," Aurox said, meeting my gaze for the first time. "Damien offered, and I did not want to be alone, nor did I wish to share a room with a stranger. The others, well, I often find them staring at me oddly."

"That would be because you can change into a bull." Stark's voice was emotionless.

"I suppose you are correct," Aurox said. He dropped his gaze from mine and went back to eating.

"Yeah, well, that brings up a subject Stark and I were talking about earlier," I began.

"Yeah, we were talking when we woke up. Together. In the same bed. Right, *roomie*?" Stark put special emphasis on the word.

My friends threw worried looks from Stark to Aurox. I frowned. "Stark, everyone knows you and I are sleeping together."

"Just wanted to be sure," Stark said, attacking his eggs again.

"Anyway," I went on, feeling my cheeks getting warm. "Stark and I were saying that it's important to be sure our red fledglings *and* vampyres"—I managed to smile at Stevie Rae—"have some-place super safe to sleep until we can get back to our tunnels."

"Rephaim and I were talkin' 'bout that when he came back to me and Shaunee's room after dusk," Stevie Rae said. "I'm thinkin' the same thing y'all are—we need to explore the school and find somewhere less aboveground for the kids."

"And you, too, right?" I asked.

Stevie Rae shared a look with Rephaim before she said, "Well, no. I'm gonna keep roomin' with Shaunee."

"Even though I tried to talk her out of it," Rephaim said.

"Hey, you know I'll be okay by myself, don't you?" Shaunee said quickly. "Last night was tough, but I'm better today. I'll miss her, but I know my Twin's in a wonderful place. She even said it before she died—her feelings were finally unfrozen. In a weird way I'm glad for her." Shaunee blinked back tears, but she also smiled.

"I know, but unless we can find a basement-like place here that has an easy exit and entrance for, well, a bird, you've got me as a roomie until we go home to the depot tunnels," Stevie Rae said.

"I remember Dragon saying something about there being stor-age for old shields and swords in the school's basement," Damien said. "So, there has to be something down there that's at least watertight enough to house Dragon's precious old weapons. You know he wouldn't let that stuff be put anywhere it would rust out and get messed up."

"Well, at least that's good news. I'll feel better with all the red fledglings and vamps underground during the day. It just seems that you guys are so exposed otherwise," I said. Uneasily, I remembered Stevie Rae's close calls with sunlight and how fried even a small bit of it could make her and Stark and the rest of them. There were new powers that came with being a new type of vampyre, but there was also a pretty intimidating list of new stuff that could kill them.

"I understand what you're saying, Z, but there is another way to look at the red fledgling housing issue," Damien said. "I know they rest better if they're underground, and safe from the sunlight, and a basement would be good for that, but they'd also all be together in a place that most likely only has one entrance and exit. That may not be such a good thing."

Stark's brows lifted. "Damn, Damien, you've got a point. At the depot we can't get trapped because there are so many ways to get in and out of those tunnels. Z, if those kids are going to spend the time from sun up to sun down in a basement, I think you and I and Stevie Rae need to sleep somewhere away from that group."

"Sounds like there's more than one way to be exposed. You guys are right. We can't all be someplace we can be trapped, and I'm thinking that the two of you, especially," I nodded to Stevie Rae and Stark, "need to be separated from the main group of fledglings. If something happens we're going to need the power of fully Changed red vampyres to help your fledglings." I sighed. "But I also don't like the idea of all those fledglings being unprotected down there while they sleep. Wonder if we could talk Darius and Aphrodite into moving down there with them?"

Shaunee snorted. "Aphrodite in a basement? Not unless you get a designer in there to fancy it up for her."

"I know you're her High Priestess and all, but she's gonna throw a major hissy fit if you try to get her to move down there," Stevie Rae said.

As much as it annoyed me to think about Aphrodite throwing a fit, I knew Stevie Rae was right. I was trying to weigh whether it would be worth the fight or not when Aurox spoke up.

"I'll stay with the fledglings," he said.

I blinked in surprise at him. "But you just said you wanted to room with Damien because the other kids looked at you in a weird way."

"That doesn't mean I want them to be without protection. I rarely sleep, so I could easily watch over them. And I like being able to help you." He hesitated, and then added, "Your grandmother helped me. It's only right that I, in turn, help you."

His moonstone-colored eyes held my gaze until Stark's voice intruded. "Sounds good. And you're right. You do need to help us out."

"How about this—I'll go with you, so we'll still be roomies," Damien told Aurox. "I seem to have a way of smoothing over awkward situations."

"He does," Rephaim agreed. "Damien helped the kids accept me. I'll bet he can do the same for you."

"That's a lovely thing for you to say!" Damien's grin lit him up from within, and I thought how nice it was to see him happy.

"So that's settled," Stark said. "Okay, Z, are you almost done eating? You said you wanted to check on Aphrodite, and I need to see Darius—he'll probably know where Dragon's storage room is. We can kill two birds and all."

I gave the rest of my psaghetti a longing look, but it didn't seem all that appetizing anymore—not with Stark glowering at

Aurox, Aurox sending me little looks, and everyone else watching the three of us. I gulped my brown pop and put on my best fake smile. "I'm done! Let's go!"

"The rest of us can round up our red fledglings," Stevie Rae said. "Since Dragon used it to store weapons, it would figure that the basement is close to the field house. How 'bout we meet in there in an hour or so?"

"Sounds good," I said. Stark put his arm possessively around me and spider monkeyed me from our booth. When we got to the cafeteria door he paused and, in full sight of everyone, pulled me into his arm and kissed me. I mean, *really* kissed me—with his tongue and everything.

Okay, I absolutely like kissing Stark, but I'm not into PDA. I mean, I like to hold Stark's hand in public. I even usually like it when he puts his arm around me (which he usually does in a nice way, and not a clingy, spider monkey way), but we don't make out in public. Ever. So my face felt really hot with mortification when he unlocked his lips from mine, put his arm back around me, and practically dragged me out of the cafeteria—while shooting a *look* over his shoulder at the table and, of course, at Aurox.

I wanted to smack him in the face.

Instead, as soon as we were outside, I untangled myself from him and held his hand. Like normal.

He didn't say anything. He just gave me his cute, cocky smile.

I stifled a shriek of irritation and ignored the hot anger building inside me. If I told him how annoying and stupid he was being, it would just cause a fight between us, and we had way more important issues to deal with than Stark acting like a jealous jerk.

Plus, I wasn't interested in Aurox. Stark would figure that out pretty soon and, hopefully, stop with his possessiveness.

But you are interested in Heath, a terrible little voice whispered inside me. *And Heath's soul is shared with Aurox.*

I reminded the whispering voice that Stark was my Warrior, my Guardian, my lover, and my friend.

And what is Heath?

Dead! I told myself sternly. But even though I tried to shut my heart and mind to it, the echo of our psaghetti song sang within me.

CHAPTER FIVE

Zoey

"She still sleeps," Darius said, keeping his voice low and closing the door to Aphrodite's dorm room softly behind him.

"It's really late. Is she okay?" I asked, feeling weird standing out in the hall and whispering.

"She will be." Darius said. "Last night was difficult for her."

"How drunk did she get?" Stark asked sardonically.

"Her father was murdered on our school's campus. She drank," Darius said evasively.

"And now she's hung over," Stark said.

"And now she must rest," Darius corrected him, seeming to stand straighter and grow taller.

Ah, crap. That's all I needed—Stark and Darius butting heads.

"Rest is a good idea." I moved so that I was standing between them. "I remember how terrible I felt after my mom was killed. You remember, too, don't you, Stark?" I asked pointedly.

"I don't remember you being drunk," he said.

"And I don't remember you being judgmental!" I'd finally had enough. "Jeesh, give the girl a break. Her dad was murdered and her mom disowned her—all in the same night. Any way you look at it, that sucks."

"Getting wasted isn't the right way to deal with it," Stark said.

"Who the hell says so? You sound like you're a zillion years old. Just leave it alone," I said.

"You're the one who said you wanted to see her. And now you're here and she's too hung over to even talk to you," Stark said.

"No, I said I wanted to check on her." I turned to Darius. "Is she going to be okay?"

"Yes, I believe so," he said.

"There," I turned back to Stark. "She's been checked on."

"I mean no disrespect, Priestess, but could the two of you find somewhere else to fight? My Prophetess truly does need to rest," Darius said.

Stark's shoulders slumped and he rubbed his hand over his face. "Z and I aren't fighting." He glanced at me and smiled apologetically. "At least, I didn't mean to start a fight. Sorry 'bout that."

"That's okay," I said. "And I don't want to fight, either."

"Good." His smile widened and he seemed his usual sweet, charming self again. "Hey, Darius, me wanting to act like a douche wasn't the reason I came over here with Z."

Darius's lips tilted up. "I am glad to hear it."

"Actually, I came to ask you if you know anything about a basement-like place here. Damien mentioned that he thought Dragon stored old shields and swords down there."

"I do know of such a place. It stretches under the main part of the school building. The entrance to it is from the hallway that runs between the field house and the stables."

"Do you know if there's more than one entrance to it?" I asked.

"I am not certain. I have only been there a few times, and then my visits were brief. I was simply returning unneeded shields to their storage place. My memory is of a long, dark room. The ceiling is low, but the floor is stone and it's as sturdily built as is the rest of the House of Night."

"Sounds perfect," Stark said. "Would you show us how to get there?"

"Of course." He hesitated and glanced over his shoulder at the closed door of the dorm room he shared with Aphrodite.

"You don't have to be gone long," I assured him. "Just show us to the basement, and then you can come back here and see if Aphrodite's ready for something to eat."

"A big, greasy hamburger and fries is good for a hangover," Stark said.

Darius smiled. "Aphrodite says girls who eat cows start looking like them."

"Of course she does," I said. "You may want to bring her back something less bovine and more sex kitten."

"Hey, I'd pay to watch what Aphrodite would do if Darius brought her a bowl of cream and a can of tuna," Stark said.

The three of us laughed as we headed from the girls' dorm to the field house. The night was unusually warm for February. I thought I might even smell spring on the soft breeze that blew through campus. I definitely heard sounds that meant spring—fledglings talking by lamplight and cats meowing at their chosen vampyre.

Cats!

"Ah, hell! Nala and all the other cats are still at the depot. They're probably totally freaked that we didn't come back," I said.

"They'll be fine for a couple of days," Stark said. "They all have those big auto feeders and they like to drink from that shower up in the depot that won't turn off, remember?"

"Their potty pans will get super nasty." I grimaced, just thinking about how uber-grumpy that would make the already grumpy Nala.

"Yeah, that's going to be disgusting," Stark said. Darius grunted in agreement. "I feel sorry for poor Duchess being stuck with all of those cats."

"Hey, she's liking the cats," I reminded him. "She was actually sleeping with Damien's Cammy cat."

"Everyone likes Damien's Cammy," Stark said, smiling.

"If we have to stay here for more than one more night, I'm going to tell Thanatos that we need to get our cats, and Duchess, no matter what the cops say about it," I said.

"We are not criminals. We have done nothing wrong and should be allowed to leave—to go on about our normal lives," Darius said. Even he sounded frustrated.

"And yet we're basically locked up here," I said.

Neither of them had anything to say about that. What was there to say? The truth was that a crazy immortal, who might still be more specter than solid body, had probably eaten the mayor. How were we going to prove that, and even if we could come up with proof, would the human police believe our evidence, or was it just too crazy? The depressing but true answer was: they weren't going to believe it, because it was super, super crazy.

Darius had remembered right—the basement was long and dark and had a cold, stone floor. There weren't any electric lights down there, just gas lanterns hanging from really old iron hooks along the stone walls between the wall-mounted swords and shields. When Darius and Stark lit the lanterns, light danced off the metal surfaces as if they were living, breathing things.

"This could totally be a setting for *Game of Thrones*," I said.

"Which is awesome," Stark said.

"If by awesome you mean dungeon-like and creepy," I said.

"But dry and underground," Stark said. "Hey, there're actually some electric outlets down here. Put up room dividers, bring down sleeping bags, beanbag chairs, and a few TVs with DVD players, and it'll be better than camping."

"That's not saying much. Almost anything is better than camping," I said.

"Getting toasted by the sun is not better than camping," Darius said.

"Gotta agree with you there," Stark said.

"Hey, are these actually real?" I asked, mesmerized by the hilt of one of the swords, which was jewel- or glass-encrusted and glittering.

"Be assured, Priestess," Darius said. "All of the stones are real."

"Holy crap!" I said. "They're beautiful and they have to be worth a fortune. Why did Dragon keep them down here? Shouldn't they be on display somewhere or locked in a vault or something?"

"I remember hearing Dragon comment that he didn't believe in displaying all of our riches for everyone to see," Darius said.

"Doesn't sound like Neferet, though. She was all about displaying riches, and Neferet was his High Priestess," Stark said.

"I am not certain if Neferet knew about this stash of weapons. It was something Dragon controlled. I do not ever remember Neferet coming here or speaking of any of the ancient swords or shields." Darius spoke slowly, as if reasoning aloud. "She took little interest in any weapon but that of her own power."

"You mean you don't think she knows about this place at all?" I said.

"She may not," Darius agreed.

"That would be really good for us," Stark said. "Not only does it mean she wouldn't know about the basement, but like Zoey said, there's a fortune in jewels and gold hanging on these walls."

"But every House of Night is independently wealthy," Darius said. "Why would we need a hidden fortune in jewels and gold?"

"Each *House of Night* is rich," I said. "But we've already begun breaking from the school by moving off campus. What if the issues between humans and vamps get worse because of the mayor's death? Does either of you guys know if the cops could have our accounts frozen?"

Darius shook his head. "I do not know."

"I have no clue, either. I still have the same debit card I used when I was at the House of Night in Chicago," Stark said. "I never even think about it."

"We need to think about it," I said. "We've all been taking for granted the way the House of Night takes care of us."

"I cannot believe the Vampyre High Council would stay silent and leave our school adrift among the human legal system," Darius said.

"But if they do, we're going to need safety and money. There's definitely money hanging on these walls, and there might even be safety down here—*if* Neferet doesn't know about it." I thought for a second and then added, "I'll bet Kalona would know for sure if she does or does not."

"Well, then, let's go ask the winged immortal," Stark said.

"I do not like thinking about breaking totally from the House of Night," Darius said grimly. "But I do agree with your reasoning. Let's talk to Kalona."

The three of us had hurried up from the basement and decided it'd be smart if we nonchalantly meandered from there to the main school building—and *then* made a big circle back to the field house area and Dragon Lankford's old office, which now belonged to Kalona.

"No need to have anyone paying attention to us coming and going from that hallway," Darius said.

"Yeah, and then calling attention to the hallway." I agreed

with him and, with what was probably more enthusiasm than necessary, forced a smile and sent a big wave to Kramisha and Shaylin as they emerged from the cafeteria. "Espionage," I muttered and sighed.

"What about it?" Stark asked.

"I'm crappy at it," I said.

He'd taken my hand and Darius was chuckling softly when we turned to our right to follow the hallway to the front of the school—and the three of us stopped, blinking dots of bright light from our eyes and gawking at the little group in the foyer.

"What's going on? Is that a camera?" Stark asked.

"This is great! There's one of the new red vampyres. Follow me!" A woman carrying a mic gestured to the cameraman and the two guys carrying the lights, and headed in our direction.

The uncomfortably bright lights closed on us, along with the woman, the cameras, and Diana, the very flustered-looking vampyre who usually served as a kind of secretary for the school—and who usually stayed calm and cool about everything.

"*Ohmygod!* I thought I saw the Fox 23 van outside, but I didn't think *you'd* actually be here!" Damien squealed as he burst into the foyer from the hallway that led to the cafeteria. "Chera Kimiko! I can hardly believe it! I am *such* a *huge* fan!"

I squinted against the camera lights. Holy crap! It was the Fox News anchor. My first thought was: *Wow, she's even prettier in person.* My second wasn't so positive: *Wow, there must be some major poo hitting the fan if Fox 23 sent Chera here.*

"Thank you so much! I really appreciate all of my fans," Chera was saying to Damien, who, totally star struck, was still grinning at her.

"Damien, why don't you tell Thanatos there's a reporter here?" I smiled and gave him a little push toward the stairway that led to Thanatos's office.

"Oh, absolutely! I'll be right back!" As Damien hurried past Chera he paused and added, "I really do just love you!"

Chera beamed a beautiful smile at him and opened her arms. "Damien, you are precious. How about a hug?"

"Ohmygod, yes!" Damien's grin lit up his face as he hugged Chera. I heard her whisper, "Adam told me to say hi."

"Oooh! Tell him hi for me right back!" Damien finished squeezing her and then he hurried toward Thanatos's office.

I swear if he'd been a puppy he would have wagged himself to death.

"You're the first red vampyre I've seen in person! Your tattoos are quite beautiful." Chera and the camera were now focused on Stark.

"Yeah, uh, I'm a red vampyre," Stark said, glancing nervously back and forth from the camera to Chera.

"Your name is Stark, right?" Chera asked him.

"Right."

Way conscious of the camera that was blinking the red RECORD light, I'd opened my mouth to try to figure out something to say that didn't end up with me hysterically shrieking, grabbing Stark, and bolting from the room, but Chera was peering up at Stark, smiling, and looking captivated as she studied his Mark. She moved closer to him. Sounding friendly and totally harmless she said, "The pattern is intriguing. It looks like arrows. You're not from Broken Arrow, are you?"

"Uh, no. I'm from Chicago."

"Are the arrows symbolic?"

"Well, yeah, I guess. I'm a pretty good archer," he said.

Chera turned her big brown eyes on me and smiled as if she and I were BFFs. "Your tattoos are amazing, too. And you have them everywhere! I think I see birds and flowers and, wow, even flames and waves within that filigree design. You must be a very special young vampyre."

I opened and closed my mouth. I had no clue what to say. If Chera had been blunt and pushy and reporter-like it would have been easy to do the whole "no comment" thing and walk away, but she seemed genuinely nice and just politely curious. Sounding as nervous as Stark looked, I said, "Well, I'm not really comfortable with the whole *special* label, even though our Goddess Marked me with extra tattoos."

"Oh, I get it." Chera motioned to the cameraman. "Jerry, cut that part." Then she turned her attention back to me. "I apologize. I'm not here to make anyone uncomfortable."

"Why are you here?" I asked.

"To get an inside reaction to the killing of Tulsa's mayor."

"We didn't kill the mayor," I said.

"I didn't mean to accuse you! Any of you! Not at all," Chera assured us, sounding as sincere as she looked.

"Is someone making accusations?" Thanatos hurried up, with Damien following closely behind.

Chera glanced at the cameraman. "Jerry, stop recording, please." She held her hand out to Thanatos. "High Priestess, I am Chera Kimiko, Fox 23 News."

Thanatos took her hand. "I am Thanatos, this House of Night's High Priestess. And I recognize you, Miss Kimiko."

"Please, call me Chera. I'm not here to accuse anyone of anything. I'm only trying to show the *whole* story, the *real* story behind Charles LaFont's death." She held out her hand to one of the guys with the lights. "Andy, let me see my iPad." The guy handed it to her—she tapped the screen and then held it up so that we could see Aphrodite's mom being interviewed by a concerned-looking man in a suit that didn't fit very well.

"Mrs. LaFont, please accept our condolences on the death of your husband, our beloved mayor," said the reporter.

"I do appreciate the sentiment, but I will not be consoled until my husband's vampyre murderer is brought to justice."

Diana and I sucked air. Thanatos seemed to turn to stone. Darius and Stark looked like they might explode. But Aphrodite's mom, Mrs. Charles LaFont, looked beautiful and devastated and mesmerizingly passionate in her sleek black dress and her pearls. She dabbed a lace handkerchief at the corners of her tear-filled blue eyes before she continued.

"So, you are sure your husband was killed by a vampyre?" the reporter prompted.

"Absolutely sure. I was there. I found his brutalized, blood-drained body." Mrs. LaFont looked from the reporter straight into the camera. "Something has to be done about the House of Night."

The interview broke for a commercial and Chera tapped the screen off.

"The only side that is being heard is that of Mrs. LaFont, and while I sympathize with her loss, I am a journalist, and I believe in telling the *whole* story."

"Miss Kimiko, there is no drama and intrigue and the story of a murderer being hidden here. There are only students and professors, and a school day that has been disrupted because of the tragic events of last night."

"Please, Thanatos, don't see me as an enemy. Allow me to tell the rest of the story and film some of your students just going about normal activities. Allow me to show Tulsa who you really are. I have always believed that fear and hatred are fueled by ignorance," Chera said earnestly, meeting Thanatos's gaze without wavering. "If our city has nothing to fear from your House of Night, allow my camera to show that. Let it educate Tulsa."

"Chera, it does seem that your intentions are good, but as I already said, our students are not going on with normal activities today."

"Excuse me, Thanatos." Damien held up his hand.

"Yes, Damien. What is it?"

"Most of the fledglings are still having breakfast in the cafeteria. That's a normal school activity."

"I would love to film your students there!" Chera said.

"Very well. Damien, you may escort Miss Kimiko to the cafeteria. I will join you, but will remain in the background so that she may film an authentic cafeteria experience."

"Ooooh! This will be fantastic!" Damien gushed.

"That is exactly what I think, too." Chera smiled at him.

"Miss Kimiko," Thanatos said. "We will only film in the cafeteria. That is as much outside interference as my school can tolerate today."

"I understand and appreciate even this small opportunity," Chera said.

"Then Damien shall lead the way to our cafeteria," Thanatos said. "Zoey, Stark, Darius, as you were."

Relieved to have the focus shifted away from us, I nodded at Thanatos and the three of us scurried out the door, though I felt Chera's curious gaze follow us.

"Do you think any publicity is good publicity?" Darius asked.

"No!" Stark and I said together.

Kalona

The winged immortal hated that the human had been killed. Not that he minded that the man had lost his life. From the information Kalona gleaned from the others, the mayor had been a weak, simpering, useless human being. Kalona only minded that it had happened while he was Warrior to the High Priestess of Death, and the human had been killed on his watch.

Kalona also hated that Neferet had so obviously been the murderer. With a grunt of irritation, Kalona leaned back in the roomy leather chair and threw a dagger into the chipped target that was mounted on the wall across from Dragon Lankford's desk. It struck true in the center of the blood-colored bull's-eye.

"I should have been more vigilant. I should have known the Tsi Sgili would find a way to regain her corporeal form and return to begin her revenge." As he spoke he threw another knife. It stuck and held beside the first. "But instead of protecting, I was *hiding*"—he said the word as if it had a foul taste—"lest the local humans be shocked at the sight of me." His laughter lacked humor. "No, instead of me shocking them, they were treated to two deaths." Kalona reached for another dagger, and his hand brushed the delicate blown glass sunflower held within a crystal vase on which was etched a likeness of Nyx, arms raised cupping a crescent moon. The movement caused the vase to rock, so that it lost balance, toppled, and fell toward the stone floor.

A ball of light, bright as the rising sun, exploded within the office. Time was suspended. The vase and flower paused in their fall, hovering just above the unforgiving stone floor.

A hand, tanned to burnished gold, reached from the ball of light, and plucked from the air first the flower, and then the Goddess-etched vase, setting them to right on the desk.

"Brother, you need a job," Kalona said sarcastically.

"I have one," Erebus said, stepping from the ball of light. He sat, slouching irreverently on the edge of Dragon Lankford's wide wooden desk. "I protect that which is exquisite and beautiful." He gestured to the crystal vase.

Kalona snorted. "Are you comparing Nyx to a vase? I'm not entirely sure the Goddess would appreciate the comparison."

"And yet it is a valid one," Erebus said. "The vase is exquisite and beautiful, and you treated it carelessly. Had I not interceded, it would have been broken."

"It was I and not Nyx who was broken."

"I stand corrected. Comparing the Goddess to a vase is foolish. Nyx could never be so easily broken, especially as she will eternally have me as her protector," Erebus said.

"You? The protector of a goddess?" Kalona's humorless laughter filled the room with the coldness of winter moonlight, causing some of Erebus's summer brilliance to mute. "Brother, you will always only be one thing, but that is not a Warrior. I was the only one of us who could fulfill more than one duty for the Goddess."

"Love is not a duty," Erebus said.

"Isn't it? I wouldn't think I knew more of love than you, but I do know that sometimes it is a duty to keep love alive, and not to allow its light to dim."

"Little wonder you could not keep her," Erebus said. "Loving a goddess should never be a duty, no matter what rhetoric you attempt to wrap that word in."

"It was *you* who couldn't keep her. Had you satisfied Nyx so fully, why did she turn to me?" Kalona smiled at his brother.

Erebus's light darkened more. "Yet now her image in glass is as close to Nyx as you can get."

"But you will not leave me in peace. Why is that, brother? Are you afraid she will turn to me again?"

Erebus slammed his hand down on the desk, burning his palm print into the wood. Kalona did not flinch, nor did he look away from his brother, though the sight of him blazing with his father's light burned Kalona's moonlit eyes.

"I am here only because you have again made a terrible mistake."

Kalona leaned back and crossed his arms over his chest. "I don't deny that I have made a long list of mistakes. Unlike you, I never claim perfection. Which, in that long list, would you like to discuss?"

"Your mistakes are, indeed, vast. Your list of wrongs against mankind as well as vampyres and the Goddess is long. But I have neither the time nor the inclination to recount them all. It is your latest mistake of which I must speak. You allowed a troubled High Priestess of Nyx to turn to Darkness and become a tool of evil. That damaged Priestess has become immortal and unspeakably dangerous."

"Neferet was intrigued by Darkness long before she knew aught of me."

"Neferet was a broken girl who became a broken fledgling. Your whispers were responsible for drawing her to this land and feeding her need for control and power, and eventually encouraging her path to immortality and her descent into madness."

"You're wrong. You know nothing of Neferet. The Priestess was broken and mad before she began listening to my whispers."

"I know that Neferet has caused the Goddess much pain, and that means she must be stopped," Erebus said.

Kalona laughed again. "And now you prove beyond any doubt you know nothing about Neferet. She has chosen the path of chaos. Not even death can dissuade her from it."

"And yet you will dissuade her."

"You fool—a week ago the Vessel Aurox, fully in the magickal form of a beast, gored Neferet and hurled her from the balcony of a building as high as a mountaintop. Last night Neferet regained enough of her physical form to manifest on this campus, cause a fledgling to reject the Change, and kill an adult human. Then she disappeared again. She is immortal. She cannot be killed," Kalona said.

"And yet something must be done with her. You opened the door to immortal power to her—you will close it."

Kalona shook his head, gathering the cold light of the moon close to him. "Who are you to command me? You are my brother, not my Goddess."

"I speak for your Goddess!" Erebus's light flared, burning so brightly that even Kalona could not help but recognize the divine and borrowed power of Nyx he wielded. "When first you Fell from the Otherworld you wreaked havoc upon the humans who attempted to succor you until Nyx heard their cries and answered the prayers of their Wise Women, calling together and allowing them to use the Divine Feminine within them. Thus was fashioned A-ya, she who entrapped you for generations."

"I remember well what happened," Kalona snarled. "I do not need you, or Nyx, to remind me of that dark time."

"Silence, you fool! I come with an edict from Nyx!" Erebus blazed. "I do not remind you of the time. I remind you of the reason behind it. You rejected your Goddess, and in your attempt to replace her you used and cast aside many women, until A-ya was created. Then you recognized the spark of Nyx within her. That is why you were vulnerable to her. That is why you loved her."

Kalona looked away from Erebus. There had been a time, in the not so distant past, when he would have arrogantly denied his brother's words and used his own immortal power to cast him from the mortal plane and back to the Otherworld.

But Kalona had changed. And the truth in what his brother said burned him more than did the harsh light Erebus had inherited from his father, the sun.

So the winged immortal remained silent, still as a statue, as Erebus's Goddess-touched words continued to batter him.

"But you would not remain imprisoned. Even entombed in the

earth, wrapped in the arms of she who was breathed to life by Nyx, still you yearned for that which your arrogance had caused you to lose. So you sent out your cloying whispers, seeking another who had been touched by Nyx—one who might fill the emptiness within you. Since the moment she was Marked, Neferet was special to the Goddess, because of, and not in spite of, the horrors she had survived. But she was, indeed, a vulnerable young fledgling. That is why Neferet was susceptible to your call. That is why, after she completed the Change, you convinced her to free you."

Kalona wanted to flee—to run from his brother's hurtful words, but something within him bade him stay and hear the edict Nyx had sent Erebus to proclaim.

"And because she, too, was only touched by the Goddess and not Nyx incarnate, Neferet failed to fill that emptiness within you. Her failure turned to poison. Do you deny that you thought you loved her, just as you believed you loved the maiden, A-ya?"

"I deny nothing, just as I acknowledge nothing. Speak your edict and begone. Your words weary me."

"Look within yourself. It is not my words that weary you. The day you can admit the truth about your past and accept full responsibility for all the evil you have loosed in this realm, is the day your load will begin to lighten." The anger in Erebus's voice softened, though the power of his Goddess-enhanced visage continued to blaze. "Then you met the fledgling, Zoey Redbird, and you were instantly drawn to, and angered by, her connection to Nyx. You wanted to seduce *and* destroy her."

"But I did neither!"

"Only because Zoey's connection to Nyx is, indeed, strong, and unlike A-ya, she is a woman, fully formed with a will of her own and, unlike Neferet, she is not damaged. Zoey Redbird's heart is loyal and true. Though your actions almost destroyed her. Do not forget you shattered the child's soul. Do not forget you trespassed into the Otherworld, risking Nyx's wrath. Because of that the Goddess herself interceded on her daughter's behalf."

Kalona looked away again, remembering that brief, bittersweet moment when he, once again, had been in the presence of Nyx.

She had not forgiven him, and Kalona had wept tears of bitterness and regret.

"Neferet trapped my soul and used the power of Darkness to command me to do her bidding. I did not willingly trespass."

"Neferet again. Your influence created that creature. She is your responsibility to stop. The Goddess's edict is thus!" Erebus made a sweeping gesture. The yellow light of the sun shimmered, and became blazing written words burned into the air:

> He who was once beloved of mine
> shall defeat she whose love for me once did shine.
> With this command I do intercede.
> Death's Warrior must protect those who are in need.
> If his heart doth open, bared again
> forgiveness may conquer hate and love win . . . win . . .

Erebus pressed his palms against the wooden desk and leaned forward so that his face and his brother's were mere inches apart. Kalona could feel the heat coming from his sunlit body and smell a summer day on his breath as he spoke.

"I would say that I hope you fail, but I need not waste my hope. An immortal cannot be defeated without a sacrifice that is equal or greater than immortality. You are capable of great anger, great violence, great battles. You have never been capable of great sacrifice. You will fail. Nyx will continue to feel the pain your mistakes have caused, *and I will continue to console her.*"

Kalona's anger finally proved too much for him to contain. With a roar he stood, knocking over his chair and bringing his hands together in a mighty clap that released a frozen blast of moonlight from between his palms. The cold, silver light extinguished Erebus's ball of sunlight. With a hiss like a sword meeting a blacksmith's forging waters, Erebus disappeared.

There was a knock on the door, and Darius's voice carried easily through the sudden silence. "Kalona? May we have a word with you?"

CHAPTER SIX

Kalona

Kalona righted the chair he had knocked over, sat, smoothed back his hair, and drew a deep breath before saying, "You may enter."

When he saw that Zoey and Stark followed Darius into the room he had to stifle a groan of irritation. Though it seemed he and Zoey had come to a truce, things were not simple between the two of them. Stark, of course, had long been an annoyance. Kalona supposed it didn't help the boy's attitude that he had skewered and killed him in the Otherworld.

"Wow," Zoey said, looking from Kalona to the glass sunflower and vase, and then to the huge tapestry that took up the entire wall behind him, which depicted a black ship with the prow of a roaring dragon. "It's super weird to see all of Dragon's stuff here, and you there." She pointed at Kalona, sitting behind the Sword Master's desk.

"It is disconcerting," Darius said softly, as if he hadn't wanted to comment, but couldn't stop himself from speaking.

"More like disturbing," Stark said. His voice was cocky, like he enjoyed baiting the immortal.

It is the sliver of immortality he shares with me that makes him so bold, and so annoying, Kalona thought. *I wonder how bold the boy would be if he knew that sliver is also a conduit I can follow to his soul?*

Kalona acted as if none of them had spoken, but made a mental note to get rid of the old Sword Master's belongings. It was past time to make room for the new.

"You said you wished a word with me, Darius?"

"I do. *We* do," Darius corrected.

"Do you know if the school has a basement?" Stark asked.

Kalona shook his head. "I have never seen it, but the House of Night is an old building and I suppose it would be logical if it did exist."

"So you and Neferet have never been down there?" Zoey asked.

He met her gaze, looking for an ancient maiden deep within her dark eyes. "Being beneath the earth has proven to be a complicated experience for me, and one I *usually* have no desire to repeat." Purposefully, Kalona made his voice teasing, deep, knowing.

"You're missing the point of the question." Stark took a protective step forward so that he was positioned between Kalona and Zoey.

Kalona's smile mocked the boy. "Perhaps you are missing the point of my answer."

"Yeah? I don't think so. I think your answers are fucked up most of the time," Stark said.

"Then stop asking for them."

As Stark moved forward, reaching for the bow he habitually carried slung across his back, Zoey grabbed his wrist, pulling him back.

"This is *not* helping," she said.

"He started it!" Stark shouted.

"He's doing it on purpose because he knows he'll get a reaction from you," Zoey told him. Then she frowned at Kalona. "Stop it.

Now. We need to talk to our school's Warrior, not a smartass with wings."

"Then first you should have muzzled your pet," Kalona said placidly.

"No, *first* I should have told you there is a Tulsa news crew in the cafeteria filming fledglings being normal kids instead of bloodsucking demons, so we don't have time to screw around with egos, which means I shouldn't have to remind you that you are oath bound to protect our school as long as Death is our High Priestess—*Thanatos is still our High Priestess; therefore you owe us your oath!*" Zoey's voice went from sounding like an irritated girl to being so filled with the power of spirit that the hairs on Kalona's forearms lifted and his skin shivered in automatic response. *"I'm here asking you a question that has to do with our safety. You will answer me and stop these stupid games."*

Kalona was careful to hide his smile. *This* was the Zoey he most enjoyed. *This* was a young, strong High Priestess who was truly fit to wield the power of Nyx.

Kalona fisted his hand over his heart and began to tilt his head in a formal bow, showing the proper respect of a Warrior to a High Priestess. He opened his mouth to speak when a sweet, achingly familiar voice whispered through his mind.

You would do well to remember she is not me . . .

Kalona's body jolted as if he'd been touched by a burning brand. He shot to his feet. There he paused, heart pumping, not knowing whether to cry out for joy or fall to his knees and weep. *Nyx had spoken to him!*

"Kalona? What's going on?"

The immortal blinked his vision clear to see the three young people staring at him. The males were watching him suspiciously, both having stepped before the Priestess. Zoey was studying him with an expression that almost appeared concerned.

He drew a deep breath. Fisted his hand and, again, bowed formally to her, and then forced his legs to relax and his body to sit. "Your words have shamed me, Priestess. I acknowledge my responsibility for the protection of this school. Please, sit." His hand shook when he motioned to the chairs that faced the desk. "Ask what you will of me."

"Okaaaay." Zoey dragged the word out, clearly not believing his attempt to cover the feelings that raged through him, but she and the young men sat, though they continued to watch him warily. "Here's the deal," she said, sounding like an ordinary girl again. "We're asking you about the basement of the school because we need to know if Neferet knows about it."

Kalona focused his chaotic thoughts on her question. "Neferet never mentioned a basement to me."

"Which doesn't necessarily mean she didn't know there was one," Zoey said.

"Actually, it does mean that," Kalona said. "As you are aware, I have an aversion to being under the earth."

"So? You two were lovers. Why would she tell her claustrophobic lover about a basement?" Stark said.

"He's more than claustrophobic," Zoey said. "His powers are different if he's under the earth. It's like the ground drains him. That's how Neferet forced him to go after me in the Otherworld. She kept him trapped underground. Right?" she asked Kalona.

"Correct. Darkness obeys Neferet. She used it to force my spirit to the Otherworld while I was too weak to fight her."

"Hey, let's be real clear here—Neferet might have trapped you and forced you to the Otherworld, but you didn't have to attack Zoey or me when you got there. That was your choice."

"You are correct as well. Though you should know that had I not done her bidding, Neferet would have kept my spirit from my body indefinitely."

"You're immortal. Unlike Zoey, that wouldn't have killed you," Stark said.

"No, it would not have killed me. It would have driven me mad." Kalona met Zoey's gaze. "I think you can imagine it. Your spirit has been shattered from your body. You know what was happening to your sanity."

The young Priestess's face paled. "Yeah, I know. It was bad. Really bad."

"Which doesn't make what he did any better," Stark said.

"It does make it understandable," Darius said. "Stark, I hear what you are saying. You want us to remember Kalona's past, but he has taken an oath that has allied him with us. We also must remember that."

"Darkness no longer does my bidding," Kalona said. "If nothing else proves to you that my allegiance lies far from Darkness, that should."

"See, you say your allegiance lies far from Darkness instead of saying that your allegiance lies with us, or even with Nyx. I gotta be honest—that bothers me," Stark said.

"Stark's right. That bothers me, too," Zoey said. "I'm not sure any fledgling at the House of Night could get Darkness to do his or her bidding, but that doesn't mean they're all on our side. Actually, we know a bunch of the red fledglings aren't."

Kalona inhaled deeply, and then, surprising himself as much as he did them, told Zoey and Stark and Darius the truth. "I have chosen the Goddess, but Nyx still turns from me. I cannot even enter her temple. She has not forgiven me." He shook his head, staring at her image etched in the crystal vase. "I do not blame her. I do not deserve her forgiveness. But that does not alter the choice I have made. I have decided to serve the Goddess again, even if it is at a distance, though it is difficult for me to speak of it." He looked up from the vase and met Stark's gaze. "You are

Zoey's Warrior. Imagine losing her. Then imagine that loss lasting eons. *Then* you might begin to know the burden I carry."

Zoey's voice broke the silence. "So, you really believe Neferet doesn't know about the basement?"

"Had Neferet known there was a basement here, she would have used it to make me more malleable, especially after I refused to call myself Erebus Incarnate."

"Since you mentioned it, why did you refuse to do that? I saw the stained glass windows in the temple on San Clemente Island, and the guy with the wings definitely looked like you. Some of the High Council were already on Neferet's side that day, most of them would've probably believed you if you'd claimed to be him," Stark said.

Kalona's snort of laughter was filled with contempt. "Because, young Warrior, Erebus is my brother and I loathe him too much to pretend to be him."

Zoey

"Your brother? Erebus? The Consort of Nyx is your *brother*?" He seriously couldn't have really meant that.

"We are twins. Not identical, but close enough. Born on the same day. I am the elder." Kalona seemed to be trying to sound nonchalant, but his fingers drumming against the desktop and his gaze looking everywhere but at me said something else besides "whatever."

"Why didn't you tell us you're Erebus's brother?" I asked.

He did look at me then. "Do you have a brother?"

"Yeah," I said.

"Yet I have never heard you speak of him."

"Her brother isn't our Goddess's lover," Stark said.

"Wait, if you're Erebus's brother, why don't we know about you? I mean, I'm not super studious, especially about creation myths and whatnot, but I should have heard *something* about Erebus having a brother." I looked to Darius and Stark for help. "Do you guys know anything about this?"

Both shook their heads and looked suspiciously at Kalona. The immortal sighed.

"Erebus is not overly fond of me, either. And, as I have already said, Nyx has turned from me. The ballads in which I was mentioned have long ago stopped being sung. Ask your studious friend Damien. He may have read rumors of me. I would have been called the Guardian of Night. Or ask Thanatos. She must know the old myths." Kalona shrugged and his raven-colored wings rustled. "That matters little today. So, what is it you want with the school's basement?"

I wanted to know more about Kalona and Erebus being brothers (OMG!), but the immortal was definitely done talking about it, so I let it go—for now. "Well, it looks like we might have to stay on campus for a few days or so, and the red fledglings rest better underground," I said. "Darius showed us where the basement is, and we're thinking about moving the kids down there."

"But we would all feel safer about the fledglings being together in one room if we knew whether Neferet knows about the basement or not," Darius said. "That is why we came to you."

"Neferet doesn't know, or she didn't when I was her Consort. I understand how dangerous she is, and why you want a safe haven for the fledglings, but I am more concerned about the dangerous factions developing within the House of Night today than Neferet's reappearance. Dallas reeks of treachery. He already hates Stevie Rae and my son. He must have encouraged Erin to break with your group. Now Erin is dead after circling with you. Dallas will conspire against you, which means he will be open to allying with Neferet, if he hasn't already done so. Your basement will not long remain a secret, especially if there are local reporters roaming the school grounds."

"They are not roaming free," Darius said quickly. "Thanatos escorts and observes them. They have been confined to the cafeteria."

"And my guess is they won't be here very long," I said.

"Long enough to combat Aphrodite's mom's hateful interview on that other channel," Stark said.

"Communication is too easy in the modern world. It is a curse as well as a convenience," Kalona said.

"I could ask Thanatos to confiscate Dallas's cell phone," I said, trying to think of something—anything—to help keep our business private.

"He'd just use someone else's, even if he had to steal one," Stark said. "And don't forget—the kid's affinity is with electronics. If he wants to communicate with Neferet, he will."

"Let us hope he and his allies are not currently in the cafeteria," Kalona said.

"Jeesh, it's such a pain in the ass to have to worry about being betrayed by one of our own." I was frustrated as hell. "I wish I could make everyone just act right!"

"This from the same young High Priestess who lectured me more than once about the importance of free choice?" Kalona's raised brows and knowing look mocked me.

"I didn't mean I wanted to take away people's free choice," I said.

"No, not as long as their choice allies with yours," Kalona said.

"That's not what she meant." Stark frowned at Kalona. "You just don't get her."

Kalona said nothing, but his eyes remained mocking ... knowing ...

Did I really want to take away free choice? No! I just wished kids would make the right choice. Jeesh, that was way different. God, this whole thing was giving me major heartburn. I'd probably have IBS any second . . .

"Huh?" I'd totally missed what Stark had been saying.

"Z, I said that Darius and I would go gather up that old stuff that we found in the basement and get it out of the way so the kids could start moving sleeping bags and TVs and things down there."

"Oh, uh, the *stuff.*" I stared at Stark. "What are you going to do with it?"

"I thought we'd box it up and ask Lenobia if she could find a place for it in one of the new storerooms she had built in the stables after the fire. Should be safe and out of the way there."

"Why not pile it up and have Shaunee set it afire?" Kalona said.

"Because we can't burn books!" I made up in a rush.

"Books?" Kalona looked super confused.

"Yeah, the old stuff is mostly books. You know, things that were probably moved out of the media center when they added the computers." I hoped I didn't sound as lame as I felt. I am absolutely a crappy liar—I'm especially a crappy unpremeditated liar.

"Well, as you say. I'll help you in gathering—"

"No!" Stark, Darius, and I said together.

Kalona's keen gaze said he thought we were up to something. I knew that even though the immortal was oath bound to be on our side, that didn't mean we wanted him to know the old stuff in the basement was worth a small, or large, fortune.

"Okay, well, here's the thing," I said, trying to start with enough of the truth that I could tell myself that I was just exaggerating a story and not actually doing a really bad job of lying. "You've got to stay here and out of sight until we let you know that the report-ers have totally left the school."

"Yea," Stark said with a smirk. "Wings are kinda noticeable to reporters."

I hurried on before Kalona and Stark could bicker. Again. "I'll tell Damien to come tell you when the reporters are gone. But then we don't need you to help us box stuff up from downstairs. See, we've already, um, talked about the Dallas issue, and we know he's trouble. So, we were hoping that you could figure out something that would keep him occupied while we clean out the basement and get the red fledglings who don't hate us settled in down there."

"Do you really expect to keep Dallas and his group from find-ing out that your fledglings have made the basement their home?"

"No, not forever," Stark said. "But it would be nice if at least the first time they slept down there we could be sure nothing would try to eat them or trap them or light them on fire or—"

"Holy crap, enough already, Stark!" He was making my head hurt. "What Stark means is that, hopefully, we're going to be able to go back to the depot soon, so if Dallas and his group could just be kinda distracted, and if our fledglings just didn't mention that they were sleeping in the basement, well, then maybe we'd have a safe spot here at the House of Night Neferet doesn't know about."

"It is always wise to have a safe place to rest," Darius added.

"So, like I said before, can you think of anything you could do to help us keep Dallas distracted and not nosing around while we get the basement cleared out and our kids moved down there?" I finished, deciding that all three of us were pretty crappy liars.

"There is the fledgling's funeral," Kalona said. "Though she used to be one of your group, everyone is aware that recently she changed her allegiance to Dallas. Would it not be a kind thing for you to ask that Dallas tend to the building and even, perhaps, the lighting of her pyre? That should keep him pre-occupied, and he would, naturally, ask his group to assist him."

"That's actually an awesome idea," I said. "It'll definitely keep Dallas and his buddies busy, and it's honestly a nice thing for us to step aside and let him publicly light her pyre and say good-bye. It'll show that we believed he really cared about her."

"If he'll do it," Stark said. "You heard him yesterday. He said he'd tell Erin good-bye in his own way, and that meant he didn't want anything to do with us."

"Which is the reason I should approach him instead of Zoey," Kalona said. "I will tell him that Zoey has declined Thanatos's invitation to conduct Erin's funeral and so the job has been left to me."

"That'll piss him off," Stark said.

"That is my intention," Kalona said. "He can direct his anger at me as I supervise the building of the fledgling's pyre." The immortal's lips turned up in a wicked smile. "I do like a good pyre. Such a shame humans ended that tradition. I can't imagine even enjoying a modern human funeral. It's sad, really."

"Kalona, it's a problem when what you say reminds me of Neferet," I said.

Kalona's smile widened, and I thought he looked like a little boy, as in the kind of little boy who would set fire to his family in the middle of the night and then say his sister's Barbie made him do it.

"Z, don't overthink it. Kalona will keep Dallas busy, and that's all we're worried about right now," Stark said.

"Except for the reporters and the police and—"

"Stark is correct," Darius interrupted me. "You overthink."

Reluctantly, I stood. "All right. I'll focus on the here and now. I'll tell Thanatos what's up as soon as the reporters are gone, and also clue in Stevie Rae. She can have the kids pack up their stuff and lay low until the basement's ready for them. Then they can come in the back way and avoid the middle of the campus grounds where Dallas and his friends should be busy building the funeral pyre."

"It will be done as you say, Priestess. Will you be moving to the basement as well?"

"No," Stark answered for me, which was super annoying.

"I'm going to stay in my old room with Stark," I continued, because I actually *can* speak for myself. "Stevie Rae and Rephaim will probably stay in the dorm, too."

Kalona nodded thoughtfully. "My son needs a place from which he can come and go easily."

"Yeah, and we decided it's not a good idea for all of us to stay in one room together," Stark said. "Especially when that one room is a basement with only one way in and out of it."

"I agree," Kalona said, standing. His hand resting on the desk drew my eye down and I noticed something weird about the wood. I kept looking and realized what I was seeing.

"Is that a handprint?"

"Is it?" Kalona replied to me. "I hadn't noticed."

My eyes met his and I realized I might not be the only bad liar in the room.

CHAPTER SEVEN

Zoey

I'd been right about one thing—Thanatos had made sure Chera and her crew interviewed a few kids, got some shots of our cafeteria—and then she'd had Damien explain (on camera) his class schedule as the Fox News team was quickly and politely herded off campus. It'd all happened in less than thirty minutes and Thanatos said our segment would air on the evening news as well as the Internet. I'd told her that it had been genius to have Damien be our school spokesman, then I caught her up on our Plan.

"And Kalona said he doesn't think Neferet knows anything about the basement, so we decided to have him keep Dallas and his group distracted while we get the place cleaned out and get our kids moved there. Hopefully, they'll have a day or two of peace, and then we'll get to go back to the depot," I finished explaining to Thanatos. "Oh, and if we're here for much more than that, someone needs to go get our cats and Duchess. They have auto feeders and water, but they'll be lonely and their litter boxes will be disgusting."

The dark-eyed High Priestess had mostly been silent while I'd done a lot of talking. I told her that the basement had been used for storing old weapons and media center stuff, and that Darius and Stark were moving all of it to one of Lenobia's tack rooms. I hadn't told her that the weapons were covered with jewels and super old, and worth, like, a gazillion dollars. And there really wasn't any media center stuff down there at all. It wasn't that I didn't trust Thanatos, but I'd decided the fewer people knew about the fortune, the better. Stark and Darius had agreed. Actually, the more I thought about it, the more I believed that Dragon could have been keeping the weapon stash a secret for a very long time, and Dragon had been one of the most loyal Warriors I'd ever known. Clearly, there was a reason he'd kept that to himself, and I'd bet it wasn't a selfish reason.

So I left the weapon/jewel/fortune detail out of my commentary.

"I am in absolute agreement with you regarding the cats—and Duchess. I will be sure they are transported here, if it comes to that. But how will Kalona distract Dallas?" Thanatos asked.

"He's going to tell Dallas that I said I didn't want to lead Erin's funeral—that I didn't even want to build the pyre. Then he's going to say you left the job to him."

Thanatos's brow lifted. "In other words, Kalona is going to bait Dallas into building the pyre."

"Yep, and hopefully leading Erin's funeral, too. After everything that happened with her I decided that it really would be best for my circle, especially Shaunee, not to get involved." I paused and added, "I hope all that's okay with you."

"When a fledgling rejects the Change and dies, it is always difficult for those left behind. In this case there were complex events surrounding this child's death. I'm going to trust your instincts, Zoey. Erin was part of your circle—you have been acting as her High Priestess. It is your right to choose her funeral arrangements."

"Thank you," I said.

"I do believe it is wise that you allow Shaunee to invoke her element during the lighting of the pyre, though. It will help what must follow to be completed more quickly. It will also help Shaunee to bid her friend a final farewell."

"Okay, yes. I'll talk to Shaunee."

"I believe you should talk with your Prophetess as well."

"Aphrodite?" Thanatos's request surprised me. "You mean about her dad?"

"Yes. Judge her mental health carefully."

"Huh? I don't think I'm qualified to judge Aphrodite's mental health." Not to mention that she might cut my heart out and eat it if I tried.

"You're her High Priestess and, if my guess is correct, her closest friend. Being Prophetess to a goddess is never an easy gift to bear, and Aphrodite lost father and mother in one night—violently and publicly."

"I already checked on her today. Darius said she was finally sleeping, so I didn't wake her up."

"Wake her. If she won't admit to needing her High Priestess, she may admit to needing her friend," Thanatos said.

"I'll do my best."

"I must also warn you to expect unrest at the school. I can feel Darkness building, and it feeds on anger and pain, fear and frustration, intensifying them, preying on their hosts, gaining power from them. Watch your circle and those who are most gifted by the Goddess carefully. Where there is great power, there also is Darkness drawn."

"At least two of my circle have just gone through big losses," I worried aloud. "And, really, Erin's death affected all of us. Now we're stuck here with kids who are also upset and pissed off.

Can't you do something to get us out of here?" I was having a hard time controlling my own frustration—I had no clue how I was going to help my friends deal with their issues.

"Zoey, I met with Detective Marx before the Fox News crew arrived. Actually, Chera Kimiko's presence here is indicative of the fact that this situation is not going to be resolved quickly."

"Didn't Detective Marx find *anything* that would prove Neferet killed the major?"

"He mentioned DNA evidence and is requesting that comparative testing begin on all our professors to rule out a match," Thanatos said grimly.

"But that's good! None of our professors killed the mayor," I said.

"Zoey, if I allow the human authorities to begin testing my professors I will be allowing them to cross a boundary that has successfully and safely separated human and vampyre codes of justice for more than five hundred years."

I shook my head. "No, I still don't see why that's bad. At least not this time."

"This time it is not bad. What about the next time a local murders a human and then stages it to look like a vampyre killing—and perhaps even has a strand or two of hair from one of our High Priestesses to leave at the crime scene. If I allow a nick in the wall that protects our kind against human persecution, how long will it be before that wall crumbles completely and The Burning Times begin again?"

I shivered. "What are you going to do? We can't just stay locked up here forever."

"I have sent a request to the High Council for a hearing this very night."

"You're going to ask them to step in with the humans?" Just the thought of it gave me a rush of hope.

"I am, and I need you here to serve as witness to Neferet's manifestation."

"Okay, sure. I'll do whatever I can," I said.

"It is now nine o'clock. I've scheduled the Skype conference with the High Council for ten o'clock, so that we will still have time this night to light Erin's pyre at midnight. Please rejoin me in one hour."

"Should I bring Stevie Rae or Aphrodite?"

"Use your own discretion, Priestess, and I will respect your decision."

I fisted my hand over my heart and bowed to her, wishing I had as much respect for my decision-making abilities as Thanatos did.

Aphrodite

"Chera's actually prettier in person?" Aphrodite frowned at Darius. He sat on the side of the bed while she sipped the iced coffee he'd brought her and caught her up on the latest disasters of the day. "Like that was a detail I needed you to report?"

"No one's beauty shines like yours," he said, smiling.

"Just tell me what kind of purse she was carrying. One of those new blue Coaches or a sparkly Valentino?"

A deep line formed between Darius's eyes. "It was made of leather."

"Color?"

"White?"

Aphrodite sighed. "No way Chera would be carrying a white purse in February. You have no clue what it looked like, do you?"

"None whatsoever, but you asking about it tells me that you are, indeed, feeling better, my beauty."

"I suppose I can't expect you to be completely perfect, but next time consider her purse a weapon. That way you'll remember to check it out. And, yes, I'm feeling better. My eyes have finally cleared, and knowing that no one expects me to sleep in a nasty basement, along with the fact that this coffee is filled with half and half and real sugar, has combined to make my headache go away." Aphrodite took another sip and sighed with pleasure. "It tastes too good to be bad."

"If it makes you feel better, that is all that counts."

"If my butt gets so big it has its own zip code, you'll take that back," she said.

Darius smiled. "You do feel better."

"Yeah, but the vision sucked. Big time."

"Are you ready to talk about it?"

"Not really."

Darius looked away uncomfortably, and Aphrodite stroked his strong arm and laced her fingers with his. "Hey, it's not because I don't want to talk to you. It's because I need to process what I saw and figure out what the hell to do about it."

"Should I get Zoey?"

"No!" she said, and then realized she'd almost shrieked the word. "No," Aphrodite repeated in a normal voice. "I don't want *anyone* to know that I had a vision yet. Darius, I just need some time to think."

"But is it wise to keep a vision to yourself?"

"Right now my gut is telling me that it isn't wise to blab what I saw."

Darius leaned forward, kissing her softly. Then he met her gaze and said exactly what she needed to hear. "Trust your instinct, Prophetess. I believe in you and your gift. I want you to know that whatever you tell me I will hold sacred and I vow, as your Warrior and protector, not to tell anyone unless you allow it."

Aphrodite slipped into his arms and felt the terrible tightness in her chest relax. She didn't have to carry the burden of her visions alone. Darius would never betray her.

"I'm so crappy at this love stuff. I'll never be able to tell you how much it means to me that I can trust you."

He stroked her back gently. "You need not tell me. You show me every day we are together."

Aphrodite closed her eyes and gathered strength from his touch and his words, praying silently: *Please, Nyx, let the days we are together turn into months, the months years, and the years decades.*

She hugged him hard, and then leaned back so that she could meet his gaze. Without any preamble she told him, "Darius, I need you to do something for me."

"Anything," he said.

"Watch Zoey."

"Watch her?"

"Yes. Watch her and see if she acts unusually pissed off."

"And if I see her being angry?"

"Come get me and I'll deal with her. Don't get Stark. He can feel her emotions and if she's the level of pissed I think she's going to be, I'm pretty sure he's going to be ready to explode, too. Plus, remember that Aurox slash Heath is stuck inside the House of Night with us. We all saw Heath's reflection. Z's pretty much avoided him since that night, but who he really is has to be affecting her. It's going to come out eventually, and, let's get serious, you know there's no damn way Stark will be cool with sharing Zoey again."

Darius nodded thoughtfully. "You're right about that. I will watch her." He paused and then added, "Your vision was about Zoey."

It wasn't a question, but Aphrodite sipped her iced coffee and then nodded. "Yeah, it was about Zoey and her anger. She was out of control."

"Why do you believe you shouldn't speak to her of this? She knows your visions are valid. Perhaps she would listen to you."

"That's what I'd think, too, but the very first thing I said when I came back from the vision was for you *not* to get Z. Darius, I was speaking from instinct—Goddess-given instinct. Yeah, I could be messed up and misinterpreting it, but that's why I think I shouldn't tell Zoey—or at least not yet."

"As I said, I believe in you. Trust your instinct and your Goddess-given gifts."

"I'm going to, but I'm also going to get some outside help, sadly from an annoying source."

Darius's brows lifted. "I assume you do not mean me."

"No, handsome, I don't mean you. I mean Shaylin."

"You're going to tell her about your vision?"

"No. I'm going to tell her an interpretative exaggeration about my vision."

"In other words, you're going to lie to her."

Aphrodite loved that he'd said it so matter-of-factly, with no judgment, and no lecture.

"Yes, that's exactly what I mean, but calling it an interpretative exaggeration sounds better."

"You're going to have her watch Zoey, too?"

"Yes again."

"Her use of the True Sight gift has, thus far, proven valid," he said.

"Which is the only damn reason I'm going to ask for her help. She irritates the crap out of me."

"And yet you are wise enough not to let that irritation keep you from calling on her gifts." His smile was full of warmth and pride. "You see, my beauty, why I trust you so?"

"I see that you and I haven't had enough quality alone time."

"We are alone now." His smile turned sexy.

"And my headache is definitely gone." She drained the rest of the iced coffee and put the glass on her marble-topped nightstand. Aphrodite draped her arms around his broad shoulders and pulled him down to her. Darius came to her eagerly. His kiss was deep and as she opened her mouth he moaned, and rolled, taking her with him so that she was on top, pressed against him while his hand found the edge of her T-shirt and began moving in hot, insistent strokes against her naked skin.

When the knocking started on the door, Aphrodite whispered against Darius's lips, "Ignore it and it will go away."

The knocking became louder, more insistent.

Aphrodite nibbled on the side of Darius's neck. "Pretend it's reality TV. Ignore it."

"Aphrodite! *Hellllo!*" Zoey's voice carried through the door. "Stark told me Darius was bringing you iced coffee, which means you're in there *and* awake."

Darius reluctantly pulled down her T-shirt. "You do need to talk with her."

Aphrodite kissed him one more time before she stomped to the door, not bothering to fix her hair, her T-shirt, or her annoyed look, and opened it, saying, "Oh, for shit's sake, come in, birth control."

"Huh? Birth control?" Z walked in.

"Never mind. Too late."

"Hi," Zoey said. "You don't look bad."

"I never look bad," Aphrodite told her.

Z rolled her eyes and waved at Darius. "Hey there, Darius. Stark said to tell you he needs help with the boxes, like, right now. Kalona's plan worked and he's got Dallas and his group piling up logs for the pyre."

"I am on my way." He paused to kiss Aphrodite quickly before leaving. "You, I will meet back here at sunrise."

"*Alone.*" Aphrodite enunciated the word carefully, sending Zoey a Look.

After Darius closed the door, Z perched on one of Aphrodite's velvet chairs. "So, if you're feeling frisky, you must not be too hung over."

"Frisky is not a verb people under the age of eighty use to describe anything except the behavior of horses, and I'm not hung over at all," Aphrodite began as she fixed her T-shirt, went to her vanity mirror, and started combing her hair. Then, watching Zoey in the reflection, she added, "Well, okay, maybe I got a little messed up last night, but sleep, caffeine, and sugar fixed that."

"Brown pop always does it for me," Z said.

"You know that's not good for your skin," Aphrodite told her.

"Like your mimosas are?"

"*Orange juice* is totally healthy. I just like mine diluted."

"With alcohol," Z said, shaking her head and trying, unsuccessfully, not to smile.

"With *good* alcohol. Like Marilyn Monroe. And you see that her skin didn't wrinkle."

"Aphrodite, Marilyn Monroe died before she could get wrinkled."

"My point exactly. Mimosas are healthy. The end."

"You're making my head hurt," Z said.

Aphrodite smiled. "You are welcome. Oh, and before Darius and I started our super hot makeout session, which was *going to* lead to super hot sex, which you totally interrupted, he told me about Chera and the jewels."

"First, eew, frisky sounded so much better than your description. Second, Chera seemed cool, but basically her being here means the House of Night is in deep poo. Third, you do understand they're not jewels—they're ancient weapons that happen to have diamonds and rubies and stuff like that set into them."

"Proving how moronic males can be. Precious gems belong draped around a beautiful woman's—meaning mine—body. Not wasted in pointy and shieldy things."

"Except for the part about them belonging just on your body, I'm in total agreement with you."

"And I agree with you that we need to keep our mouths shut about them."

"Yeah, that's what my gut told me to do, but it felt awkward keeping it from Thanatos."

"If Thanatos didn't mention the weapons to you, that means Dragon was the one keeping them from her, not you—not us. I say box them up and hide them in one of Lenobia's tack rooms. I'm pretty sure if I tried to use my mom's gold card today, it would tell me I'm shit out of luck, so I say yes to having a financial backup plan."

Zoey's gaze met hers in the mirror. "Last night was bad. I'm really sorry about your dad, and I'm sorry about the stuff your mom said to you, too."

Aphrodite bit back the sarcastic reply that came so easily to her, drew a deep breath, and was honest with her friend. "I knew my mom never really cared about me, but knowing it and having her put it out there for everyone else to know are two different things—two different feelings. It hurts. A lot."

"Yeah," Z said softly, her eyes getting watery. "I know what you mean."

Aphrodite turned the little stool around so she could face Zoey. "You know what one of the first things I was happy about when I got Marked?"

"Having awesome hair?" Z smiled through her tears.

"No, stupid, I already had awesome hair," she quipped, and then her voice changed and she stared down at her lap. "One of the first things that made me happy was that I learned vampyres can't have babies, so I knew there was no way I'd slip up and accidentally get pregnant and then be a shitty mom and make some poor kid as fucking miserable as my mom made me."

"Hey, that's not going to happen."

Aphrodite wiped her eyes and looked up at Z. "Yeah, not as long as I keep having super hot sex with a vampyre it won't."

"Well, that's as true as it is gross, but it's not what I was talking about. That's not going to happen to you because *you aren't like your mom*," Zoey said carefully. "You're good and loyal, and you wouldn't hurt someone you love."

"Thanks," Aphrodite managed to say, wiping her eyes again.

"And don't call me stupid," Z said.

"I didn't call you a retard. I was being nice *and* politically correct." Aphrodite turned back around and started fixing her smeared mascara.

"And yet you still found a reason to say the r word." Zoey sighed. "So, you really are okay after losing your dad?"

"Are you really okay after losing your mom?"

Z looked surprised at the question. "I guess I will be. I mean, like you, my mom hadn't done much mothering in a long time. I was used to her not being around already."

"Then I guess I will be okay, too."

"If you need someone to talk to, you know you can talk to me, right?"

"Right. Same for you with me. I know you and the bumpkin are close, but she has the perfect mamma and daddy," Aphrodite put on Stevie Rae's accent.

"There's nothing wrong with having good parents. It's actually normal."

Aphrodite snorted. "We'll have to agree to disagree about that, but that's not my point. I'm just saying if you need someone else to talk to who has at least one dead parent, I'm here for you."

"Thanks, I think." Z grabbed a Kleenex and blew her nose loudly. "Why don't you get all snotty and ugly when you cry?"

"Because I am not as disgusting as you are," she said.

"Can I take back that nice stuff I said about you?"

"You can try. You'll be unsuccessful, but you can still try." Aphrodite pulled a pair of skinny jeans from a hanger and flipped the switch that started her electronic shoe cabinet to begin turning so that a neat row of boots appeared. She grabbed the red-soled Louboutins. Looking over her shoulder at Z's gawk she said, "What? You can't tell me these boots aren't perfection."

"I can't even look at your boots because your closet is freaking me the heck out."

"Which is just one reason you are a fashion disaster."

"How did you even think of having that done to your closet?"

"Oh, for shit's sake, my mom was a night*mare*, not fashion im-*paired*." Aphrodite rubbed her forehead. "Jesus Christ, that was a slant rhyme, and I did it on purpose. Let's go. I need a drink and a look at the boy stuff that's holding our jewels hostage."

"Okay, but if you're not nicer this time, I'm gonna tell Kramisha you like to rhyme, 'cause it makes you feel divine, and it keeps you from livin' a life of crime." Zoey grinned at her. "Heehees!"

"I have no words." Shaking her head, Aphrodite followed Zoey, who was giggling like a third grader, down the hall. "And she wonders why I drink . . ."

CHAPTER EIGHT

Neferet

Mortals would describe what Neferet did as dreaming. They would say they had been having nightmares so vivid that, upon waking, the dreams had stayed with them and even seemed real.

Cocooned in the den of the fox, clothed only in blood and Darkness, Neferet expanded her consciousness, sifting through levels of the seen and unseen worlds, in a quest for survival.

No, the immortal did not dream.

In truth the Tsi Sgili was re-experiencing her life, one event after another—reliving the moments that had culminated in the birth of an immortal, and by thus reliving she hoped to rediscover that which the vision in the mirror had shattered: her purpose and her true self.

Neferet began with the night reflected in the mirror, the moment her innocence had been lost. She once again became sixteen-year-old Emily Wheiler—daughter of a mother who had died just six months earlier—and she relived the night her father had attacked and raped her.

She could smell him: brandy, sour breath, sweat, cigars, and lust. She felt the disgust of knowing what he intended, and the terror of realizing she could not escape him. Then she experienced once again the pain of her beaten and torn body.

Still Emily Wheiler, she fled, bleeding and desperate, to be rejected by her fiancé, but at the same moment saved by the Tracker who Marked her as fledgling and forever altered her destiny.

Safely within the Chicago House of Night, her body healed under the watchful eye of her first mentor. But her mind could not recover. Emily needed vengeance to fully heal. Her mentor's voice was as clear as it had been that night in 1893.

". . . An insatiable need for retribution and vengeance becomes a poison that will taint your life and destroy your soul . . ."

Her mentor had explained to Emily that she faced the choice between forgetting what her father had done to her and moving on with her new life as a fledgling—or wallowing in self-pity and carrying the scars of what that monster had caused, unable to forget and forgive.

The fledgling who used to be Emily Wheiler did not take either choice.

The Tsi Sgili's body twitched spasmodically. Her breathing quickened, though she did not awaken. She remained deeply unconscious and utterly in another time—another place—and relived the birth of Neferet, Queen of the Night.

She returned to Wheiler House, the home of her father, as avenger, strangling him to death and claiming her new name, and her new life—without forgiveness, doubt, or self-pity.

Neferet's hands twitched as the specter of her past fingered the strand of pearls, smooth and deadly, and relived the exhilaration she had felt when she had ended Barrett Wheiler's pathetic life.

Neferet relived something else as well—she was again filled with the flush of that first kill. She hadn't tasted his blood. The thought had not entered her mind then, but she had felt the power of ending his breath, of stopping his heartbeat, of knowing she had caused his spirit to flee that broken, mortal shell.

The chill that had paled Neferet's flawless skin warmed, though ever so slightly.

She relived her escape from Chicago by train, accompanying a small group of vampyres who were scouting new House of Night sites in the west. At the train's first stop, Emily Wheiler buried her journal. In the dirt of the land that would become Oklahoma, she entombed the only record of what had happened to her. She remembered cutting into that earth with a spade, and opening a wound that was the red of dried bull's blood and carried with it the scent of the end of all things. With the burial of that sad, pitiable account of innocence lost and rape revenged, Neferet's new life blazed.

It was not an easy life.

But always within that comet of rebirth was a dark center of comfort that never forsook Neferet. Night was her world, and the shadows in the deepest corners of her world held solace and acceptance and comfort.

The Chicago School Council had decided it was unsafe for fledgling Neferet to return there, and she had been transferred to St. Louis's Tower Grove House of Night. There her gifts scorched through her.

Neferet curled tightly into herself, reliving the next moment that had defined who she would become.

The cat had been a small, shorthaired black and gray tabby. She would have been too small, too ordinary, too unattractive, for Neferet to have noticed at all, had it not been for her keen intelligence, and the additional toe she had on both of her front paws. It had been winter in St. Louis, frigid and snowy, and young Neferet had thought the little tabby had appeared to be wearing mittens.

The school's ill-tempered cook had named the cat Chloe, after a human thief who had been caught trying to burgle the school, because she had been unable to keep the feline from breaking into her kitchen, no matter how often she locked windows, and kept a keen eye on the scullery maids with their lackadaisical habit of forgetting to close doors. That day Chloe had pried open a window, scaled a ceiling beam, leaped on the cooling table, and gorged herself on a fresh kidney pie. The vampyre had been throwing the beast from the pantry when Neferet had happened by.

"How ever did she find a way to wear mittens?" young Neferet had exclaimed, as she rescued little Chloe from the snow bank she'd landed in, brushing wet white flakes from dusky fur and smiling as the cat batted at the ties on her ermine-lined cape.

The cook had laughed at Neferet mockingly. "I know you are young, but that is no reason to sound like such a simpleton. Chloe is polydactyl—six toed. Surely you've seen our High Priestess and her mate's cats. All polydactyl. This ugly little runt must be related to them, though I don't see the resemblance, except in those paws." The old vampyre had turned away, still cackling, shaking her head, and muttering, "Mittens on a cat. The child is pretty, but empty-headed . . ."

Neferet remembered how her face had burned with embarrassment and anger, until Chloe had looked up into her eyes.

Then Neferet's world had changed. She relived the thrill of it—of *knowing* what was within the cat's mind. She didn't hear actual words—cats don't think in words. She heard emotions, and the emotions told stories. Chloe beamed mischief. Her belly was full and warm and she was sleepy. But most important, the cat looked into her eyes with love and loyalty and joy, and chose Neferet as her own for life.

Pandeia, longtime High Priestess in St. Louis, had not called her a simpleton. Nor had she mocked Neferet when the young fledgling had gone to her, holding a sleeping Chloe, and describing with breathless wonder the dream images she could pull from the little feline's mind.

"And, High Priestess, I can touch your cat's mind, too!" Neferet had gushed, pointing to the vampyre's plump calico lazing on the windowsill. "She is happy, very happy, because she is pregnant!"

The High Priestess's smile had almost outshined the cook's mocking. "Dear Neferet, Nyx has granted you a wonderful affinity, a special attachment to cats, the animal most closely associated with our Goddess. Nyx must value you highly to award you such a gift."

The glorious day faded and Neferet's experience changed. Months passed as quickly as the Tsi Sgili's rapid heartbeat.

She was still a fledgling, but older. Her council was valued—first because of her connection to the felines that roamed freely at the House of Night as companions of the fledglings and vampyres. Then because though her affinity had begun with cats, soon it had become apparent that Neferet was able to touch people's minds almost as easily as she did cats'.

Images lifted from the past, one after another, dizzying in their speed:

"Neferet, it would be helpful if you came to town with me. I need to know if the town is growing restless again at the thought of our full moon rituals," her High Priestess had asked.

She had gone with Pandeia, opening herself to the onslaught of fear and hatred and envy that the local humans directed at the High Priestess, though they either simpered and tipped their hats to her, or averted their eyes and pretended not to see her.

Neferet began to loathe going to town.

"Neferet, the human Consort of our new professor seems sad; it would be helpful if you could tell me if he wishes to leave, but is fearful to ask," Pandeia had asked at another time.

Neferet had slipped within the man's mind. The human hadn't

been sad. He had been unfaithful to his vampyre, and had been sneaking away during the daylight hours while she slept to gamble and whore on riverboats.

The professor had sent him away and quickly forgotten him, moving on to another, more loyal Consort within a fortnight.

But Neferet had found it hard to forget what she had touched within the man's mind. Lust and envy—greed and desire. It had sickened her.

Seeing how much their High Priestess valued her counsel, others came to her, always seeking the answers hidden beneath the masks of others.

As Neferet relived the experiences, she felt the resentment that had begun within her then. They were all so needy! Even the High Priestess.

"Neferet, tell me if that Son of Erebus Warrior thinks I'm truly beautiful . . ."

"Neferet, I want to know if my roommate is telling me the truth about . . ."

"Neferet, tell me . . ."

"Neferet, I want . . ."

"Neferet, why does . . . ?"

The Tsi Sgili shivered, though still she did not awake as experience after experience, memory after memory, assaulted her so rapidly that they bled into one another, becoming a collage of need and greed, desire and betrayal, lies and lust.

Darkness saved her. As when she had been Emily, she was drawn to the night-blooming gardens of Tower Grove. The most shadowy places in her House of Night were familiar friends to her. There she could disappear, calling the night to her, so that others looked right over and past her, and never seeing . . .

Chloe understood. She was intelligent and precocious, and no matter what insipid thought Neferet had overheard, she found a way to make her smile. She whispered to the cat the feelings she was learning never to say aloud—never to show to other fledglings—never, ever to reveal to any vampyre.

"I hate it when Pandeia asks me to listen in to a human's mind, especially a male human," young Neferet had told her purring feline. "They are all vile. Their thoughts are obsessed with our bodies—with possessing us—even though their fear is so strong it almost has a scent: sour breath, sweat, and insatiable desire."

Chloe had touched noses with her and rubbed her face against her cheek, filling her with unconditional love and acceptance.

"When I am High Priestess I will only use my powers when *I* want to. I do not agree with Pandeia and the rest of them. Just because I'm gifted, that doesn't mean I must be at their beck and call. *I* was given the power, not them. It should be *mine* to do with as I wish."

Instead of snuggling against her, as usual, the little cat's ears pricked and she stood, perching on Neferet's lap and peering out into the night-cloaked gardens of the House of Night.

In her den, the Tsi Sgili moaned aloud, not wanting to relive what happened next, but not able to escape from the visions of her past.

The Tower Grove House of Night had lush grounds that stretched for more than two hundred secluded acres around the main campus. The grounds were, of course, meticulously tended, but it was the early twentieth century, and St. Louis was still known as the gateway to the wild west. The gardens were home to more than water features and night-blooming flowers.

Chloe scented the air.

Neferet breathed deeply with the little cat. When she arched her back, growling ferociously, Neferet had bared her teeth, too, sharing her rage that an intruder had entered her House of Night.

It wasn't until Chloe had leaped from her lap that Neferet had come to herself and knew fear. She raced after her cat.

The bobcat had been hunting rabbits and had chased one to ground not far from the dark corner in which Neferet and Chloe had been sitting. Frustrated at losing his prey, the big male had sprayed around the clearing, marking it as his own.

Chloe burst into the male's territory. Shrieking a warning, the bobcat faced the little tabby. Yowling and spitting, Chloe flew at the male, all claws and teeth.

"No!" Neferet screamed along with Chloe as the bobcat struck once, twice, swatting the little cat as if she were an annoying insect, and slicing her belly, neatly disemboweling her.

The huge beast, easily three times the size of Chloe, was closing on where the tabby lay gutted, twitching and bleeding, when Neferet reached the clearing.

Rage filled the fledgling, and she charged the animal, screaming in wordless hatred, hands raised in claws, and teeth bared.

The bobcat's ears flattened against his skull. His yellow eyes met Neferet's blazing emerald gaze. What he saw there gave him pause. As quickly as his instinct to kill had been ignited, his instinct for self-preservation took over, and the feline backed away, fading into the foliage.

Neferet rushed to her cat. Chloe was still alive. Her little heart raced and she was panting in panic and pain. "No! Goddess, no!" Neferet ripped her dress and tried to push the intestines back into the cat's belly, and staunch the terrible flood of blood. "Help her, Nyx! Please, if I am as important to you as everyone says I am, please, I beg of you, help her!" Filled with her cat's pain and her own despair, Neferet cried into the night. "Help her, Goddess! Please help!"

The air above the clearing had shimmered with silver light that glittered like stars come to earth, and a woman materialized beside the dying cat. Her hair was long and as white as the full moon. She wore a dress the color of dusk and a headdress covered in gossamer silver strung with diamonds.

Within the den, the Tsi Sgili's restlessly twitching body stilled. Her breathing became shallow. Her naked skin was chill and so pale she seemed almost transparent as she relived her first meeting with Nyx.

"Daughter, you are important to me," the Goddess had told her. "And not only because I can see great power within you. I love you, as I do all of my children, because of your true self— that within you which is vulnerable and wounded, yet brave enough to continue to live and grow and love."

"Then please, Goddess. Save Chloe. She is the most important thing in my life. I love her," Neferet had begged.

Nyx had raised her arms, and the silk that draped them had shimmered like moonlight on water.

"I give you one final gift—that of the ability to soothe others' pain with your touch. Let it teach you compassion to temper the budding power within you." Nyx pressed her hands over her heart, and then she bent forward and placed her palms against Neferet's head.

Within the cold, dark den, Neferet relived the infilling of that divine touch and her breath stopped in remembrance. The Goddess's touch had not filled her with power. It had filled her with gentleness.

"Oh, blessed be, Nyx!"

"It is the Goddess! Blessed be, Goddess of Night!"

Joyous cries came from all around Neferet as vampyres and fledglings, following her calls for help, had found the clearing.

"Blessed be, my daughters. Merry meet, merry part, and merry meet again," Nyx had greeted the others, smiling beatifically before she disappeared into a ray of moonlight.

Neferet had not watched Nyx go. She had been focusing all of her being on her cat. She pressed her hands against her bleeding body, channeling the magickal touch of the Goddess.

Neferet felt the difference instantly. Chloe's panting ceased. Her heart slowed. Her pain-glazed eyes cleared, for just a moment, and they met hers as the little cat beamed love and joy and relief. Then, completely happy and utterly relieved of pain, her cat curled around her hands. Purring contentedly, she nuzzled Neferet, and died.

"No! No! I was supposed to be able to save you!" Neferet had pulled Chloe into her lap, and begun to keen over her lifeless body when pain exploded across her forehead. Still cradling Chloe's body, Neferet had crumpled, until her face was pressed into the grass and the blood and earth absorbed her sobs.

"Neferet, child! I am here with you. All will be well!" It was the High Priestess, Pandeia, herself who lifted her. "Oh, blessed Goddess, thank you!" Pandeia had exclaimed as Neferet raised her face. "Not only did Nyx gift you with a healing touch, she also blessed you with the Change this night."

Still crying and clutching Chloe's body, Neferet was dizzy with confusion.

Pandeia's gaze went from the new Marks that decorated Neferet's face, proclaiming to the world that she was an adult vampyre, to the body of the little cat. "Oh, it is Chloe. I grieve with you, Neferet." The High Priestess stroked the cat's motionless head. "But your touch healed her pain and she went on to the Otherworld, where she frolics with the Goddess."

In the den, the Tsi Sgili drew a deep breath, and then spoke the words aloud, just as she had done in the past.

"I didn't heal her. Chloe is dead."

Pandeia's gaze had been kind, her voice understanding. "I know it is a terrible loss, and difficult for you to bear right now, but when you can think of this night clearly, you will realize that the ability to touch her spirit and to soothe little Chloe's passing more fully healed her than would mending her physical wounds. Nyx has richly blessed you."

In her den, Neferet whispered aloud the words she had only been able to think silently those many decades ago: *Nyx has taken from me the only thing I love.*

Anger stirred the Tsi Sgili, moving her toward consciousness. Her breath quickened, and she almost opened her eyes. But before she could fully rouse, time moved forward, taking her to the next defining experience in her past. The day she killed her lover and began hearing the seductive whispers of the winged immortal—the liar and betrayer, Kalona . . .

CHAPTER NINE

Zoey

"Zo, Thanatos sent me to find you. The conference with the High Council has begun," Aurox said.

"Oh, crap! I totally lost track of time."

"High Council conference? WTF?" Aphrodite said.

"Yeah, again, crap." I checked my phone: 10:10 PM. Yep, I was ten minutes late. "Sorry, with all this basement moving stuff I forgot to tell you guys. Thanatos is going to ask the High Council to intercede with the TPD because she thinks the humans are going outside their boundaries in the investigation. She wants me to join her so we can tell them about Neferet materializing and being all super crazed and our circle kicking her out, which is what set up the fact that she ate the mayor." I paused, and sent Aphrodite an apologetic look. "Sorry for saying it like that."

She shrugged. "You're just telling it like it is."

"Well, she should say it in a nicer way," Stevie Rae said, sending me a frown.

"Bumpkin, nice has never been something I give much of a shit about. Z should just tell it like it is."

"Hey, we all know you got so wasted last night you couldn't function most of today. There's no point in pretending like nothing can bother you," Stark said. He aimed his comment at Aphrodite, but he wasn't even looking at her. He was watching Aurox and frowning.

"Stark, two words: shut it," Aphrodite said. "Oh, and two more words: jealous much?"

Goddess, I was sick of their bickering. "Aphrodite, since you're okay talking about your dad, I want you to come with me to Skype the High Council." I spoke quickly before Stark could say whatever petty comment he had opened his mouth to say, whether it was to Aphrodite or Aurox. "Stevie Rae, you come with me, too."

"Okie dokie," she said.

"We better get going. Thanatos sent Aurox on a fetch mission for you, so that means you're late," Stark said, grabbing my wrist and sounding super douchey.

I raised my brows at him and pulled my wrist from his grasp. "*We,* meaning Aphrodite, Stevie Rae, and I, are going right now. And yeah, I'm late because I got all caught up in a zillion petty fires that need to be stomped out around here. While we're talking to the High Council I need *you* to be sure the red fledglings have gotten all their stuff moved into the basement, then help Darius and Damien gather everyone together to go to the funeral. I'll meet you there."

"But I wanted to—"

"To what?" I knew I was sounding like a bitch, but my patience was gone. It was obvious that what he wanted to do was to be sure he was stuck to my side if Aurox was anywhere around. "Stark, you didn't see Neferet materialize. That's what the High Council is going to want to hear about."

"I just thought you might need me to—"

I cut him off again. "I need you to *not* argue with Aphrodite or me, and just be sure Erin's funeral doesn't turn into a stupid gang fight."

Aurox cleared his throat. "I'll go ahead of you and let Thanatos know you will join her momentarily."

"Yeah, thanks Aurox," I said absently as the kid took off, obviously glad to get away from the tension he'd accidentally caused.

I could see that I'd embarrassed and probably even hurt Stark, but I really didn't have the time or the energy to baby his feelings. So I didn't say anything. Stark didn't say anything. No one said anything. Until Stark fisted his hand over his heart, bowed formally to me, said, "It will be as you command, Priestess. I hope your conference with the High Council goes well," and walked away, with silent Darius and Damien following him.

"Okay, awkward," Aphrodite said. "You know Stark is just being possessive because of the Aurox slash Heath thing. No need to hammer the kid in front of Bull Boy."

"I didn't hammer him!"

"Actually, Z, you sounded pretty mean," Stevie Rae said.

"Are you going to tell me you're always super sweet to Rephaim, even when he's annoying the crap out of you?" I said, feeling kinda sorry that I'd lost my temper at Stark, especially in front of my friends, but also still feeling annoyed at him.

"Yeah, I can tell you that I've never been mean to Rephaim on purpose," Stevie Rae said.

"That's probably because he's only a boy half the time. It's pretty tough to get mad at an effing bird. It's gotta be like dating a dog. I'll bet he's happy and wiggling like he had a tail every time he comes back to see you," Aphrodite said. "Jesus, it exhausts me just thinking about it."

"You, I'm used to being hateful, so I'm not gonna say anything 'bout you bein' mean. Her, I'm not." Stevie Rae turned her back on Aphrodite. "Is somethin' wrong with you, Z? You're jumpy as a cat on a hot tin roof."

"Elizabeth Taylor was a goddess," Aphrodite said. "Batshit crazy, but a goddess."

"What are you talking about?" I said.

"The movie. Ask Queen Damien. I'm sure he wishes he had been Elizabeth Taylor."

"Aphrodite, sometimes I think you're speaking another language, but officially here's what's wrong with me: I'm tired of everyone bickering. I'm tired of Stark acting weird about Aurox. I'm tired of not knowing how *I'm* supposed to act around Aurox because of the Heath thing. I'm tired of people getting eaten. I'm tired of worrying about what the hell Neferet is going to do next. And I'm super effing tired of being stuck at the House of Night like a prisoner."

Aphrodite and Stevie Rae looked at me like I'd grown wings.

"Damn, Z. You need to start drinking," Aphrodite said.

"Does Xanax work on fledglings?" Stevie Rae asked her.

"It's worth a try," she said.

"I'm right here. I don't like to drink, and I don't want a Xanax."

"I'll grind one up if you sneak it into her brown pop," Aphrodite said.

"Deal," Stevie Rae said.

Then they both started laughing.

I shook my head. "You two aren't funny, and we're late." I walked away from them. They trailed after me, still giggling at my expense.

I was surprised to see Kalona standing behind Thanatos, arms folded over his bare, muscular chest, looking like the statue of an avenging angel.

Why doesn't he ever wear a shirt? flitted through my mind. Then Thanatos gestured at us to join her, saying, "Ah, good. Here is Zoey.

I am glad to see she is accompanied by the young High Priestess Stevie Rae, as well as our Prophetess, Aphrodite."

Kalona stepped back so that the three of us could be seen by the computer camera, along with Thanatos. The large screen showed the High Council Chamber in the temple at San Clemente Island, just off the coast of Venice. Seven stone thrones, each ornately carved, were on a stage-like area. Six of the thrones were occupied. I knew the seventh belonged to Thanatos. I wasn't sure how I felt about the fact that they hadn't filled her spot on the High Council. I liked that Thanatos was here with us, yet still had enough power to maintain her seat on the High Council. I didn't like that that might mean she could be yanked back there at any time.

I realized no one was saying anything and everyone was staring at me. My face flamed with heat and I fisted my hand over my heart, bowing quickly. "Merry meet, High Priestesses. I'm sorry I'm late. I was, um—" I paused, totally losing whatever excuse I was going to babble.

"She's stressed out because we're all stuck here," Aphrodite finished for me. She performed a cursory bow. "Merry meet. It's me, Aphrodite."

"We remember who you are, Prophetess." Duantia spoke first. "It would be rather difficult for us to forget our first human Prophetess." She was sitting in the most ornate of the thrones and, obviously, was leading the High Council. Then Duantia turned her dark eyes on me, and I could feel their power even with thousands of miles separating us. "Being late is sometimes inevitable. Stress is also inevitable. Learning to limit one and handle the other is part of being a High Priestess." Before I could start to apologize again, she looked from me to Stevie Rae. "Merry meet, Stevie Rae. When events allow, the Council and I would like to extend an invitation to you and your unusual Consort, Rephaim, to visit San Clemente Island. We are intrigued by the two of you. It is true that the boy actually shifts his form from human to raven daily?"

"Merry meet," Stevie Rae said, bowing formally. Then she smiled a little shyly, but answered Duantia's question with no hesitation or embarrassment. "Yes, ma'am, Rephaim's just like a normal boy at night, but as soon as the sun rises he changes into a raven."

"He has no recollection of the hours when he is a beast?" another High Council member asked.

"Not really, no. Or at least if he does he hasn't told me. Rephaim doesn't like to talk about it much."

"We will speak more of this when you and your Consort visit us," Duantia said.

"Better get one of those really big dog travel crates," Aphrodite whispered to Stevie Rae.

I elbowed her.

"Now, back to the subject at hand," Duantia continued. "Thanatos has summarized last night's events. Aphrodite, the Council extends our condolences to you. A parent's death is never easy."

"Thank you."

"Zoey, Stevie Rae, Aphrodite, you were present when the apparition manifested on your campus. Thanatos reports to us that you believe it was Neferet. Are the three of you in agreement on this?"

"We are," I said. "Aphrodite and I saw the spiders first. I knew it was Neferet then. She's manifested as spiders before, here at the House of Night, and when she fell from the balcony it looked like her body disintegrated into a whole nest of spiders."

"It was obvious from the beginning the spiders weren't normal," Aphrodite added. "And it only got more obvious when Z started casting the circle."

"As I already said, I had felt a change in the school's energy just before Zoey called me to report what was happening. My initial thought was that I was sensing the approach of death, and death did visit our campus that night, but upon reflection I believe I also sensed the approach of the Tsi Sgili. Her power is derived from death and Darkness—it is what has fueled her immortality. I agree with Zoey and her circle. Neferet attempted to manifest."

"We saw her," I said, not liking that the Council members looked undecided. "It was definitely Neferet's body that almost reformed before the elements threw her off campus."

"Not far off," Aphrodite said. "She killed my father at the school's main entrance. That's probably as far as she could make it without draining someone."

"We also believe Neferet could be responsible for the fledgling's rejection of the Change that night," Thanatos said. "Her specter passed through the girl as she fled the circle, and the fledgling died mere minutes later."

"Yes, the child with the water affinity," Duantia said. "Such a shame to lose a Goddess-gifted fledgling."

"Though it does make sense that an immortal who feeds from death and Darkness could cause a fledgling's death in such a way," said another Council member. "That could be what gave her the power she needed to fully manifest."

"Neferet killed Erin and Aphrodite's dad," I said firmly. "We even tried to tell the detectives that, but no way can we explain the whole truth to them. No way are they going to believe us."

"And now they are asking for us to begin DNA testing with my professors to compare with the evidence they found on the mayor's body," Thanatos said.

I heard Aphrodite's surprised intake of breath and realized I should have warned her about that detail. Crap! I really had to start managing my time better.

"Humans want to investigate this murder within your House of Night." Duantia didn't make the statement a question, but Thanatos answered her anyway.

"Yes, which is in direct contradiction to our traditions. I will not give the permission to invade this school. That is why I have asked for your intercession," Thanatos said. "All the human authorities need to understand is that the vampyre community has charged Neferet with the death of the mayor, and that we are working diligently to find her and to bring her to justice. They can end their investigation and lift the restrictions on our House of Night. In return our oath is given that we will be quite certain Neferet will pay for her crimes."

"And yet the local humans believe Neferet has been the victim of violence herself," Duantia said.

"Because we couldn't explain to them that she used Darkness to kidnap my grandma, so we had to use magick to save her!" I hadn't meant to yell, but I was just so frustrated at how unfair the whole dang thing was!

"There is much that cannot be explained to the humans, Zoey," Duantia said. "Your mother's death at Neferet's hands is another sad example of this."

I nodded, not trusting my voice.

"Zoey, if the restrictions are lifted from the House of Night, are you and Stevie Rae still determined to continue to live off campus, separated from the school?" a Council member who had been silent until then suddenly asked.

"Yes," I said. "The tunnels under the depot are more comfortable for red vampyres and fledglings."

"Yet you are neither."

I frowned. "Well, I'm not a normal fledgling either." I raised my hands, palms outward, so that the lattice tattooing the Goddess had placed there was fully visible to the camera.

"And I'm not a normal Prophetess of Nyx," Aphrodite said. "So, I'll be going with them."

"I'm the first red High Priestess," Stevie Rae said. "That's not normal, either, and I'm with Zoey and Aphrodite. We're not meanin' to make trouble, but it is what it is—we're stickin' together."

"I don't get the problem with us living at the depot. You guys were okay with it before," I said.

"Yes, that was *before* Neferet was provoked enough to kidnap your grandmother and kill a fledgling and a human, and bring the local authorities into your House of Night," said the same Council member.

I could hardly believe what she was saying. "That was *not* our fault!"

"No one is blaming you," Duantia said quickly. "We are only attempting to sift through the many recent tragic events." Suddenly she shifted her attention. "Kalona, you are the only immortal here. What is your opinion?" Duantia's question seemed to surprise all of us. Thanatos shifted in her chair, and Aphrodite and I moved aside a little so that Kalona could stand between us and face the High Council.

He bowed, fisting his hand over his heart, before answering. "I see no problem with Zoey and her group, and that includes my son, Rephaim, living in the depot. They are guarded by strong, loyal Warriors, and the tunnels provide safety for them. As to the murders, I have no doubt that the creature, Neferet, manifested and caused both deaths, and that humans cannot begin to make her pay for her crimes."

"Kalona, we have accepted you as part of our community because of the oath you swore to Thanatos, but we are all curious about your answer to one question in particular," Duantia said.

Kalona's wings rustled and his body tensed, but his voice was steady. "I will answer any questions you might wish to ask, High Priestess."

"Though you never fully admitted being Erebus come to earth, Neferet presented you to us as such. She said you tricked her into believing it."

"And yet I never claimed to be Erebus, and here I stand, sworn Warrior to a member of your own Council, as Neferet gets away with murdering children and humans."

"Yes, it is an interesting turn of events. Our question is, who are you?"

Everyone, even Thanatos, was gawking at Kalona. Was he going to tell them that he was Erebus's brother? Holy crap!

"I have been many things—a god, a lover, a destroyer, a savior. Now I am Death's Warrior," Kalona said. "It is fitting that I am also an immortal."

I thought about speaking up and telling everyone that he was Erebus's brother, but was he *really*? I'd already been late, looked irresponsible to the Council, and they had to know I was annoyed as hell at them. I didn't need to spout out a claim like that and then have Kalona say nothing. Or worse, deny it completely. So, for a change, I kept my mouth shut.

"Kalona, I have prayed to Nyx and asked her to speak to me of you, and tell me if you present a danger to Thanatos, or to the House of Night," Duantia said.

"And what did the Goddess say?" Kalona asked.

"Nyx has remained silent."

"I think that is an answer itself," Thanatos said. I thought she sounded pissed. She and Duantia had a silent stare down, which ended in Duantia looking away to address her Council. "Priestesses, has anything you heard here tonight changed your previous judgment on Thanatos's request for us to intercede with the Tulsa humans?"

The five High Priestesses spoke creepily as one, "No."

Duantia faced us again. "Then it is decided. What is happening in Tulsa has already caused unrest between vampyres and humans, as well as between fledglings and vampyres within the Tulsa House of Night itself. Part of you have broken from the whole, and it is clear to us from the recent events that this break is not a healthy one for the vampyre community. We have shunned Neferet. She is no longer our concern. It is not our responsibility to bring her to justice."

"But Neferet's the one causing the problems. She's the one the humans need to blame—she's the one you need to blame." I practically choked trying to keep from yelling at them.

"She is immortal. As Kalona said, she cannot be brought to justice by humans," Duantia said.

"You expect us to bring her to justice," Kalona said.

"Yes, we do," Duantia said. "Therefore, we will not intercede with the local humans. Nor will we any longer recognize the separation of fledglings and vampyres from your House of Night."

"Sgiach is a vampyre High Priestess and she lives separately from you—and you've allowed that for centuries," I tried to reason with them.

"Sgiach is not causing unrest with humans. Sgiach is not coming to us asking for our aid," Duantia said.

"You know what, it makes perfect sense now why she stays on a booby-trapped island and ignores you," I told them.

"Perhaps it is time Tulsa became an island as well." Thanatos sounded grim and powerful. "I abdicate my position on the High Council effective immediately."

"Thanatos, you cannot mean to lead your House of Night into breaking with the High Council!" Duantia stood. The rest of the Council were looking either super shocked or super pissed.

"I mean to change and adapt. I mean to remain here as High

Priestess of Tulsa's House of Night. I mean to support these two unusual High Priestesses and this Prophetess in their desire for a place of their own. And, most importantly, I mean to bring Neferet to justice *without allowing an invasion of my school.*"

"But that is not—"

"That is my oath; so mote it be!"

Then Thanatos clicked the disconnect button. Skype made its funny little hang-up sound, and the screen went blank.

CHAPTER TEN

Aphrodite

"Holy fucking shit. Thanatos, you have balls. Great big ones," Aphrodite said.

Thanatos raised her brows. "I shall ignore the vulgarity and accept the compliment, Prophetess."

"Just so you know, it's a massive compliment," Aphrodite said, bowing her head respectfully to Thanatos.

"You really stood up for us. Thanks, High Priestess," Stevie Rae said.

Kalona and Zoey exchanged looks. "So we are left to deal with Neferet and the local authorities on our own," he said.

"Again," Zoey added. "It's not like this is the first time the High Council has left us hanging like this."

"They mean well," Thanatos said, sounding somewhere between sad and cynical. "They think they're doing what is best for the vampyre community as a whole, and that is what the Council was created eons ago to do."

"They're stuck in the Dark Ages!" Zoey blurted.

Aphrodite watched her closely. Yeah, the High Council had been assholes, but they still had Thanatos—the power of their circle—two Prophetesses (even though Shaylin was a pain in the ass), a Bull Boy, and an immortal on their side.

"I say good riddance. They're a bunch of old women—no offense, Thanatos," Aphrodite said. "Z, the only thing they could really do for us is to *maybe* get the TPD off our backs. We don't need their permission to create our own place in the world. It's our world, too, and we'll *make* our own place."

"Yep, that's what I'm thinkin', too," Stevie Rae agreed.

Zoey crossed her arms over her chest. "So, we're all stuck here together, doing nothing."

"Until we catch Neferet, I'm afraid we are," Thanatos said.

"Catch her? What good will that do?" Zoey said.

Aphrodite saw that she wasn't the only person watching Zoey closely. Thanatos's brows lifted and she cocked her head to the side. "Priestess, we have all agreed Neferet is responsible for the deaths that happened last night, have we not?"

"Neferet did it," Z said.

"So Neferet must be found and turned over to the authorities. Until then, the truth is that the human authorities will find no proof that will place blame on any of us, as we are innocent."

"Hang on. Does that mean you're going to let our professors start being DNA tested?" Zoey asked.

"No. That means we are going to find Neferet and provide her *matching* DNA to the human authorities."

"Neferet is a powerful immortal. She's not going to let us catch her, let alone take her to the cops."

"Zoey, you say that, yet you and your circle managed to defeat that powerful immortal and rescue your grandmother from her."

"We beat her before. We'll beat her again." Stevie Rae sounded way more positive than Z.

"Actually, all we have to do is find Neferet. Get her to a public place and start nailing her with hard questions. She's going to lose her temper and do something batshit crazy, especially if a detective asks her for a DNA sample," Aphrodite said. "Yeah, it's going to suck for us when she explodes into spiders or eats some locals or whatever, and humans start to understand that there's more going on here than vampyre versus human, but that won't suck nearly as much as being under house arrest and blamed for shit no one here did."

"I believe it is time humans understand there are more forces at work than just those of human and vampyre." Kalona surprised Aphrodite by agreeing with her. "Evil is always stronger when it is underestimated."

"You're going to let humans see you?" Zoey asked Kalona.

"I am going to bring Neferet to justice and protect this school. If that means I show myself to humans, then so be it."

"I have a question." Stevie Rae half raised her hand.

"Yes?" Thanatos said.

"How're we gonna find Neferet?"

"That will be the easy part. We will remain here, stay on the path of our Goddess, and wait for Neferet to reveal herself," Thanatos said.

"That's crap!" Z sounded like she was ready to explode. "When Neferet kidnapped Grandma I was sitting in the tunnels in the kitchen. I was just waiting and whining to Nyx to help me save Grandma. And, guess what? The Goddess appeared to me and basically told me that a child sits around and cries. A High Priestess actually does something. So, now you're telling me that our big decision is to sit around and wait?"

"No, what I'm telling you is that we are going to show wisdom and act with patience. We have one of our own to bury, and then we are going to resume classes, and our lives, and not allow our school to be overrun by angry locals or ourselves to drown in Neferet's Darkness. I expect you and Stevie Rae to show your leadership skills and to help me, and the rest of the faculty, keep everyone calm and on task. And now, if you are done attempting to lecture me about a Goddess I have served faithfully for centuries, I have a funeral over which I need to preside." Thanatos's tone said she'd heard enough from everyone—especially Zoey—and she stood. With Kalona following in her shadow, she left the room.

Aphrodite stepped between Zoey and the door. "At the risk of sounding more like you than I'd like to sound, I'm going to tell you that you need to adjust your attitude."

Z narrowed her eyes. "This situation doesn't piss you off?"

"Of course it does, but snapping at the one *grown* High Priestess who is actually on our side is just stupid."

"Z, you did sound kinda snappy." Stevie Rae looked uncomfortable, but that didn't stop her from speaking.

Zoey drew a deep breath and let it out slowly, fingering the Lifesaver-looking Seer Stone that dangled from a long silver chain around her neck. "It's just so damn frustrating to have Neferet doing crap *again*, and have us just hanging out, waiting for her next move."

"Okay, you said 'damn' and 'crap' in one sentence, so I'm starting to feel hopeful that perhaps the mental breakdown you're obviously having might cause an update of your boring non-curse curse words," Aphrodite said. "Other than that, I still say you need to check your attitude. This isn't the same old, same old with Neferet. She's been shunned by the High Council."

"Yeah, even if they're too chicken to go after her themselves, it's a big step that they've shunned her," Stevie Rae added.

"I'd call them something more descriptive than chicken, but the point is still made. And we have an entire school going against her. Neferet can't hide forever—like we've all already said, if nothing else, she's just too damn crazy to go unnoticed for very long."

"No," Z said. "That's part of the problem—the entire school

isn't against her. Dallas and his friends have definitely been on her side, and are definitely not with us."

"But, Z, Neferet killing Aphrodite's dad changes everything." Stevie Rae glanced at Aphrodite. "Sorry again." Aphrodite shrugged and Stevie Rae rolled on. "What she did this time was real public. *She ate the mayor.* The cops are involved. Thanatos is going to make sure they get evidence that will prove what she did, and Dallas is not gonna want to get smacked with a murder charge, or even a helpin' a murderer charge," Stevie Rae said.

"Dallas and his disgusting friends would not do well in jail. They're going to sit tight and shut up. Sure, they're going to be a pain in the ass to be around, but that's really no different than normal school," Aphrodite said.

"Yeah, I guess you guys are right," Z said. "Sorry about the Negative Nancy thing. I really just want to do something that will fix everything. You know, make everyone be nice and stop calling Darkness and whatnot."

"That's not being Negative Nancy. That's being Deluded Debbie. People suck. They do stupid things and they're not nice. The end," Aphrodite told her. "As proof of my point, let's go to Erin's funeral. She didn't act right, and I'm pretty damn sure her funeral is going to suck."

Aphrodite was seriously sick of attending funerals. Not only was it bad when someone decent, like Dragon Lankford or poor little gay Jack, died, it was sad and sucked and couldn't even be made better by wearing awesome clothes. Black. Boring. Depressing.

And to put a cherry on the shit sundae of an event, Zoey was definitely having anger control issues. She'd snapped at the High Council. She'd snapped at Thanatos. That was not Zoey-like behavior. And she'd failed to mention to his own daughter the little detail about the cops having DNA evidence on whoever killed her dad. Aphrodite glanced over at Z. She was walking beside Stevie Rae and nodding at something the bumpkin was babbling on and on about, but she didn't have her usual *I'm smiling at my BFF* look on her face. Z was frowning. She looked tired. No, actually, she didn't look tired. She looked annoyed. Or pissed. Yeah, Z definitely looked pissed.

Aphrodite didn't know what the fuck to do.

Maybe Zoey needed to hear about her latest vision, the one that starred Out of Control Angry Z and ended with her in jail and a bunch of people being eaten.

But Aphrodite's instinct was still telling her that this wasn't a Zoey who could be reasoned with—or at least not right now she couldn't be.

Maybe after the funeral was over. Maybe Z was just super tense because funerals were awful.

The three of them had gotten to the middle of campus—the all too familiar pyre/funeral area in the center of the giant oaks that ringed the school. Thanatos and Kalona were at the head of the pyre, standing by Dallas, who looked stone-faced, but was nodding at whatever Thanatos was saying to him. His friends made a little semi-circle of fashion disasters behind him.

Darius's wave caught her attention. "There are our boys," she said, and they changed direction to meet their Warriors, the rest of their circle, and Stevie Rae's red fledglings who were making another semi-circle on the opposite side of the pyre.

Darius hugged her and Aphrodite let herself rest in his arms, wishing they were already alone.

"Thanatos and Kalona look grim. Did the meeting with the High Council not go well?" he whispered into her ear.

"Train wreck. I'll explain later," she whispered back, and then the professors were there, filling in the missing parts of the semicircles to form one complete circle, making it appear as if the school were one, united, group. Which was, of course, totally not true.

Thanatos spoke first. Her voice was strong and clear—she was actually a pretty good speaker, but when she started a prayer that rhymed, Aphrodite's attention wandered.

She watched Dallas. As far as she was concerned, he'd always been too short and his eyes had seemed beady—even before he'd lost his mind and gone red. Tonight he stared at the pyre and Erin's shrouded body, wiping his eyes on the back of his sleeve every once in a while. Technically, he was crying, but mostly he looked mad. Aphrodite's gaze went to the red fledglings behind Dallas. None of them were crying. Most were either looking at the pyre or at Thanatos. Well, a few were gawking at Kalona, but kids always gawked at Kalona.

Aphrodite's eyes traveled around the circle, and she noticed that Nicole hadn't joined Dallas's group. She was standing next to Lenobia and Travis in the middle of a clump of professors. As if she had felt her gaze, Nicole looked at Aphrodite. It wasn't a bitchy look, but it wasn't friendly, either. Aphrodite thought if a look could speak it would say, *WTF?*

Aphrodite held her gaze a little longer, then let her eyes continue to move around the circle. Her gaze halted again when it came to Shaylin. She was standing next to dickhead Erik. The fact that Shaylin always seemed to end up next to Erik made her wonder about the girl's judgment. Erik was undeniably hot. If he hadn't been hot Aphrodite wouldn't have been there, done him, but she'd also moved on. Of course she hadn't seen Shaylin and Erik doing any face-sucking. He'd never even held her hand in public. Maybe it wasn't Shaylin stalking Erik. Maybe Erik hung around her because she'd been the first fledgling he'd Tracked. That was a possibility.

Shaylin was supposed to be able to read people's auras or colors or whatever she called them, and tell what a person was really like on the inside, so it was also a possibility that Erik was becoming less of an ass, and Shaylin could see that, though that possibility seemed unlikely.

Aphrodite flipped her hair back. Shaylin had read her colors. She'd pissed Aphrodite off, and been a bitch at first, but later she'd apologized. And the truth was that Shaylin had been right when she'd told Aphrodite: *You do have a flickery yellow light inside your moonlight light . . . It's part of your uniqueness—your warmth . . . it's small and hidden, because you keep how warm and good you really are hidden most of the time. But that doesn't change that it's still there.* Remembering, Aphrodite flipped her hair back again. As annoying as it was, her instinct was telling her that Shaylin was the real deal—that she did have True Sight and a Goddess-given ability to interpret it.

Aphrodite glanced at where Zoey was standing over by Stevie Rae and Rephaim, between Stark and Shaunee. Naturally, Shaunee and Stevie Rae were bawling their eyes out. Z wasn't, though, and that seemed weird. Z usually snot cried at funerals, and as messed up as Erin had gotten before she'd died, she had been part of Z's original circle.

When Aphrodite looked back at Shaylin, the girl wasn't watching Thanatos anymore. She was watching Zoey and her expression said she didn't like what she was seeing.

That's when Aphrodite made her decision.

Then her attention was pulled back to the funeral as Dallas lifted the blazing torch while Thanatos raised her arms and her voice, commanding, "Dallas, it has been entrusted to you to light Erin's pyre, and it is my decision that Shaunee use her Goddess-given gift to aid our fallen daughter's body as it returns to ash and earth." Thanatos gestured for Shaunee to join her beside the pyre.

Shaunee's cheeks were washed with tears, but she didn't hesitate. She walked to the pyre and as Dallas touched the torch to the dry logs, she called into the night, "Fire, come to me!" Her long, dark hair lifted on the heat thermals that surrounded her. "Set my Twin's body free! So I ask, and so mote it be!" There was a great *whooshing* and the pyre exploded in fire. Everyone except Shaunee was forced to take several steps back from the blaze. Aphrodite shielded her eyes with her hands, unable to look away from Shaunee. She was still crying, but she was also smiling as her element did her bidding.

Aphrodite thought she looked like a fire goddess. Not that she'd ever tell Shaunee that, but still . . .

As Thanatos closed the circle and bid everyone to blessed be, Aphrodite whispered to Darius, "Gotta do something real quick. I'll meet you back in our room." She kissed him and then ducked through the crowd, trying to catch sight of Shaylin, and wishing the girl wasn't so effing short.

Distracted, she almost ran into a damn tree. Good thing she didn't because on the other side of it, Rephaim was holding Stevie Rae, who was still bawling her eyes out and totally soaking the front of his T-shirt.

"I know it's hard, but Erin is with Nyx," Rephaim was saying to Stevie Rae. He glanced up as Aphrodite stumbled around the big oak.

She put her finger to her lips and mimed a *shhh* motion, shaking her head. That's all she needed—Stevie Rae expecting Aphrodite to be included in her blubberfest. Luckily, Rephaim didn't pay any attention to her, and went right back to overcomforting Stevie Rae while Aphrodite tiptoed away.

She felt a shivery, *not right* feeling and froze. Her gaze found Dallas immediately. He couldn't see Aphrodite, though. The tree was in his way, but Aphrodite didn't think he would have noticed if she'd stomped around unattractively like a heifer. He was too busy staring at Rephaim and Stevie Rae. The hatred in his gaze was frightening. Silently, Aphrodite worked her way around the tree, moving closer to Dallas. He was saying something, muttering to himself. Aphrodite concentrated, watching his too-thin lips and listening with all of her focus.

"It ain't right. Mine is dead and hers ain't even human. It ain't right . . ."

That was it. That was all Dallas was muttering. Aphrodite waited, watched, ready to warn Rephaim and yell for Darius if Dallas actually tried anything, but the kid just kept saying the same shit over and over, even as he walked away.

Aphrodite shook her head. Dallas was seriously not right. Z might be having a mental breakdown, but she had a point about not wanting to be stuck at the House of Night with him.

"Okay, see ya tomorrow, Erik!"

Hearing Shaylin's voice, Aphrodite sighed in relief, and hurried to catch up to her as she waved bye to Erik and started meandering toward the girls' dorm.

"Pssst!" Aphrodite called after her.

Shaylin glanced back, questioningly.

"There. Now." Aphrodite pointed to the shadows outside the flickering gaslights that illuminated part of the sidewalk.

They got to the dark part of the pathway together. Shaylin crossed her arms over her chest. "You can't boss me around."

"And yet you just did what I told you to do."

Without saying anything Shaylin spun around and started to walk away.

"Hang on! I was just kidding. Come back." When Shaylin didn't stop walking, Aphrodite sighed and added, "Please."

Shaylin immediately came back to her. "Please was all you needed to say. Next time try it first."

"Fine. Fine. Whatever."

Aphrodite looked at Shaylin. Shaylin stared back at her. Aphrodite flipped her hair. Shaylin's eyes widened. "Are you nervous?"

"I never get nervous."

"You're fidgeting with your hair."

"I'm *flipping* my hair."

"You need something from me." Shaylin smiled.

"No. *I* don't need anything from you. *Aphrodite, Prophetess of Nyx,* needs something from you."

"If you start talking about yourself in the third person I'm going to get very creeped out."

"Just shut it and listen: I had a vision, and it had to do with Zoey losing control of her temper, and bad stuff happening because of it."

Shaylin's smile disappeared. "Did you tell Z?"

"I don't think I should. Or at least I don't think I should right now."

"Have you prayed about it and really listened for an answer from Nyx?"

"Yes, moron. Of course I have. The answer I got is why I'm standing here talking to you and not Zoey."

"Don't call me a moron," Shaylin said.

"Then don't sound like one. You already know something's up with Z."

Shaylin chewed her lip.

"Well?" Aphrodite pressed.

"I'm not comfortable talking about this with you."

"Forget you're talking to me. Pretend like we're one Prophetess talking to another Prophetess about our High Priestess, because that's actually what we are." Aphrodite met her gaze. "This isn't gossip. This isn't mean. This is us doing our jobs."

"Her colors are getting weirder and weirder," Shaylin said quietly.

"Weird*er*? Like it's *been* happening?"

"Yeah, I talked to her about it in the tunnels. I noticed her colors were getting murky, swirling together, and I told her that it seemed to me that she was confused about something."

"And then what?"

"She said I was kinda right, and basically, that I shouldn't blab her business around to everyone."

"Yeah, I can understand why she'd say that," Aphrodite said.

"And now I've blabbed and I feel crappy about it."

"I'm not going to say anything to anyone—not even Zoey. Shaylin, are Zoey's colors still murky?"

"Very, and they're swirling, almost like the beginning of a whirlpool or the tip of a tornado."

"What the hell does that mean?"

"Anger. Confusion. Frustration. Basically, not good stuff. Okay, here's an example: Dallas's colors are *always* swirling."

"Shit! Are Zoey's always swirling?"

"No, that just started, and it doesn't keep going. She was swirly when she first came up to the circle tonight, but as Thanatos talked and prayed, she got more and more still and clear. By the time Shaunee lit the pyre she was back to her normal purple with silver flecks. Sorry, I know it's super confusing," Shaylin said, shaking her head.

"Actually, I think you're doing a good job of describing it." When Shaylin blinked at her in surprise Aphrodite added, "I told you she's Aphrodite, Prophetess of Nyx, right now."

"Third person—creepy."

"Get used to it. Here's what *the Prophetess* wants you to do— keep watching Zoey and tell me whenever she starts to swirl."

"Like, right away?"

"Yes, moron. Right away."

"You're sounding a lot more like Aphrodite than *the Prophetess* right now," Shaylin said.

"That's because she and I have mind melded. Just do what we say and no one gets hurt," Aphrodite said.

"You're so damn strange," Shaylin said.

"Normal is overrated. Do we have a deal?"

"Do you promise not to tell anyone except Zoey and Nyx what I tell you?"

Aphrodite hesitated, then nodded. "I promise. You have my oath on it. I wouldn't gossip about Zoey."

Shaylin studied her. "I believe you. Both of you."

CHAPTER ELEVEN

Aurox

Aurox wondered if funerals ever got easier. Would it be less sad if he had lived decades of life first? If he had friends he could talk with afterward?

He walked away from the main group, heading nowhere in particular. No one spoke to him. No one noticed him. But Aurox noticed everything and everyone.

Shaunee remained beside the burning pyre, crying softly, though the heat of the flames dried her tears almost instantly. Thanatos stood as close to her as she could bear. The winged immortal remained as well, standing statue-like in the shadows, eyes scanning the area around the pyre as if he expected an enemy to appear from the fledgling's ashes.

Aurox moved swiftly and silently, staying out of Kalona's line of vision. He didn't know what to make of the immortal. Was he friend, foe, or simply a god whose purpose was to observe them and laugh?

Aurox continued to move through the shadows. Rephaim was comforting Stevie Rae. Aurox envied their closeness—especially the way Stevie Rae was able to accept Rephaim completely, without judgment or hesitation.

He noticed Dallas as well. The young red vampyre seemed

miserable, filled with anger and envy. Aurox did not like how he stared at Stevie Rae and muttered to himself. Perhaps he should speak with Thanatos about him, though the High Priestess, as well as the rest of the House of Night, seemed well aware of Dallas's potential for violence.

Aphrodite flitted off. Aurox saw her calling to Shaylin. It felt right that the two Prophetesses would seek one another out, especially during such trying times.

He should have continued to walk away—continued to fade into the night and wait until Stevie Rae's red fledglings were settled for the daylight hours in their new lair in the basement. Then he could reappear to stand guard. To protect. To remain silent and vigilant, and to want no more than to serve this House, and through this House, the Goddess Nyx.

But, as always, Zoey drew his gaze. Aurox paused, and from the darkness allowed himself a moment to watch her. Stark was holding her hand as she talked with Damien and Darius. She kept glancing from whomever she was speaking to, to Shaunee. Zoey was nodding, and engaging in the conversation, but Aurox could tell that most of her attention was on her friend who stood so close to the pyre, weeping.

Zoey will probably remain until Shaunee is ready to say her final good-bye, Aurox thought. For a moment he considered remaining as well—waiting with Zoey. Perhaps there would be something he could say or do that would help.

No. Stark would be with Zoey, and Stark could only abide Aurox's presence if Zoey wasn't near.

And yet Aurox felt drawn to Stark as well as to his young Priestess. He honestly liked the Warrior. There had even been moments today when he had been helping Stark and Darius ready the basement for the red fledglings that they had worked easily together—companionably. Aurox had almost felt as if he belonged. Then Stark and Darius had sent him on an errand and Thanatos had called him—asked him to find Zoey—she was late for a meeting.

Aurox had found Zoey easily. He thought he could always find Zo.

But Stark had been with her, and suddenly the Warrior had become strange, cold, freezing him out and causing Zoey to berate him in front of the others.

He's jealous of me, Aurox thought, though he knew there was no reason for Stark to feel the slightest bit of jealousy.

Zoey paid no attention to Aurox. She rarely even glanced in his direction. Earlier, it had seemed as if she could hardly bear to share the same table with him in the cafeteria.

Aurox knew that within him there was supposed to be the soul of a human boy named Heath. This boy had been Zoey's love—her intended Consort—even though she was bonded to an Oath Sworn Warrior.

Aurox had asked Damien about it, and Damien had explained the situation to him with patience and kindness, though his explanation hadn't really helped.

It wasn't that Aurox didn't understand that it was acceptable for a fledgling or a vampyre to have a human Consort as well as a Warrior or even a vampyre mate. That made sense to Aurox. Love was too complex an emotion to be constrained and given limitations.

What Aurox didn't understand was how he could possibly host a human boy's soul.

Where was this Heath?

Aurox had tried to reach him. Tried to talk to him. He never received any answer. Yes, once in a while he had odd dreams where he was fishing or playing sports. Or kissing Zoey.

No, that dream wasn't from something within him. He

dreamed of kissing Zoey because *he* wanted to kiss Zoey. She was beautiful. She was powerful. She had believed him to be more than a vessel of evil before he believed it himself.

Aurox mentally shook himself. It mattered little what Zoey was because of what she was *not*. She was *not* interested in him because the terrible truth was that sharing the soul of her human love was not enough to make Zoey forget how Aurox had been created. He had come into being through the death of her mother.

He couldn't forgive himself for that. How could Zoey?

But I didn't murder her mother! Aurox's mind cried.

Had her mother not died, I would not exist! His conscience reminded him.

Not my choice! Not my fault!

Yet, still, I am held responsible for the death!

Because I am a product of that death!

Mentally exhausted by the internal debate that never changed—never could be won—Aurox did the only thing that he knew would silence the struggle within him. Unnoticed by anyone, Aurox made his way to the stone wall that encased the grounds of the House of Night. It stood twelve feet tall and two feet wide. With preternatural strength, Aurox leaped to the top of the wall, dropping quietly over the outer side. The wall was exactly 6,823 feet long. Aurox knew this not because he had looked up its length in the school's registry. He knew it because he had covered each of those feet, shadowing the great wall, running, running, running, around and around the school grounds in the darkness outside the wall, until all he knew was the struggle for breath, the pounding of his heart, the burning of his body, and the war within his mind finally ceased.

So Aurox ran.

There were lights hung high on iron arms that jutted in regular intervals from the wall. Those lights were the only electric spotlights the House of Night owned, and they were aimed outward, effectively blinding any humans who might attempt to peer into the gaslit, shadowy school grounds. Those spotlights also created the shadow at the base of the wall in which Aurox ran, unseen, more swiftly than any human, any vampyre, could ever run.

The night before, after the fledgling and the human had died, it had taken ten laps around the school for Aurox's mind to quiet. He thought tonight it might take several more.

He breathed deeply, steadily, pumping his arms and driving his body unmercifully.

Aurox's left shoulder skimmed the stone as he followed the first curve around the northwestern part of the school.

He didn't see the metal barrel. He didn't see the humans. He did collide with both humans and metal and fall, end over end, rolling several feet before he could stop himself.

"Fuck! Vampyre!" a male voice yelled.

"We didn't see anything!" another male cried.

Dazed, Aurox stood, turned, and faced the danger. Already he was reaching out for the fear that was wafting from the two males, readying himself to draw the emotion to him, to fuel his change into a creature that would battle them—that would protect the House of Night.

Two teenage males had scrambled away from Aurox. They were holding red plastic cups that had had been full of liquid before Aurox had slammed into them. Together they had grabbed the little metal barrel and were trying to drag it away with them as they backed away from him.

"Hey, that's not a damn vampyre," one of the boys said.

The other squinted at Aurox, staring at his unmarked forehead. "Damn, you're right, Zack."

They stopped dragging the barrel. "Shit, man, you made us spill our beer. You almost made us run off and leave the keg."

"Yeah, that's not okay," the other boy said, shaking his head and wiping at the liquid that had spilled down the front of his shirt. Then he paused. "Hang on—he was runnin'. Is a vamp chasing you?"

"Chasing me? No," Aurox said.

"Then why the hell were you runnin' like that?"

"Because I wanted to," Aurox answered truthfully.

"Dude, next time *look* where you run."

Completely confused Aurox said, "What are you doing here?"

"Shit, man, same thing you are. Trying to get a look at some vampyre pussy."

"Vampyre pussy?"

The first boy sighed. "Look, we ain't showin' you unless you can keep your mouth shut."

"Vampyre pussy," Aurox repeated, not sure whether to crack their skulls together or laugh.

"Just show him, Jason. It's not like he's one of them. And if he tells anyone it'll fuck this up for him, too."

Jason shrugged. "Okay, but *don't say shit.*"

"I won't say shit," Aurox said.

"Right. Check this out." Gesturing, Jason had Aurox follow him to the wall. He stopped and pointed at the metal barrel. "Bring the keg. It's too high up to see without it."

Aurox lifted the metal barrel and took it to Jason at the wall.

"Damn, man, you're strong. Fucking keg weighs a ton," Jason said appreciatively, rolling it so that it was positioned against the stone wall. Then, carefully, he stood on it, balancing by finding finger holds in the stones. "Right here. You can see in." The boy pressed his face against the wall, his eyes disappearing as he peered. "It's damn dark in there, but sometimes, usually about now, you can see vamps. And it don't matter how cold it is—they don't wear much. I've seen some serious vampyre leg and tit." He hopped down. "Check it out."

Feeling surreal, Aurox followed Jason's lead. He balanced easily on the metal barrel and there, at eye level, was a fist-sized hole in the school's wall. Through it Aurox could see the sidewalk that stretched between the girls' and boys' dormitories. As he watched, two female fledglings came into view. Their voices carried to him, but the words were lost in the night. He could see them, though he didn't recognize the two girls. With a little jolt of surprise he realized they were wearing skirts that showed their legs and little tops that stretched tightly over their breasts.

Aurox got off the barrel and faced the two boys.

"Did you see any of them?" Zack asked, eyes bright with excitement.

"No," Aurox said.

"Well, shit. There's been all sorts of action going on in there tonight, but we haven't hardly been able to see nothing," Jason said. "So, want a beer? We got another cup."

Not sure what else to do, Aurox nodded.

"I'm Jason, and this is my cousin Zack," Jason said, opening a spout on the keg, and then handing him the full cup.

"To hot chicks!" Zack said, as he and Jason lifted their cups. Both boys looked at him expectantly.

"Yes!" Aurox tried to sound normal and enthusiastic. When the two boys upended their cups and gulped down the liquid, he followed suit and took a long drink from the plastic cup. The beer was cold and a little bitter, but he liked it. He liked it a lot.

"Drink up," Jason said. "We have a shitload of beer. The other guys who were supposed to meet us here turned out to be dickless no-shows."

"Hey, all the more for us!" Zack said.

Aurox drank with them, thinking that there was something very relaxing in just standing there with the two boys, and not having them look at him like he was a freak.

Aurox took another long drink, finishing the cup. He wiped the foam from his mouth with the back of his hand, and then he heard himself blurting, "I'm Heath. Do you guys come here often?"

Jason refilled all of their cups, then the two boys sat on the grass, their backs against the wall. Aurox sat across from them.

"Nah, we just found this place a few nights ago."

"How?" Aurox asked and drank.

"Well, we was drivin' by, mindin' our own business, and Zack says to stop—he sees lights *through* the wall," Jason said. "I thought he was crazy."

"You thought I was drunk," Zack corrected him.

"You were both, dude," Jason said, and laughed.

"Yeah, but I was right. When we got out and I gave him a leg up, Jason found the hole."

"It was easier to see before. They had a bunch of Christmas tree lights strung all over the campus in there. Got a good look at some vampyre pussy. Damn, those girls are hot."

"Fledglings," Aurox corrected him automatically.

"What's that?"

"You probably didn't see vampyres. You probably saw fledglings."

"Like I care? I saw leg and tit and it was hot," Jason said. "So, did you find a hole, too?"

"No," Aurox said.

"Damn! I was hoping you found somethin' with more to see," Jason said.

"Hey, dickhead, you need to be happy with what I found. This is the best look we've had at *real* vampyres," Zack told his cousin.

"Fledglings," Aurox corrected again, holding his cup out for another refill.

Jason opened the spout again, refilling his cup, but Zack was watching Aurox carefully.

"How do you know so much about them?" Zack asked.

Jason sat up straighter. "Hey, are you one of their donors? Like, do you let them suck your blood?"

"And fuck you?" Zack added.

"No. No," Aurox said, shaking his head, noticing that it was feeling strange—woozy—and the ground seemed to be swaying a little under him.

"Look, we won't say shit to anyone if you tell us how to get that gig," Zack said.

"Seriously, nobody. Not one person will know," Jason said.

"I'm not anyone'ssss mate," Aurox said and belched. Then he laughed. His speech was giving him trouble, but he felt good. Really good.

"Dude, why are you laughing?"

"It's not fucking funny that you're keeping this shit to yourself."

Aurox finished the third cup of beer in one long gulp. "I was laughing at the bubbles in my head."

Zack frowned. "Lightweight. You better not have far to drive to get home."

"Don't have to drive," Aurox said happily.

"Then you *do* stay here!" Zack said.

Aurox blinked several times, trying hard to focus on the boy. "Sssometimes I do," he slurred.

"Okay, look, we're not kidding. We could be into the blood-sucking. They don't even need to pay us," Jason said.

"But not with guys. I can't go there," Zack said.

"Oh, for sure. Not guys," Jason agreed. "But chicks, yes. Totally yes."

"So, what do we have to do?" Zack asked.

Aurox's head was filled with amazing little bubbles, and his legs felt funny—like they were too heavy. But his mind seemed to be working fine. He knew the boys shouldn't be out there, and he knew he—for sure—shouldn't have run into them. But all that came out of his mouth was, "Wwwwait. Thinking."

Jason sighed and took another swig of beer. "Maybe having his blood sucked so much fucks up his alcohol tolerance level."

"I don't give a shit, as long as I get more than my blood sucked," Zack said.

"I hear ya on that," Jason said.

They stared at Aurox.

Aurox was considering and rejecting options. While he considered, he held out his cup to be refilled.

"Are you sure? You're gettin' pretty wasted," Jason said.

"Thinking," Aurox slurred.

Zack shrugged. "Give him more. He said he's not drivin'."

Aurox thought about his options while he drank. He could morph part way into the bull creature and scare the two boys away. Or, he could just pick them up and toss them toward the road, and growl. Either way they'd be scared way.

He'd keep their beer, though.

But as he thought about it more Aurox realized scaring the boys was probably a bad idea. The House of Night was already on lockdown. It wouldn't be good for the school if the boys were scared enough to go to the human authorities.

What Aurox needed was to turn back time and *not* to have run into them. He'd still like to keep the beer, though. He really liked the beer.

Everything else needed to be wiped away from the night. Gone. Forgotten. Never happened. Except for the beer.

Zack leaned closer to Aurox. "Hey, you okay in there?"

"You want to give us a number to call or whatever? Like we said, we won't tell nobody."

That's when Aurox got the idea. It was a good one, too. It would fix the problem with the boys who had found the hole, *and* it would show Stark that he wasn't his enemy—that he actually wanted to be his friend. Plus, he'd get to keep the beer. He grinned at the boys. "No number. Wait here. I'll bring 'em to you."

"Seriously!" Zack said.

"Vampyres?" Jason seemed more skeptical.

"Not females. I'll bring vampyre-donor-ssspecialist vampyre," Aurox stumbled over the words.

"Uh, we said we weren't into guys," Jason said.

"No, dude, shut up! He's gonna get the guy who'll take us to the chicks," Zack said. "You just can't walk in and do this shit like it's nothing. There's rules that have to be followed. Right, Heath?"

"Yes," Aurox said. "We will follow the rules." He stood and held his cup out for another refill. Then he pointed at Zack and at Jason. "You. And you. Stay. I'll be back with the vampyre and the rules."

Holding his full cup carefully, Aurox crouched, and then sprang up to land on the top of the twelve foot wall.

"That was awesome!" Jason said.

"No wonder they keep this shit quiet. If everyone knew that you got, like, superpowers from vamp sucking there'd be a line around the fucking school to get in!" Zack said.

"Stay," Aurox said. Holding the red cup carefully, he dropped down into the school grounds.

He meant to run swiftly to the field house. That was where the entrance to the basement was, and that was where he thought Stark would probably be, helping the red fledglings get settled in. But Aurox's run was more of a sideways jog. And instead of a swift, stealthy entrance to the field house, the doorknob was turning wrong and when he finally managed to open it, Aurox's momentum had him stumbling inside, staggering across the sand and into the hallway that led to the door to the basement and somehow bumping up against Kramisha.

"Damn, Aurox! 'Scuse yourself," she snapped at him.

"I didn't mean—I couldn't get the door—well, sorry," he finally managed. He saw that she, and the group of fledgling behind her, were staring at his beer. He followed their gazes, looking down at an almost full cup. When he looked up it was to grin at her and slur, "I didn't sssspill any!"

"You's shitfaced," Kramisha told him. Then she turned toward the open door to the basement and shouted, "Z! Your boy's out here makin' an ass of hisself!"

"Noooo! Not, Zo, I need—" Aurox tried to whisper to her, but Kramisha waved a hand in front of her face, screwed up her nose, and backed away from him.

"Shewww!"

"Kramisha?" Zoey was coming up from the basement. Aurox was relieved to see Stark right behind her.

"*That* smells nasty." Kramisha pointed at Aurox. "He been drinkin'. A lot. I ain't entirely sure what he is, but I'm sure gettin' shitfaced can't be good for him." The other fledglings were still staring at Aurox, and she motioned for them to follow her. "Let's get settled. And leave Z to her own business."

Watching them go, Aurox said, "I'm not a *that*."

Zoey and Stark walked up to him. Zoey sniffed and looked from his almost full cup to his face. Her big, pretty eyes got bigger, but not really prettier. "Holy crap! You're drunk!"

CHAPTER TWELVE

Stark

"Drunk?" Aurox said. He looked confused and, well, drunk. "Drunk," the kid repeated. Then he nodded with exaggerated seriousness. "Yes. Drunk."

Zoey opened her mouth, no doubt to ask Aurox what the hell was going on, but he ignored her, stepped into Stark's personal space, and in a gush of beer breath spoke way louder than the whisper he'd been trying for, "Stark, you come with me. You have to pretend to be vampyre-specialist-donor vampyre and make them forget vampyre pussy."

Zoey made a noise that sounded like she might have been choking. Stark couldn't look at her. He was too busy trying not to bust out laughing. Aurox was totally wasted! And he'd just said vampyre pussy—out loud. Man, Zoey was gonna shit kittens! The whole thing was awesome.

"Aurox, how many of those have you had?" Stark pointed at the almost full red Solo cup.

Aurox squinted at the cup. Stark watched him count on his fingers. "One, two, three, four. This is four, and I didn't spill it, even though I jumped on *and* off the wall. Stark, beer is good!"

"My head is going to explode," Zoey said.

"No! No! No!" Aurox assured her, sloshing beer all around

them. "Nothing bad will happen. Stark will make the human boys forget."

Suddenly, Stark didn't think Aurox was so funny. "Hang on—what human boys?"

"The ones with the keg who're looking for vampyre pussy," Aurox said, totally matter-of-factly.

"What in the hell is going on!" Zoey shouted.

"Jeesh, Zo, take a chill pill," Aurox said. "Me and Stark can handle it."

For just that instant Aurox sounded so much like Heath that Stark watched Zoey's face pale. Her hand went to the Seer Stone around her neck and she fingered it nervously.

"Zoey." Stark spoke softly, trying to radiate calm to her. "It's going to be okay. Whatever's going on, *Aurox* is right. He and I can handle it."

Zoey met his gaze and nodded, not saying anything. Stark turned back to Aurox. Damn, it was so fucking weird! The kid looked *nothing* like Heath. He usually sounded and acted *nothing* like Heath. And yet here was Heath's spirit, all bathed in beer, shining through Aurox so brightly it almost blinded them.

"Give me that." Stark took the beer from Aurox and tossed it onto the sandy floor of the field house. Aurox watched it spill as if Stark had wasted water in the desert. "Now, tell me exactly what's going on."

"I drank beer with them. It was good, and they were nice, but they shouldn't be here. I didn't want to scare them and make them tell other humans about," he paused, and did his exaggerated whisper again, "*you know, my bull.* So, I told them to wait and I came to get you so that you could make them go away and forget."

"There are human boys here somewhere?" Zoey asked.

Aurox's face scrunched up as he frowned at her. "Not *here.*

Outside—out *there*." He pointed in the general direction of the door to the field house behind them.

"Outside the field house!" she almost yelled.

"Zo, sometimes I think you don't listen so good," Aurox said. Still frowning at her, he continued speaking slowly, as if trying to get her to understand a foreign language. "Two boys. *Outside* the wall. With the keg. And cups. They. Want. Hot. Vampyre. Chicks."

"Okay, I think I get it." Stark grabbed Aurox's arm and started to drag him toward the door and away from Z before she went for his throat, although that would have been funny as hell. "You found two kids, with beer, trying to get over the wall, right?"

"See, you listen better." Aurox patted him on the back, almost knocking Stark over. "But they're just looking through the hole for vampyre pussy, not trying to get over the wall."

"If you say pussy one more time I'm going to smack the crap out of you," Zoey said, coming after them.

"You can't come!" Aurox stumbled to a stop. "You have legs and tits!"

"Oh. My. Goddess. I'm going to kill him!"

Stark stepped between the two of them. He faced Zoey. She'd gone from pale to bright red in zero-point-nothing seconds. "Z, I think this is something that a Warrior needs to handle."

Behind him, Aurox belched, sending a wave of beer air wafting over them.

Zoey narrowed her eyes and pointed at Aurox. "You have never been able to drink!" Then she spun around and stomped back to the basement entrance, slamming the door behind her.

"She seems mad. Should we bring her a beer?" Aurox said.

Stark covered his laugh with a cough. "Ur, no. Z doesn't like beer."

"Doesn't like beer? She should. It would make her head feel bubbly and happy."

Stark didn't bother to cover his laugh a second time. "I wish it worked that way with her, but it doesn't."

"Because she has legs and tits?"

Stark knew it was wrong, but he couldn't stop himself. "I'm not sure. Maybe you should ask her next time you see her."

Aurox nodded, looking as serious as a drunk could look. "I will."

"That should be fun. But until then, show me where these humans are, and while we're going there, start back at the beginning and tell me exactly what happened before and after you were introduced to the red Solo cup."

Zoey

Aurox was Heath. Annoying, stupid, beer-soaked Heath. *Vampyre pussy—who the hell even says something like that?* I knew the answer to that ridiculous question: drunk teenage boys.

"Well, they look snug as fleas on an old dog," Stevie Rae said, cutting into my internal dialogue and pulling my attention, thankfully, away from drunk Aurox/Heath and the fact that neither he nor Stark had returned to the basement yet.

"How long until dawn?" I asked her.

"Little less than an hour," Rephaim said.

"Hey, is Stark back yet?" Aphrodite asked as she, Darius, and Shaylin joined us.

"No. Not yet," I said. "But Aurox was pretty messed up. He may be awhile." Kramisha had told everyone about Aurox being drunk. I'd said that Stark was sobering him up, which I assumed he was doing *after* he messed with the minds of the kids who had gotten Aurox drunk. But I hadn't mentioned that part to anyone. They'd had enough stress for one day—hell, for one year—and I hadn't wanted to freak anyone out for no reason. And Stark was usually right—he could handle almost anything, so I was letting him handle it.

Of course I was going to want to hear every single tiny detail when he got his butt back to me. I also had a few choice words ready for Aurox/Heath, *after* he sobered up. Moron.

"I gotta agree with Kramisha. Aurox drinkin' is probably not a good thing," Stevie Rae was saying.

"Typical boy behavior," Aphrodite muttered.

"Well, Heath was a drinker. Remember when he showed up drunk at that—" Stevie Rae began, but broke off when Aphrodite elbowed her. "Oh, uh. Right." Then she very obviously changed the subject. "Hey, y'all did a really good job down here!" She hugged Rephaim and smiled at Darius.

"Yeah," I chimed in, glad she'd changed the subject. "Everything looks really good—cozy and nice." Stark, Darius, and Rephaim had done most of the hard work—then Stevie Rae's red fledglings had quickly and quietly carried sleeping bags and pillows and such down to the basement after the funeral (and while Dallas and his friends had retreated to Goddess only knew where).

"Thank you." Rephaim grinned.

"It did turn out well," Darius said, nodding in appreciation.

"It's like a big slumber party!" Stevie Rae said.

"Which is exactly why Darius and I are *not* staying," Aphrodite said. "Actually," she made a big show of yawning, "I do believe I am ready for bed. What about you, handsome?"

"Your wish is my command, my beauty," Darius said, kissing her.

"It is probably a good idea for all of us who are still staying in the dorm to head to our rooms—*obviously*," I said.

"Has anyone seen Dallas and his idiot friends?" Aphrodite asked.

"No, but they have to be on campus somewhere," I said.

"I say we should just be happy that they haven't been hangin' 'round here," Stevie Rae said. "Maybe Dallas went back to his room 'cause he's feelin' sad about Erin. She was his girlfriend."

"Last time I saw him he was feeling mad, not sad," Aphrodite said.

"What do you mean?" I asked her.

"After the funeral I caught him watching Stevie Rae and Rephaim," Aphrodite said.

"His colors are bad," Shaylin said. "Swirls of anger. I agree with Aphrodite. He's mad, not sad. I hate to say this, but if he and his awful friends are hiding out in his room it's not because they're trying to make him feel better. I would bet he's going to want revenge and not healing."

"Then he needs to go after Neferet. If anyone's to blame for Erin's death, it's her," I said.

"His colors say he doesn't think like that," Shaylin said. "He's mad. Period. And he's going to want to strike out at someone who's in front of his face."

"We need to watch him," Aphrodite added. "Especially you, Shaylin. If you see his colors doing some unusually crazy swirly shit, be sure you let one of our Warriors know—fast. And then find Thanatos or Z."

I looked from one Prophetess to the other. "I like that you two are working together."

"Me, too," Stevie Rae said.

"We're just doing our jobs," Aphrodite said. "No need to get all huggy-kissy. And speaking of jobs—has anyone checked on Shaunee?"

I sighed. "She's probably still by the pyre. Why don't we all walk up and get her. She's going to need a shower and some sleep."

"Okie dokie," Stevie Rae said. "I'm glad I'm roomin' with her. I'll make sure she gets somethin' to eat before she goes to bed, too."

"Okay, I gotta ask—how in the hell does Rephaim get back inside your room? Do ya just leave the window open, or what?" Aphrodite said.

"Are you askin' just to be mean?"

"No, bumpkin. Not this time. I'm asking because I'm curious."

I didn't say anything. The truth was that I was curious, too. Shaylin and Darius stayed quiet as well. Okay, because *it's weird that Rephaim turns into a bird every day and we were dying to know the details.*

"She does leave the window open, but only a little," Rephaim answered for her.

"Huh," Aphrodite said. "So you fly in and out?"

"Just in, usually," Rephaim said. "I walk outside just before dawn. I fly back as the sun sets."

"What about your clothes?" Shaylin asked the question I wanted to ask, but didn't because I couldn't think of a High Priestessly way to phrase it.

"He takes 'em off right before the sun rises," Stevie Rae said. "And I bring them to our room. Then he puts 'em back on when he's himself again."

"I'll bet it would suck if you timed that wrong," Shaylin said.

Rephaim smiled. "You're right. I'd hate to have to hang from that third-floor window, yelling, until someone heard me and helped me in."

Stevie Rae giggled. "You'd be naked."

"It'd be like one of my naked-at-school-in-the-middle-of-class nightmares," I said.

"I have those, too!" Shaylin said. "They're awful. And I can never find my shoes. Like I'd care about my shoes if I was naked at school?"

"I'm glad you're just a tall, handsome, muscular Warrior," Aphrodite told Darius, tiptoeing and kissing him. "The naked bird thing would stress me out."

"He's not naked when he's a bird," Stevie Rae said. "He has feathers."

"Let's go," I said, before the two of them could give me a headache.

We waved good-bye to the group of kids that were snuggling down on mounds of sleeping bags, blankets, and pillows, all huddled around the biggest flat screen that would fit down the narrow basement stairs. Following us up the stairs was the crazy opening song of *Django Unchained*. "I can't figure out if I like that movie or not," I said.

"Z, Quentin Tarantino is a genius. Obviously crazy, but still— genius," Aphrodite was saying as we closed the door to the basement.

"Unlike you. You're just crazy," Shaylin told her.

Stevie Rae was giggling at Shaylin when Nicole stepped from the field house into the hallway, cutting her giggles off like she'd flipped a switch. With a rustle of wings, Kalona appeared behind her.

"What's she doin' here?" Stevie Rae ignored Nicole and spoke to Kalona.

"She found me and told me that she was looking for you," Kalona said.

"Spying's more like it," Stevie Rae said.

"Spying? Seriously? That's stupider than calling Tarantino a genius," Nicole said.

Aphrodite made a sound like a hissing cat.

I stepped forward, feeling Darius move to my side. "What do you want, Nicole?"

The red fledgling met my gaze steadily. "I have something to say to Stevie Rae."

"So say it," I said. "She's right here."

Nicole drew a deep breath, and then she walked up to Stevie Rae. Rephaim was watching her carefully, and Kalona was right behind her. I tensed, ready for anything crazy she might do, but I felt a touch on my arm.

"No," Shaylin said quietly. "It's nothing bad."

And Shaylin was right. Nicole stopped in front of Stevie Rae, fisted her hand over her heart, and bowed respectfully. "What I want to say is that I'm sorry for the crap I caused before. I'm sorry I tried to hurt you. I don't have any excuse for what I did. It was wrong. I've changed, and I want to change sides, too. I want you to be my High Priestess."

I could tell that Stevie Rae was shocked—I think we all were shocked. Well, maybe not Shaylin, but the rest of us definitely were. Stevie Rae looked at me. I shrugged. She looked back at Nicole, asking her, "Why should I believe you?"

"Well, I thought about that before I came to talk to you, and I couldn't come up with any for-sure answer, so I figured I'd just take a chance that you actually would believe me because I think High Priestesses just *know* things. If that's true, then you'll know you can believe me."

"Consult your Prophetesses," Kalona said.

"Hey, I got nothing. No vision. No woo-woo feeling either way. Nadda," Aphrodite said. "Ask Shaylin."

Stevie Rae looked at her other Prophetess. "What do ya see?"

"Her colors are pretty. She's not red at all anymore. She's pink, like a flower. She's not hiding anything except that she's way more nervous than she seems." Shaylin paused and smiled at Nicole.

"Sorry about that last part, but I have to tell Stevie Rae the truth."

Nicole's mouth was pressed in a straight line. She nodded, and then spoke quickly, "I understand. And you're right. I am nervous."

"Where's Dallas?" Stevie Rae asked her.

"Last time I saw him I was on my way to my room. He said he was going to the guys' dorm for a *Resident Evil* marathon in his room. I told him I couldn't make it. I'd had enough blood and death for a while," she said.

"So, you're not going to hook up with him again?" Aphrodite asked her.

Nicole faced her. "I don't want anything to do with him."

"Because you're still pissed he cheated on you with Erin?" Aphrodite prodded.

"Because I don't want to be with someone who is mean. Dallas is mean," she said.

"She's telling the truth," Shaylin said.

"You have a responsibility to give her a chance," Kalona said.

At first I thought it was a strange thing for him to say, but then I *really* thought about it. If anyone would know about second chances, it was Kalona.

"I think he's right," I said. "You are the only red High Priestess she has, and if she's swearing allegiance to you, then you have to accept her and give her a chance to prove that her oath is actually worth something."

"Is that what you're doin'? Swearing your allegiance to me?"

"Yes."

"Well, then, I'll give you a chance," Stevie Rae said.

I watched a flush of color come over Nicole's face, and she blinked her eyes real hard, like she might cry. Stevie Rae obviously noticed, too, because when she spoke to Nicole again, her voice had softened. "I have to be sure Shaunee's okay, so I'm going to have Shaylin take you to the rest of the kids."

"In the dorm?" Nicole asked.

"No, my red fledglings are curled up in the basement," Stevie Rae said.

"A basement? Really?" Nicole smiled. "That's awesome!"

I felt my lingering leeriness about Nicole relax. She honestly looked like she didn't have a clue about the basement.

"Shaylin, are you okay with takin' her down there and helpin' her settle in?" Stevie Rae asked.

"Absolutely! I'm staying down there anyway. Come on, Nicole, let's go catch the rest of *Django Unchained*. It's blood and guts, too, but at least there's a happily ever after."

Before Nicole walked away, smiling, with Shaylin, she fisted her hand over her heart and bowed to Stevie Rae again. "Thank you, High Priestess."

Stevie Rae inclined her head gracefully in response and, sounding exactly like a full-grown, awesome High Priestess, said, "Blessed be, Nicole."

CHAPTER THIRTEEN

Shaunee

"You don't need to stay," Shaunee said to Thanatos. She didn't look at the High Priestess. She kept her attention focused on the burning pyre. "I'll keep vigil. I think I should, plus it's something I really want to do."

"You were a good friend to her," Thanatos said.

"I hope I was. I tried to be, but things got real messed up and nothing's turned out like I expected it to."

"Daughter, that's life: messy, confusing, heartbreaking, but wonderful. All any of us can do is to try to be our best, and to learn from our mistakes, as well as our victories."

"Well, right now my best is to stay here, with Erin, and watch over her until dawn."

"It is an ancient tradition that those who most loved the dead remained by their beloved's pyre from its first flame until after the first flame of dawn. I shall leave you to your vigil, wishing you to blessed be, Shaunee."

Shaunee fisted her hand over her heart and bowed to Thanatos respectfully before turning back to watch the pyre blaze.

"You don't need to stay, either," Shaunee spoke to the immortal she knew was watching from the shadows. "Stevie Rae and Zoey will need you. I'll be fine."

"I did not like how Dallas looked tonight. He wants retribution for this death, which is impossible," Kalona said.

"He looked sad when he lit the pyre. Maybe that's all it is—she was his girlfriend," Shaunee said, wanting to believe it.

"If he had truly loved her, he would be keeping vigil as are you." Kalona said what Shaunee hadn't wanted to think about.

"Everyone grieves differently," she said.

"I recognize his way of grieving, and know it will turn to anger. He will lash out, trying to erase his pain with violence and vengeance."

"Is that what you did?" Shaunee looked from the pyre to Kalona. The winged immortal's beauty was almost as bright as the flames, though his brilliance held an Otherwordly silver light.

"Yes," he admitted slowly. "Yes, that is what I did. That is why I recognize it in Dallas. That is also why I understand how dangerous he could become."

"Here's what I don't understand," Shaunee said. "How can losing love make you want to destroy people? When Erin and I weren't Twins anymore I was sad and lonely. But I didn't think about doing anything mean to her, or to Dallas, even though I didn't think he was good enough for her." When the immortal didn't answer, Shaunee turned to face him, though she kept one hand raised, pointed palm forward, at the pyre, controlling her element and allowing its familiar heat to soothe the sadness within her.

"I believe your question can be answered only by each individual."

"So, you're not going to answer me?"

Kalona hesitated, and Shaunee could see several emotions crossing his handsome face: sadness, doubt, and even annoyance. His wings lifted restlessly, but finally he did answer her. "When I lost Nyx the only way I could bear it was to replace all the love I'd felt for her with anger. As long as I burned with anger I made myself believe loving the Goddess had been a lie." Kalona met Shaunee's gaze, and she thought she could see eons of misery in his amber eyes. "Maintaining that anger came with a price, and that price was violence and destruction, death and darkness."

"But wouldn't it have made more sense if you'd just gone to Nyx and admitted you didn't want to live without her?"

Kalona's smile was infinitely sad. "My pride kept me from seeing any way back to her."

"Does it still?"

"No. It is Nyx herself who keeps me from her side now," Kalona said.

"I don't think she always will," Shaunee said.

"You are young," he said. "You haven't lived long enough for life to kill your ability to hope."

"Well, I don't know Nyx as well as you do, but I absolutely believe that she's a just, forgiving goddess. She's proven that time after time. I've seen it, and I'm only eighteen." Shaunee paused. "Maybe it's not about how long you've lived, or having the ability to hope, even when things seem hopeless. Maybe it's just about how much faith you have."

"I do have faith, young fledgling. I have faith that Nyx forgives those who deserve her forgiveness," he said.

"You don't think you deserve her forgiveness, do you?"

"I know I do not." He bowed his head slightly to her. "Stand watch over your friend. I will disturb you no longer." Then he faded into the darkness.

Shaunee turned back to the pyre and raised her other hand. She took a step even closer, closed her eyes, and let her element flood through her, and as she did so she spoke a prayer that lifted with the smoke to Nyx.

"Goddess, this is my good-bye to Erin. I know she's with you, and finally at peace. Thank you for loving her and taking care of her. Also, thank you for loving Kalona and taking care of him, too, because no matter what, I know you don't just turn your back on the people you love."

"You think you're so fucking much better than me, don't you?"

Dallas's voice jolted her, and Shaunee couldn't say anything for several moments while she controlled her element. The flaming pyre reflected her shock, and had Shaunee not focused and brought it under control, its natural course would have been to consume Dallas.

When she had her element under control again and was able to turn her attention to Dallas, the stupid kid was just standing there, smirking at her and looking like the dickwad he was, totally oblivious to the fact that she had just saved his idiot life.

"No, Dallas, I don't think I'm better than you. The truth is, I don't think much about you at all," she said.

"Erin thought you were an uptight bitch," he said.

Shaunee bit her lip instead of lashing out at him. She could have fried him with her fire, *or* with her words. But she didn't want to do either, especially over Erin's pyre. So, she thought about it for a long, uncomfortable moment, and then said the nicest thing she could think of. "Are you sure you knew what Erin really thought about anything?"

"I fucked her! Of course I knew what she thought." He took a couple of steps out of the shadows toward Shaunee, and his smirk became a sneer. "Unless you're tellin' me you used to fuck her, too."

Shaunee stared at him, too shocked by the mean ignorance in his words to know what to say.

"Shiiiiit! I knew you two were abnormally close. You did fuck her! And she didn't even tell me. That's a damn shame. The three of us, we could've had a good time."

The flame that had been building inside Shaunee turned white hot. Her mind cleared. She trapped Dallas with one look.

"I didn't like you when you were with Stevie Rae. You always felt wrong to me. Plus, you're too short," she couldn't help adding. Then she refocused and made herself tell the truth, without name-calling or spiteful comments. She channeled fire, but instead of burning him, Shaunee scorched him with the truth. "For her entire life, Erin's biggest desire was to find anybody, anything, who could make her *feel something*. You were just the last in a long list of anybodies. I understood how vulnerable and messed up she was, and I really cared about her, even after she wasn't my best friend anymore. If you really cared about her, you'll show it by staying here with me until sunrise and respecting her memory, even though she's gone."

Dallas couldn't seem to look away from her. His eyes filled with tears and then overflowed. Shaunee thought she might have glimpsed the real boy for a second—the boy who might have actually been able to love Erin. Then he blinked and wiped his cheeks with the back of his sleeve. His lip curled. "You're as stupid as Erin used to say you were. I can't stay here until sunrise. I'm a *red* vampyre. The sun will burn me up."

Shaunee's element filled and calmed her. She would not return his hateful words with more poison. "You always know when it is dawn. You could stay until just before the sun rises, and then leave. I'll wait the rest of the time with her. Erin would appreciate it."

"I thought you said I was just the last in a long list of anybodies," he said.

"I shouldn't have said that—it was mean of me, and it's not right to fight over Erin's pyre. Dallas, I'm sorry."

His laugh was sarcastic. "You're not sorry, you're *weak*. Erin knew that when she left you. Just like I knew it when I left Stevie Rae."

"You didn't leave Stevie Rae. Stevie Rae fell in love with

Rephaim. She left you, and you couldn't handle it. That's when you turned to Darkness, and you're still turned there."

"Fuck Stevie Rae! Fuck all of you! Your friends are the reason Erin's dead!" Dallas yelled, taking a threatening step toward her.

Shaunee lifted one hand. A wall of heat channeled through her, crackling between them. Shielding his face with his arm, Dallas staggered away. "You'll pay for what you've done! You'll all pay for what you've done!"

Stark

"That kid is gonna be hurtin' for certain tomorrow," Stark said as he came into Zoey's old dorm room. There were only ten minutes or so until dawn, and he felt dragged to the ground by weariness deep within him.

"That took you forever. I was really getting worried you wouldn't be back before sunrise," Zoey said, sitting up in bed and putting down the book she'd been reading.

"Yeah, sorry. I couldn't just leave him all messed up like that." He smiled at Z and went over to the sink. "Is Shaunee okay?"

Zoey looked annoyed at the question. "Yeah, she seems fine. Well, she's sad and all, but that's normal. She's staying with the pyre until after the sun rises. I guess Dallas came by and made some kind of stupid scene, which is totally like him, but Shaunee handled it."

"You didn't think you needed to stay with her?"

"Shaunee? At the pyre?" Zoey frowned at him.

"Yeah. You are her High Priestess."

"Well, technically, as long as we're stuck here at the House of Night, Thanatos is her High Priestess, not me. And Shaunee said she told Thanatos she wanted to stay by the pyre by herself. Thanatos respected her wishes—I figured I should, too. Do you have a problem with that?"

Stark cupped water in his hands, rinsing soap out of his face while he tried to figure out how to talk to Z. She'd been so damn touchy since the whole thing on the balcony had happened showing that Aurox was Heath and Heath was Aurox. It made him feel like he was living with a porcupine!

"No," he finally said. "No problem with it at all. Z, I wasn't trying to fight with you. I just wanted to know about Shaunee."

"Erin's funeral's over. Shaunee's fine. That's about it. I want to know what really happened with Aurox and those human boys. I couldn't tell what the hell Heath was talking about."

Stark's stomach tightened. "You mean Aurox."

"Yeah, Aurox." Zoey frowned. "That's what I said. So, what's going on?"

Stark was too tired to argue with her, so he ignored her Freudian slip, even though it made his heart hurt. "Two guys somehow found a hole in the school's wall—not very far from here, actually. They were drinking and looking for hot vampyres." That's about it." He repeated her words, pulled his shirt off, and started to brush his teeth.

"Stark, seriously? You're leaving out massive details."

He shrugged, and spoke through the toothbrush, hoping she'd get the clue and stop with the interrogation. "No big deal. I used my red vamp superpowers to make them believe I was a cop and that they got lucky. I didn't haul them to jail, charge them with public intoxication, and call their parents. And they think the House of Night is on my patrol, so I'll be looking for them every night from here on out, which means they won't be back."

"Well, that's good."

She didn't say anything else for as long as it took him to finish brushing his teeth and get in bed, but he knew from the way she was chewing her lip and scrunching her forehead that she had lots more to say. Plus, he could feel her tension. He could always feel her tension. He realized he should rub her shoulders and try to get her to relax, but he couldn't quite get past the *reason* for her tension.

Aurox was Heath. Zoey loved Heath.

And that hurt Stark's feelings and made him feel like shit.

So, he lay down next to her and blew out the little flicking gas lamp, wishing with everything inside him that Zoey would curl up on his shoulder and put her arms around him and tell him he didn't need to worry about her wanting to be with Aurox or Heath or *anyone except him.*

Instead, from the darkness, Zoey said, "Why was he out there?"

Stark sighed. "He was running around the school wall. I didn't really get why, and he was too wasted to explain it to me."

"Running shuts off his mind," Zoey said.

"How do you know?"

There was a short silence, and he could almost hear her thinking, then she said, "It's what Heath used to do when he had a problem. He'd run himself exhausted and it would shut off his mind."

"Oh," Stark said, feeling shittier by the moment.

"Where is he now?" she asked.

"In the basement passed out," Stark said.

"I didn't think he slept."

"He may not, but I can promise you he passes out."

"Did you turn him on his side so he won't choke if he pukes?"

"No, but feel free to go tuck him in yourself if you're so damn worried about him."

"Stark, I was just—"

"I know what you were *just.* I know the whole thing, Zoey. That's the problem."

"You don't need to get mad at me," she said.

"I'm not mad. I'm tired. The sun's coming up and I gotta sleep. Good night." Stark rolled on his side. His back to her, he curled in on himself, wishing that she'd put her arms around him and pull him to her and tell him everything was going to be okay—that they'd figure this thing out *together*.

Instead he heard her say a soft, " 'Night." He felt the bed shift as she rolled away from him.

Stark had never been so glad to give himself over to the pull of the sun and the dreamless sleep dawn brought with it.

Stevie Rae

It was always so dang hard to say bye to Rephaim. Stevie Rae rolled over, alone in her bed. She was exhausted—the sun had risen a few minutes ago, and every moment she fought the need to sleep it drained her. But she was really having a hard time shutting off her mind. She couldn't stop thinking about how much she wished that Rephaim was there with her. She didn't mean to be ungrateful, but after Erin's funeral, Thanatos breaking with the High Council, Nicole swearing allegiance to her (*her!*), not to mention Neferet being who-the-heck-ever-knows-where, she would've really, *really* liked to snuggle up in Rephaim's arms and feel safe and loved.

Instead she'd said bye to him outside a little bit before sunrise and then come up to the room she was sharing with Shaunee. Stevie Rae had taken the bed nearest the big picture window, even though that wasn't the smartest choice. Their room faced east and got full sunshine in the morning. If they didn't have blackout drapes she'd be like bacon frying in a skillet.

But they did have blackout drapes—big, thick dark ones. They were so heavy and so firmly tied together that even though Stevie Rae left the window open all day long while she slept, the strongest breeze didn't cause them to move. That was a good thing, because she would always leave her window open. What if Rephaim needed to come to her? What if he got in some kind of trouble when he was a raven and needed a safe place to hide? She wanted to believe that something of the boy she loved remained deep within him, even when he was a beast.

That's why she wished he'd let her stay and watch him change into a raven. She'd thought a lot about it, and she might try to touch him—to tame him. *"After all,"* she'd told him the day after the Goddess had forgiven Rephaim and gifted him with the form of a human boy during the hours between sunset and sunrise, *"I tamed a beast once before. Maybe I can do it again!"* She'd expected Rephaim to smile and laugh, like he usually did—he seemed so happy around her. But he hadn't. He'd gotten all serious and taken her hands in his and said, *"When I was a Raven Mocker I had some humanity within me. You have to remember I am different now. When I'm a boy, like now, I'm completely human. When I'm a raven, I'm nothing but a beast. I don't know you. I don't know me. I know only the sky and the need to ride the wind."*

That had scared her. And she'd told him so. She didn't hide stuff from Rephaim—they were too close for that.

"But you always come back to me. Doesn't that mean something of you is still inside the raven?"

He'd looked sad, but he'd told her the truth like they'd promised. *"When I am a raven I am a beast. I don't know love. I don't know you. Please don't make it into something it's not."*

"But you come back to me!"

"Stevie Rae." He'd cupped her face in his hands. *"I think that's just because of Nyx's magick."*

"Like she put a GPS in you so you could find me?"

"GPS?"

"Modern magick that helps you find your way home."

He'd grinned. *"Yes! Nyx put a GPS inside me so I can find you."*

Stevie Rae kicked off her blanket and looked at Shaunee's empty bed. She should try to stay awake and be sure Shaunee was okay. It would be terrible to lose her best friend, and even though Erin and Shaunee had been having problems, that didn't change the fact that up until just a few weeks ago, they had been inseparable for the entire time they'd been at the House of Night. There was a big difference between fighting with your BFF and having your BFF die.

Stevie Rae's mind automatically went back to the night Erin had coughed up her life's blood and died. Zoey had been with her every second. It'd helped. Shaunee being there for Erin had to have helped her, too. And now Shaunee was doing the right thing— she was watching over her friend's pyre until after dawn.

Stevie Rae rolled over and stared at the blackout curtain, trying to keep her eyes open—trying to fight the energy drain that happened naturally to red fledglings and vampyres when the sun was in the sky. It wasn't *impossible* for her to stay conscious during the day. It was just hard. Really hard. Her eyelids fluttered. Maybe she'd rest for just a little while. She'd hear Shaunee come in and wake up again and check on her . . .

The door opened so quietly that it almost didn't wake up Stevie Rae. She lay on her side, facing the window, struggling to come fully awake. *Shaunee's being so quiet,* Stevie Rae told herself groggily. *Maybe she doesn't want to talk. Maybe she just wants to sleep.* Stevie Rae decided that she'd roll over and open her eyes, but not say anything—just let Shaunee know she was there and awake (kinda) if she needed to talk. She started to turn over and suddenly there was a weird crackling sound just above her shoulder. She tried to sit up and the crackle changed to an even weirder hum as an electric shock, like static electricity on steroids, zapped through her, pressing her down on the bed.

Instantly awake and completely freaked out, Stevie Rae tried to sit up again, saying, "Shaunee, somethin's wrong over here."

Even though there was nothing above her, electricity shot through her again! Still on her side, Stevie Rae pressed herself into the bed, trying to stay away from whatever invisible danger was hovering above her. "Shaunee!" she yelled. "Help me!"

"She ain't here. She's still bawling at Erin's pyre. Fucking hypocrite."

Stevie Rae's breaths came in little pants of panic as she recognized his voice. "Dallas, what are you doin' in here?" Automatically, Stevie Rae began reaching out for the protection of her element, but Shaunee's room was on the third floor of the dorm—too many feet above the earth for her element to help her without the aid of a cast circle and Zoey's boosting power.

He stepped into her view, a dark silhouette against the black drapes. She could see that he was holding one of his hands up, palm open, toward her. That palm was glowing. With his other hand he reached out to grasp the thick cord that knotted the drapes in place. "Let's just say I'm here to start my payback."

Stevie Rae tried to get off the bed. An electric field crackled and zapped through her, making her cry out in pain and cringe back. "Dallas, this is crazy! Shaunee's going to be here any second."

"It'll be a second too late for you. And don't worry, I'll make sure Shaunee gets what's coming to her, also. First, it's your turn." His eyes were flat. His voice was filled with hatred. "I'll kill her fast, with just one quick zap. But not you—you deserve to suffer. You cheated on me with a fucking freak of nature—now fry for it!"

Dallas tugged hard at the cord, untying the blackout drapes.

Pulling his half of the curtain open, but being careful to keep himself covered, he stepped back.

Daylight flooded into the room through the open, uncovered window, directly onto Stevie Rae.

It was like she had stepped into the mouth of a furnace. The electrical field pinned her to the bed as the sunlight began burning her skin. Stevie Rae covered her face, writhing in agony, and she began to scream.

Then everything turned super crazy.

There was a terrible screeching, so loud that it penetrated through Stevie Rae's agony.

"Ahhh! Get the fuck off me!" Dallas was yelling and staggering around the room.

The electric field that had kept her prisoner evaporated and Stevie Rae rolled off the bed. She pressed herself against the side of the bed, escaping into the cool shadow.

Dallas lurched past her, obviously trying to get to the door, but the huge raven's attack was relentless. Completely shocked, Stevie Rae watched the bird draw Dallas's blood, raking claws over his upraised arms as he beat the air with massive wings and shrieked in anger.

The door burst open and Shaunee ran into the room.

"Stevie Rae! What the ___"

Dallas grabbed her, holding her before him, using her as a shield.

"No, Rephaim, don't hurt Shaunee!"

The raven drew its claws in at the last second, just grazing the side of Shaunee's face as the momentum of his attack had him hurtling past her and into the wall.

Dallas shoved Shaunee away from him and at the bird and then he ran, darting through the door and slamming it closed behind him.

Shaunee scrambled across the floor to Stevie Rae. "Ohmygod! Your skin! Oh, Stevie Rae, you're burnt bad! Don't move—don't move. I'll close the drapes and get help."

Stevie Rae grabbed her hand. She was panting in pain, but she forced the words. "Let Rephaim out first. He'll be scared."

Shaunee didn't have to look for the raven. He flew at them, skimming above them so close that Stevie Rae felt the air he stirred. He landed on the footboard of the bed. Perching there he peered down at Stevie Rae, cocking his head.

"Go on," she said, trying to sound calm and normal. "I'm okay. Go on outside." Stevie Rae lifted her hand, making a weak gesture toward the open window and ignoring the fact that her hand—her arm—and she was sure her face—were all scorched bloody. "Shaunee'll take care of me now. I'll see you at sunset."

He cocked his head again and made a soft croaking sound.

Stevie Rae thought he was the most beautiful bird she'd ever seen.

"I love you, Rephaim," she said. "Thank you for saving me."

As if that had been what he'd been waiting for, the big raven spread his wings and soared out the open window.

Shaunee ran to the window, closed it, and then tugged the blackout drapes together, tying them quickly and securely.

She crouched beside Stevie Rae. "Want me to lift you into bed?"

"No. Just get help."

As Shaunee sprinted from the room Stevie Rae pressed her face against the floor and prayed that she would pass out.

CHAPTER FOURTEEN

Neferet

Nyx has taken from me the only thing I love. In her den, the words whispered around her, causing the tendrils of Darkness to quiver against her skin. Cocooned in their cold, sharp touch, Neferet's consciousness traversed time and dimensions, skipping like a stone over a still lake, as she touched the past.

As a fledgling she had already been respected and valued. After her Change to vampyre, it was inevitable that Neferet would become a High Priestess. She hadn't had to seek out the title. It had come to her effortlessly, as she so richly deserved.

So, too, did the Warrior come to her.

His name had been Alexander. She remembered her first sight of him at the Summer Games. He'd become a Sword Master that day and defeated all challengers to take the crown that was an olive wreath woven with scarlet ribbons. As the youngest High Priestess of the House, Neferet had placed the wreath on his head and bestowed the ceremonial kiss of victory on his lips.

She remembered she could smell his sweat mixed with the blood of the opponents he had defeated. His eyes had followed her the remainder of the ceremony. Later he told her that he never would have attempted to seduce her that night—not when he was unclean, still covered with gore from the competition pit. But

Neferet had seduced him—had not allowed him to wash and prepare himself for her.

He would smile and retell the story over and over—how his High Priestess had been so desirous for him that she hadn't wanted to wait for him to bathe. What Alexander had not understood until it was too late was that Neferet had been so desirous for him *because* of the blood and sweat in which he had been covered.

Over the course of the rest of the Summer Games, Alexander became infatuated with her. So infatuated that he petitioned for a transfer from the New York House of Night to St. Louis's Tower Grove School where Neferet taught the Spells and Rituals class. As newly crowned victor of the Summer Games, his transfer request was granted.

Neferet would have discarded him soon after his arrival, as she had all of her previous lovers, had it not been for the kitten.

Alexander had, of course, heard the tale of Chloe's death and the great "gift" Neferet had been granted by Nyx that night. So after he arrived at Tower Grove, he took to his knee, bowed reverently before her, and reached into a knapsack slung over his back to pull forth a mewing black kitten who batted at his hand with sharp little claws that glinted from all twelve of her toes.

Neferet reached for the kitten. "A polydactyl! Wherever did you find her?"

"From the wharf on the Manhattan bank of the East River. The sailors prize six-toed cats. They swear they kill twice the rats as normal-toed cats. When I found her, I knew you should belong to her—just as I knew you should belong to me."

Entranced by the kitten's mischievous gaze, Neferet had not discarded Alexander.

He was a powerful Warrior. Alexander's talent with the sword almost matched Neferet's talent to heal. Neferet liked the irony in his loving her. He could cut men down. Neferet could heal them—

even if that healing was no more than a touch that soothed their way to the Otherworld.

Of course Alexander did not cut men down—not unless he or the House of Night was threatened, and in 1899 there were few who would dare threaten the powerful and wealthy Tower Hill House of Night.

Bored, Neferet began ignoring Alexander. She had little Claire—another loving, mischievous cat as her own. She had her duties at the House of Night. And, most important, she had powers that were growing almost daily. Each of those things was more interesting than honorable, dependable, boring Alexander. She hadn't even needed to use her skills as an empath to predict his declarations of eternal love. She had needed to use her skills in diplomacy not to yawn her way through them.

Early in the year of 1900 Neferet received an unusual invitation. She was the youngest High Priestess to be invited to the Gathering at San Clemente Island during which the High Council would lead a discussion on the direction vampyre society should take in this new century, wherein they believed inventions, science, and technology would advance at an unheard-of rate.

Alexander begged Neferet to allow him to accompany her. She had adamantly refused. She had no intention of tolerating his constant, cloying attention when there would be so many new Warriors from whom to choose. After all, the *most* decorated and powerful and experienced Warriors were always chosen to protect the Vampyre High Council and the San Clemente Island House of Night.

She did allow him to drive the carriage that would take her to the Mississippi River and the House of Night–owned steamboat that would transport her in the style of a queen—no, better yet, a goddess—to the port at New Orleans. There she would join many other High Priestesses for the Atlantic Crossing.

They had just arrived at the riverboat wharf when the thieves attacked. Mistaking the House of Night's rich mahogany carriage for that of a wealthy gambler, the six humans, enticed by only one driver and no additional guards for such an opulent carriage, descended upon Alexander. In the darkness they did not see the elaborate tattoos that Marked him forever as vampyre. Too late they did see his sword.

Neferet watched from the window of the carriage, spellbound as Alexander killed all six of the attackers—quickly and brutally. Neferet had thought the sound his sword made as it sliced the air must be like the singing of the mythic Valkyries as they hovered over a Norse battlefield, waiting to choose the dead warriors they would take to Valhalla.

Dripping in gore, he strode to the carriage door, and wrenched it open. Breathing heavily he said, "My Priestess! Thank the Goddess you are unharmed."

"I shall thank you instead." She had taken him there, covered with blood, still carrying the sweet stench of battle, his blood and hers burning hot from killing.

Afterward he had fallen to his knees before her and bowed, saying:

"High Priestess Neferet, love of my life, I pledge myself to you as your Warrior, body, heart, mind, and soul. Please accept me!"

"I accept your Oath," Neferet had heard herself saying while her body still pulsed from his touch. "From here on you shall be my Warrior."

It took exactly one full day and night for her to regret accepting Alexander's Oath. Thankfully, Neferet's empathic gifts enabled her to dam the emotional tide that usually flowed between a bonded Warrior and his Priestess. Alexander bemoaned the fact that he could not sense her needs or hear her emotions. He fretted aloud that should she be in danger, he would not know it as would any other Oath Bound Warrior.

Neferet had only shrugged and said it was an irony that her empathic abilities had somehow negated the Warrior-Priestess psychic sharing. He had been such a fool to believe her. How could he not have seen that it was *she* who controlled their bond? Had she cared more, Neferet would have explained to him that he should be grateful he couldn't know her real thoughts and emotions. By the time they reached Venice, Neferet had thought about casting him over the side of the ocean liner a total of three hundred and sixty-one times, though he sailed on, blissfully unaware of the truth.

Neferet had been right about the San Clemente Warriors. They were spectacular. And outshining them all was Artus, the High Council's Sword Master.

Artus carried himself like a god. He was aloof and untouchable. His word was law with the Sons of Erebus. He answered only to Duantia, Leader of the High Council.

Most important, he loved battle. He was merciless, only ending a training session after he had drawn blood at least thrice from each opponent and making each of them yield formally to him.

Artus was not handsome—he was glorious. He was tall. His muscles were long and lean. His skin was black as a raven's wing. Unlike Alexander, whose muscular young body was smooth and free of scars, Artus was covered with evidence that illustrated a life of violence.

But it wasn't simply his appearance that attracted Neferet. It was what simmered beneath. She used her gift and probed his mind, read his desires, knew his needs. Artus thrived on pain. It was why he pushed his Warriors so hard. It was why he had become the leading Sword Master of the old century, and had remained so for the new one. It was also why he hadn't bonded with any High Priestess. He hadn't wanted any of them to know his true self—to discover his true needs. Instead of taking a vampyre lover, Artus chose human prostitutes to sate his desires. Surprisingly, Neferet heard little gossip about Artus's choice in bed partners. The other High Priestesses found him off-putting. He was too aloof, too serious. He did his job and did it better than any other Warrior in the world—that was all that concerned the San Clemente vampyres. That was all the others understood about him. But Artus could not hide himself from Neferet. To her he was a scroll, written in blood, easily read, easily enjoyed. Neferet desired him more than she had ever desired anyone. She set about having him.

Seducing Artus was more difficult than Neferet had expected. Even among the unworldly beauty of the most powerful and important High Priestesses of their time, Neferet outshined them all. But Artus seemed impervious to Neferet's beauty.

His aloofness had served only to flame her desire for him.

She had studied him. She learned his habits. Neferet took to wearing the traditional ceremonial garb of Italy's ancient High Priestesses, which left her breasts bared, her hair adorned with flowers and ivy, and her lush hips draped in transparent fabric the color of a maiden's blush. Then she made certain she led the casting of the circle that daily asked for Nyx's blessing on the Sons of Erebus Warriors.

She could feel Artus's eyes on her body, but when she tried to meet his gaze and draw his attention more fully to her, he always looked quickly away.

Unfortunately, Alexander did not look away from her. Ever. Her Warrior mistook the reason she was lavishing so much time and attention on the Warriors and at the field house as devotion to him. He strutted about, enjoying the envious glances of his new Warrior friends. He boasted that Neferet's power was as great as her beauty. He fulfilled her every whim like a lap dog. Alexander baffled her as much as he irritated her. How could he not see that he was only an afterthought to her? She probed the Warrior's mind for subterfuge, and found none. His feelings were true. He was completely enamored with her and utterly deluded into believing that she felt the same for him.

Alexander could not have been more wrong.

Neferet yearned for something darker, more sensual, more fulfilling. She yearned for Artus. The next time she led the Warrior Prayer and Artus's eyes grazed her body, Neferet had focused the full force of her gift and delved deep within his mind. She was richly rewarded. She had discovered exactly how to seduce the aloof Warrior.

Neferet had set the stage carefully. She waited until it was just after dawn. She knew Artus would be finished drilling the Warriors. He would be in his quarters in the rear of the field house, preparing to rest for six hours. Then he would take the most uncomfortable guard shift, during the time the sun was brightest in the sky.

The High Priestesses assumed Artus took that shift because of his devotion to them. Neferet knew the truth behind that convenient belief. Artus thrived on the physical pain that uncomfortable shift and the sun caused him. Neferet had kept that delicious secret close to her as she plotted and planned his seduction.

First, she got rid of the fledgling Warrior who served as Artus's aide. That was the simplest step. She allowed the fledgling to caress her—she pretended to desire his youth and his perfect body—she made him believe she would send a fledgling in his place that dawn to serve Artus, *if* the boy would rendezvous with her at a discreet inn on nearby Torcella Island.

Of course she would deny trying to seduce him. Actually, it had amused her to consider the punishment Artus would mete out to him after he discovered why the boy had shirked his duties.

Next, she slipped away from Alexander. She thought of sending him into Venice to find her a perfect piece of silk in an impossible color, but she hadn't wasted the energy on fabricating a fool's mission. Instead she'd waited until his attention was elsewhere, and called fog and mist, shadows and darkness to her so that she faded away from him before he'd even known he needed to look for her. And look for her he would, she was quite sure. He always looked for her. She'd curled her lip in distaste. Why had she let blood and lust shackle her to such a predictable bore? Neferet shrugged off the unpleasant thought of Alexander and his devotion. She wouldn't think about him at all—she didn't want to taint the pleasure of what she was certain would come.

Flushed with excitement, Neferet made her way invisibly to the field house. She entered through the rear door—the one nearest Artus's quarters. Then she waited.

Neferet hadn't had to wait long. As she already had learned, Artus was a vampyre of habit. When his fledgling didn't appear at exactly thirty minutes past dawn, he opened the door to his quarters and gruffly called, "Salvatore! Boy! Where are you?"

"Salvatore is not here. No one is here except for me and you," she'd said.

He was frowning when he emerged from his quarters, hair wet, chest bared, with only a towel wrapped loose and low around his slim hips. "Priestess, have you misplaced your Warrior?"

Neferet had lifted her chin and made her voice flint. "Warrior, have you misplaced your respect? I am a High Priestess. I expect to be greeted as such."

Artus had lifted one dark brow, but he had complied, fisting his hand over his heart and bowing to her. "What can I do for you, Neferet?"

"Ah, you *do* know my name."

"Everyone on San Clemente Island knows your name. What can I do for you, Neferet?" he'd repeated.

"I am here for a lesson," she'd said.

"Your Warrior is a talented Sword Master. Why not take a lesson from him?"

Her full lips had curled up and her voice had purred, "Oh, but you misunderstand me. I am not here to take a lesson. I am here to give one."

His dark eyes widened as she pulled a leather strap from the folds of her dress and lifted the dagger she had been hiding behind her. Then she tugged at the tie at her shoulder, and her gown slithered down her body. Naked, she walked to him, not speaking until she was within reaching distance. "Hold your hands before you and put your wrists together."

"Neferet, what are—"

"I didn't say you could speak! Do as I command!" When he just stood there, statue-like, she raised the dagger and touched it to his chest.

His intake of breath was sharp, but he didn't move, didn't look away from her.

Neferet had smiled, though she'd made her voice sharp, cruel. "Obey me!"

"Yes, High Priestess." His voice had gone deep. He raised his hands, pressing his wrists together.

Neferet wrapped the leather strap around them, tightening it until she could see that it was uncomfortable. Artus's breath was coming fast. Sweat began to bead across his ebony body.

"Good, but you didn't obey me quickly enough. I must punish you, but only if you beg me to."

Their eyes met. In his she saw shock and then understanding and desire. "Please, Neferet, punish me," he begged.

She had been happy to comply.

In her den, Neferet's body warmed in remembrance at how she had punished him. She had been mounting Artus, imagining herself as an ancient goddess mounting a sacrificial bull, when Alexander had found them. He'd cried out her name, sounding like a heartsick schoolboy. Utterly in the throes of ecstasy and pain, she'd whirled from Artus to face Alexander, and dropped the barriers she'd fashioned between them.

"See who I really am! See what I really think of you!"

Her emotions had battered Alexander. She remembered how colorless his face had been when he'd sobbed and fled the field house.

Almost as colorless as it had been when he'd been found the next day after he'd fallen on his sword, ending his miserable, boring life.

She had had to pretend public heartbreak, of course, though not for the first, nor last time in her life. She fabricated a story that portrayed Alexander as a disturbed young Warrior. She'd sobbed and said she had accepted his oath because she'd believed in her ability to heal him. Her concern for his unstable emotions was why she had been spending so much time at the field house—why she had insisted she lead the Warrior Prayers.

The High Council had responded with compassion, praising her for her attempt to heal one who had been so obviously broken. That hadn't been a surprise. Neferet was adept at manipulating High Priestesses. Artus's response to Alexander's suicide *had* been a surprise.

She'd gone to him the next dawn, cloaking herself in darkness and sneaking into his chamber. He had utterly rejected her. His words had been respectful, but she had seen within him. *He had been disgusted by her.*

Neferet had cut through his subterfuge as cleanly as she had his skin.

"Tell anyone why Alexander really killed himself, and I will explain in detail to the High Council about your need for punishment. You know what they would do. That's why you hide your desires with human prostitutes, paying for their silence. Should they discover you, the High Council would, correctly, believe your need affects you as a Warrior and dismiss you from your post."

"You are utterly devoid of compassion." Neferet never forgot the loathing in his voice.

"We each wear our masks, don't we? Keep my secret and I will keep yours."

Neferet had left San Clemente Island the next day, immediately after lighting Alexander's pyre. The High Council had been understanding and compassionate. Of course she should return to her House of Night immediately. The loss of an Oath Bound Warrior was life altering for a High Priestess!

Artus had remained silent.

One year later Neferet heard how shocked the High Council had been when his body had been found floating in the Grand Canal. There had been no sign of violence on his body, only his many scars. Apparently, he had drowned himself. Neferet had smiled at the news.

Alone on the return voyage Neferet had fallen into despair. She'd begun to believe that there would be no male, human or vampyre, who could possibly be her equal. Her despair had grown greater as she drew nearer the end of her voyage. With the ocean, waves of Neferet's emotions had surged before her, washing against the shoreline, penetrating the ground and soaking across the land.

That was when the dreams had begun. She had dreamed she'd been wrapped in power, folded into greatness, cherished beyond pain and pleasure.

"No mortal male could be your equal because you deserve to be mated to a god!" his beautiful voice had whispered, and Neferet had begun listening.

CHAPTER FIFTEEN

Zoey

"Ah, shit. She looks worse than I expected." Aphrodite said.

"Yeah, she does." My voice sounded shaky as my friends and I looked through the big window into the ICU cubicle of our infirmary. Shaunee had gotten Stark, me, Aphrodite, and Darius. On the way to the infirmary she'd quickly filled us in on what Dallas had done. I'd told myself I wouldn't cry—that I'd be a strong, mature High Priestess and set a good example, but one look at Stevie Rae had totally scared the crap out of me and made me want to burst into tears. She'd had her oversized Kenny Chesney concert T-shirt on, but everywhere the shirt hadn't protected— her face, arms, and legs—were bright red and covered with angry-looking blisters that oozed blood. Margareta, the vampyre in charge of the infirmary, said that she hadn't completely gained consciousness yet, and that wasn't good because Stevie Rae needed to drink blood, or else she wouldn't even begin to heal.

"Can't they give her a transfusion or something?" Aphrodite said.

"I already asked that," Shaunee said while I wiped my eyes and sniffed. Stark handed me a Kleenex. "Vampyres aren't like humans. An infusion won't work. We have to absorb blood through our mouths, and throats, and well, you know—everything—for it to heal us."

"I hope you know how nasty that sounds," Aphrodite said said.

"Aphrodite, I'd chew poo and spit it down Stevie Rae's throat if it would make her better," I said.

"That won't be necessary." Thanatos's voice had us turning toward the entrance to the infirmary. She'd opened the door. Kalona stepped inside. Rephaim was on his heels. Barefoot and pulling on his shirt, he sprinted past his father.

He went straight to Stevie Rae. We crowded around the door, watching and waiting.

"Stevie Rae, it's time to wake up now." Rephaim sat beside her on the hospital bed. Tears dripped down his cheeks, but his voice didn't shake. He sounded calm and sure of himself. "I got here as soon as I could. I am sorry you had to be like this for so long, but you know the problem I have during the sunlight. I'm not really myself." He tried to laugh, but it came out as a sob instead. He cleared his throat and wiped his eyes, saying, "It's not as bad as your problem with the sun, though." He reached out like he meant to touch her cheek, but flinched at the rawness and blisters. Instead he rested his hand on her chest, over her heart. "Hey, I need you to wake up now," he repeated, his tears falling faster and faster.

Kalona pushed past us to stand beside his son. "Rephaim, you must make her drink from you. You are bonded to her, and within your veins pulses the strength of immortals. Only you can heal her."

Rephaim looked up at his dad. "She's not conscious. She won't wake up."

"Then you must force her to drink."

Rephaim nodded. He lifted the hand he'd been pressing over Stevie Rae's heart and bit himself. Hard. Right on his wrist.

I didn't need to see the blood seeping through the bite. I could smell it. It was super weird. In a way it was kinda stinky, like mold or newly dug-up dirt, but there was something else in it, too, that reminded me of dark chocolate and spices and a cool, moonlit breeze in the middle of a sweltering summer night.

"Wow, that's bizarre smelling," Stark murmured.

I didn't say anything because I couldn't stop my mouth from watering. All I could do was watch in envy as Rephaim leaned forward and gently cradled Stevie Rae's head while he pressed his bleeding wrist to her slack lips.

"Drink, Stevie Rae. You have to," Rephaim pleaded.

Stevie Rae didn't react at all. Rephaim's blood ran from the corners of her mouth and pooled scarlet against the white hospital sheets, looking delicious . . . irresistible . . .

"Zoey! Help her."

I realized I'd been staring, spellbound, at Rephaim's blood when Kalona's voice jerked me back to myself. "H-how?" I stuttered.

Thanatos answered for him. "Call spirit. Have it strengthen and infill her. Her body will heal if her spirit awakens so that she may drink from her mate."

"Of course—I understand, sorry." I cleared my throat and drew a deep breath, ignoring the new rush of blood scent that filled my lungs. "Spirit, come to me!" I felt better when my favorite element responded—more myself—more in control. Grounded again, I commanded, "Go to Stevie Rae. Fill her and strengthen her so that she comes back to us!" My hair lifted as spirit left me and poured into Stevie Rae. Immediately, she took a deep breath, coughing as blood choked her. And then her eyes opened and she clamped her hands around Rephaim's arm, sucking from his wrist—drinking deeply.

"Not so much that she weakens you." Kalona put his hand on his son's shoulder. "She will need to drink from you again, and often, until she is completely healed, and you must be strong enough for her to do so."

Rephaim nodded and gently put his hand over Stevie Rae's. "Stevie Rae, you have to stop. You can have more later."

I saw her eyes when she looked up at him. They were red-tinged. Her expression was feral.

"Uh-oh," Stark said. He and Kalona tensed at the same time, but Thanatos's voice was like balm, soothing the tension in the room.

"Let her be. Stevie Rae is a vampyre—a High Priestess. Trust her. She will find herself."

And, sure enough, Stevie Rae blinked several times and her eyes faded back to normal. She pushed Rephaim's wrist from her mouth, wiping blood from her lips and looking like she was going to cry. "Did I hurt you? I'm so sorry, Rephaim!"

"Shhh," he soothed, pulling her into his arms. "You would never hurt me."

Suddenly she sat back, staring up at Rephaim. I was amazed to see that her skin was already less boiled looking. "You saved me! When you were a raven!"

"You needed me. I could feel your pain. I came to you."

Shaunee had already told us her version of what had happened, but hearing it from Rephaim was surreal. I mean, the kid was a bird during the day. He wasn't supposed to be anything *but* a bird. Yet he'd saved Stevie Rae's life.

"You're the most wonderful guy in the universe!" Stevie Rae smiled love and joy at him. "Do you remember it?"

Rephaim wiped tears from his eyes and smiled back at her. This time he was able to lightly touch her red cheek. "I only re-member that you needed me and then the raven's anger."

"Well, that's good enough for me," she said. Then she turned her attention to Thanatos. "Dallas tried to kill me *and* Shaunee."

"Oh, Goddess!" Shaunee said. "I knew he was mad when he came back by Erin's pyre, but I didn't know he was crazy."

"He's not crazy," Stevie Rae said. "He's mean."

"And he's powerful," Thanatos added. "Capture him," she ordered Kalona. "Bring him to me. The High Council may have turned from us, but Death can still judge and can still mete out justice."

Kalona fisted his hand over his heart in acknowledgment of her command. As he strode from the room Stark said, "I'm going with him."

"Do so, and be sure you don't allow the immortal to kill Dallas. I want him returned to me very much alive," Thanatos said.

"Yes, High Priestess." Stark bowed quickly to her and then to me before hurrying after Kalona.

"My red fledglings," Stevie Rae said. "Are they all okay?"

Thanatos nodded. "Kalona and Aurox guarded them while they slept peacefully during the day."

"And Darius went directly to the basement to join Aurox as soon as Shaunee told us what had happened," Aphrodite said.

I was surprised to hear Aurox's name. Now was definitely not the time to mention it, but hadn't he been super drunk and then passed out all day?

"So it was just Shaunee and Stevie Rae who were his targets?" I asked.

"I don't know," Shaunee said. "He seemed pissed at all of us. Well, I mean all of Zoey's circle. I think he blames us for Erin rejecting the Change."

"Yeah, he told me he was just beginning his payback by killing Shaunee and me," Stevie Rae said, leaning against Rephaim like she was absorbing strength from his touch.

"That's ridiculous," Aphrodite said. "If anyone's to blame it's Neferet."

"We made more convenient targets," Shaunee said.

"No one is going to be targeted again—not while Death reigns as High Priestess here," Thanatos said. "But until Kalona and Stark find Dallas we will all be on high alert." She turned to me. "Zoey, I know we have all had concerns about the fledglings sleeping in one place together, but I am going to command that you and your circle—along with your Prophetesses—rest with the red fledglings. That gives us two lines of protection. The first will be Darius and the Sons of Erebus Warriors. The second will be your circle itself."

"You just mean Stevie Rae's red fledglings, right?" I said. "Dallas has that whole other group who follow him."

"And are equally as hateful," Stevie Rae added. "Just last night that little red fledgling, Nicole, you know the one who helped Lenobia save the horses when the stable caught fire?" Thanatos nodded and Stevie Rae continued. "Well, she officially left Dallas's group and swore herself to me—basically because of how hateful Dallas and his group are."

I was opening my mouth to agree with Stevie Rae—no way did I want to be stuck in a basement with those jerks Dallas called friends—but Thanatos spoke first.

"When my judgment of Dallas is finished, there will be no fledglings who follow him." Her voice was like ice.

I wondered how Thanatos thought she was going to get the jerk red fledglings to be nice, but she had, like, a zillion years of experience and was super powerful. Who knew what kind of magickal vampyre stuff she could have up her sleeve? I hoped it was something uber mean. The truth was that after what had happened tonight, I was done being patient with anyone who wanted to hurt my friends or me—and if that meant Thanatos was going to use the vampyre equivalent of old school corporal punishment, then so be it. Dallas and his friends deserved whatever they got.

"Zoey, would you go check on my kids? Tell them that I'm gonna be okay? You know Kramisha and Shaylin are gonna be freakin' out when they hear what happened." Stevie Rae's voice was getting weaker and weaker, and even though she was smiling at me and holding Rephaim's hand, she'd laid back on her pillow, looking exhausted and broiled.

"No problem," I assured her. "I don't want you to worry about anything except getting well. Aphrodite and Shaunee and I will all go see the kids and make sure they know you're gonna be just fine."

"Good. While you're speaking to the red fledglings you can tell them that even though it is Saturday I have decided the House of Night needs an extra day of classes to make up for all the school time we have missed. I have already notified the professors. I will make a schoolwide announcement in a few moments. I expect everyone in their first-hour classes at eight P.M., sharp. Tardiness is unacceptable. Violence and hatred will not throw my House of Night into chaos," Thanatos said.

"Oh, for shit's sake—school—ugh," Aphrodite muttered under her breath.

"I think that's an awesome idea," Stevie Rae said. "Take notes for me, Z."

"Okie dokie," I said, thinking that I'd get Damien to take notes for her. "I'll come see you after class."

"We all will," Shaunee said.

Aphrodite grunted.

So, Stevie Rae had been totally right. Her red fledglings were freaked. Kramisha descended on us the second we entered the basement.

"If she ain't okay I'm gonna shank Dallas my own self."

"Stevie Rae's going to be fine," I assured her and the other kids who were clustering around.

"He really tried to kill her, didn't he?" Everyone turned to Nicole, who was standing off from the group, with only Shaylin near her.

"Dallas tried to kill Stevie Rae and Shaunee," I said, meeting her gaze and looking for any clue that she'd known what he'd planned.

Nicole's expression didn't betray anything except disgust. She shook her head. "He got worse and worse, but I didn't think he'd try anything right here at the House of Night."

"You used to be like him," I said.

"You're right. I *used to be*. Not anymore. Not for a while now."

"How do we know you're telling the truth?" Shaunee asked.

"I believe her." Shaylin spoke with no hesitation. "I've watched her colors change."

I looked to Aphrodite. "You're still sure about her?"

"Who her? Shaylin or Nicole?"

"Both," I said.

Aphrodite's gaze flicked over Shaylin before coming back to me. "I trust Shaylin's judgment. If she says the girl's changed, then I say believe her."

"She used to be Dallas's girlfriend, and Dallas just tried to kill Stevie Rae and me!" Shaunee blurted. "I'm not being a bitch—I'm just telling it like it is."

I heard a few of the kids mutter in agreement with her. Nicole's face had paled, but she'd lifted her chin and faced Shaunee. "Erin was Dallas's girlfriend and you still cared enough about her to stand by her pyre until after dawn."

"I knew Erin a long time," Shaunee said. "I've known you for, like, two seconds."

"Was Erin perfect for that long time you knew her?" Nicole asked.

Shaunee looked away from the red fledgling. "No. No, she wasn't."

"I wasn't perfect in my past, either, but I'm asking for a second chance."

I'd heard enough. My Prophetesses and my gut had convinced me. "That's good enough for me," I said loudly. "And it needs to be good enough for the rest of you, too. If we held the past against everyone, then Kalona wouldn't be our High Priestess's Warrior, and Stark wouldn't be my Warrior. Hell, Stevie Rae wouldn't even be my BFF."

"I would have been shunned and cast out of the House of Night along with Neferet," Aurox said. I hadn't noticed him before. He was standing behind us, just inside the basement entrance.

I didn't look at him, but I did nod in agreement. "And if Aurox hadn't been given another chance my grandma would be dead. Shaunee, we need to be on the same page about this. Too much crap has happened for us to start mistrusting each other."

Shaunee looked at Nicole briefly, and then her gaze met mine. "Okay, you're my High Priestess. I trust you."

"Thank you," I said. I looked around the group. "Anyone have anything else to say?"

"Is Stevie Rae gonna be okay?" Kramisha asked.

"Completely," I said.

"Did Rephaim really save her when he was a bird?" Shaylin asked.

I smiled at Shaunee. "Tell 'em the story, but be fast. Remember that Thanatos said she wants today to be a make-up day and everyone has to be in their first-hour class when the bell rings at eight."

There were a bunch of groans at that news, but they were cut off by Shaunee's retelling of what had happened earlier. I took the opportunity to exit to Darius, who was standing at the upper entrance to the basement. Aphrodite, of course, came with me.

As I passed Aurox I glanced quickly at him. The kid looked rough. His eyes were bloodshot and puffy and his perfect skin looked kinda chalky and damp. "Hangovers suck, huh?" I couldn't stop myself from quipping, though I didn't wait around to hear if he answered me. Aphrodite snickered all the way up the stairway.

"Kalona and Stark are searching for Dallas?" Darius asked as we joined him.

"Yeah," I said. "Thanatos wants him brought back for judgment. She said she's done with his red fledglings, too."

"It's going to be real interesting to see what she does with all of them," Aphrodite said. "Well, *if* they manage to find Dallas. He's gotta seriously *not* want to be found."

"The immortal will find him, have no doubt of that," Darius said.

"Did anyone do a roll call and see if any of his friends took off with him?" I said.

"I did a quick check after I made sure our fledglings were safe. Dallas is definitely gone, but I don't believe anyone left with him," Darius said.

"I hope whatever Thanatos does makes him leave us alone for good," Aphrodite said.

I sighed. "I don't know how you'd even begin to lock up a kid who can control electricity. It's depressing to start thinking about how many ways he could escape."

"Thanatos is wise. She will pass a righteous judgment," Darius said.

"I'm worried that righteous and doable are two totally different things," I said.

"As your Warrior isn't present to say this, I will stand in his stead and tell you not to worry so much," Darius said.

"She's hardheaded. She's not going to listen," Aphrodite said, kissing his cheek. "But thanks for trying."

He smiled at her. "I am used to dealing with a hardheaded woman."

"Have you been cheating on me with a stubborn skank?" Aphrodite said, pretending to be pissed off. "Don't make me claw some poor, less attractive girl's eyes out."

Darius laughed and pulled her into his arms. I rolled my eyes. "I'm going to see if I can get lucky two days in a row and get psaghetti for breakfast. Bye, Darius. Aphrodite, I'll see you in first hour."

I'd just decided to detour to my dorm room and actually attempt to brush my hair and fix my face before going to the cafeteria when his voice called my name. Truthfully, I didn't want to stop. I wanted to pretend like I hadn't heard him and scurry to my room and keep avoiding him for as long as possible. But I'd seen the kid run. It's not like he couldn't catch me. I drew a deep breath and stopped, waiting for him.

"Zoey, may I speak to you for a moment?" Aurox asked as he caught up with me.

He sounded so un-Heath-like and formal that I relaxed a little. "Yeah, of course."

"I believe I owe you an apology."

"For what?"

His smooth brow furrowed. "I believe I said something impolite to you last night."

"You believe?"

"My memory seems impaired. I can only remember pieces of what I said."

"Aurox, getting wasted does a lot more than just impair your memory. It can make you sick and make you do and say stupid things. You don't need to apologize to me, just don't get drunk again."

He sighed and rubbed his forehead as if he had a headache, which I was pretty sure he did have. "But, Zo, beer's really good."

I felt like he'd smacked me in the gut. "How do you do that?"

His hand dropped from his forehead and he gave me a totally confused look. "Like the taste of beer?"

"No!" I threw my hands up in frustration. "Sound just like Heath."

"Do I?"

"Not most of the time, but you did just then, when you called me Zo."

Aurox blinked a few times, then he said, "I am sorry I offend you."

"You don't offend me. You confuse me," I said.

"You confuse me, too," he said.

"Why?"

"Because I feel things for you that I know are wrong."

"Wrong feelings? Like what?" I held my breath while he answered.

"I am drawn to you. I care about you. I think about you. Often," he said slowly. "And I know those feelings are wrong because you loathe me."

I opened my mouth to tell him that I didn't loathe him, hell, I didn't even dislike him, but he held up his hand, stopping my words.

"No, I understand why you loathe me. It's not because you are a bad person. You are a really good person—a special person. It's not your fault you feel like you do." Aurox started to back away from me. "I just wanted to apologize for anything impolite I said last night. I'll leave you alone now."

"Aurox, hang on. Don't go anywhere. I need to say something to you." I motioned for him to follow me over to one of the many stone benches that were positioned under the huge oaks on the school grounds. "Okay, sit with me a sec and let me figure out how to say this right."

He sat beside me. Well, not really beside me. Mostly he perched on the very end of the bench, as far away from me as possible. I sighed.

"All right. Here goes." I took a long breath and blurted, "I feel as drawn to you as you are to me. I think about you. Wait, no, that's not right. I make myself *not* think about you because I'm thinking about you." I sighed again. "Like that's not confusing. Anyway, here's the deal—I'm seventeen, and inside of you is the soul of the kid I've loved for almost half of my life. But *you're* not that kid, which is what I tell myself all the time, and mostly I can believe it. Then you'll do something like sing the psaghetti song, or call me Zo with that one tone of voice that only Heath had, or get stupid drunk and say something that's totally Heath-like, and I'm scared I can't make myself believe it anymore," I finished in a rush.

"It?"

I frowned at him. "See, that's exactly what Heath would have said. I used a complex sentence and lost you."

"Sorry, Zo."

"You just did it again! And the *it* I'm scared of is that I can't make myself believe that you and Heath aren't turning into the same kid."

"Oh." He paused and I could practically see the wheels turning inside his head. "You still love Heath?"

I met his gaze and told him the absolute truth. "I'll always love Heath."

He didn't look away from me, so when his grin started I saw

the beginnings of it and how it made his eyes sparkle with familiar Heath mischief. "That's good," he said.

"No, that's confusing, especially because Stark is my Warrior as well as my boyfriend," I said.

"But did you not love Heath and Stark together before?"

"Well, yeah, but it was pretty complex. And stressful. For all three of us."

"Yet you still loved them."

He hadn't phrased it like a question, but I answered anyway. "Yeah, and what I'm trying to get you to understand is that I think it's just too hard to love more than one guy at the same time. I can tell you for sure what Stark would say about me trying that again."

"Stark was kind to me last night."

"Well, Stark and Heath ended up being friends. Sort of."

"Then perhaps we can all be friends again," he said.

Friends sounded safe. Who doesn't need more friends? "We can try."

"You could suck my blood if you wanted to."

"Aurox! No. No, I do *not* want to suck your blood," I lied, remembering how utterly, overwhelmingly awesome it had been to suck Heath's blood *and* how much Heath liked it when I did. I narrowed my eyes at the kid. "Aurox, you don't have Heath's memories, do you?"

He shook his head. "I don't think so. Sometimes I say or do things that surprise me because I cannot remember how I know them. There is only one thing I am certain that I have from Heath."

I knew I shouldn't ask, but I heard my mouth saying, "What's the one thing?"

"His love for you, Zo."

CHAPTER SIXTEEN

Stark

"Are you sure we're still on his trail?" Stark asked the winged immortal's back between the panting breaths he was taking as he raced after Kalona.

"Can you not scent his blood?" Kalona glanced over his shoulder and then, obviously seeing that Stark was struggling to keep up with him, slowed to a jog and pointed to the grass of someone's well-maintained lawn they were cutting through. "There, see where the vampyre's blood has spattered the ground because it still seeps freely from him? My son did well in clawing his head—head wounds bleed easily and are difficult to staunch."

"Yeah, especially if you're moving as fast as he is." Stark wiped the sweat from his forehead, jogging beside Kalona. "Who knew Dallas could run like this? I would've definitely thought we'd have caught up to him by now. He didn't have that big of a lead on us. The kid can *move*. I always thought of him as one of those video-games-hands kids—soft and weak unless they're pretending to be Zorg from the Planet Org, then they can destroy whole worlds with their fat fingers."

Kalona furrowed his brow. "Your world still confuses me sometimes, but I can tell you I know why Dallas moves so quickly. He is fleeing for his life."

"Hey, Thanatos specifically said you're *not* supposed to kill him."

"That is a shame. It would be just that I finish what my son began," Kalona said.

"Can't say I disagree with you."

Kalona held out his hand, stopping Stark. They'd been following Dallas's trail that led steadily west, and had run straight into busy Riverside Drive. "There." Kalona pointed across the street to where the slick surface of the Arkansas River glistened in the moonlight. "He thinks to use the water to spread the scent of his blood downstream, and wash away his trail."

"Thinks? You mean that won't work?"

"Not for me it won't. Blood still seeps from him—it is him I scent as surely as I scent his trail."

"Huh. That's good," Stark said. Following the immortal across the four lanes of Riverside Drive, he was glad it was late and cold enough that joggers and bikers weren't around. Sure, Kalona had put on a long coat, but those wings weren't exactly inconspicuous.

Kalona paused after they'd crossed the asphalt bike path, bending to look more closely at the foliage. "Here is where he climbed down to the river."

Stark looked at the weeds and sniffed, trying to pick up the sight or scent of Dallas's blood. All he could smell was the muddy, fishy river. But the immortal seemed sure of himself, so Stark shrugged and followed him down to the river. When they reached the bank, Kalona paused again. This time he squatted. He seemed to be gulping big breaths of air while he stared across the lazily moving water. It'd been pretty dry since the ice storm in December, and the river was shallow, showing big stretches of sand bars between the sluggish water.

"I didn't know you were such a good tracker," Stark said, crouching beside him.

"I spent eons tracking evil beings that far surpassed this one small vampyre's ability at subterfuge. It is a skill not easily forgotten," Kalona said.

Stark watched him from the corner of his eye and wondered, not for the first time, just exactly what Kalona had done for the Goddess before he'd Fallen. And if he'd been so damn good at his job that centuries later he could still track scarily well, why had he Fallen at all?

"There!" Kalona pointed. "Do you see him, there, on the log near the far bank?"

Stark smiled. "I don't need to see something to hit it. Just give me a little room and get ready to retrieve the asshole after I shoot him, 'cause now I get to do what *I'm* scarily good at." He stood, notched an arrow, and drew the bow back. *Bury the arrow to the feathers in the thigh of the vampyre named Dallas,* Stark focused his specific thought—his specific purpose—and let fly the arrow.

It shot from the bow with a satisfying thrum, whistling through the air, invisible but deadly.

"Aaaah!" Dallas's scream carried easily across the water.

Stark smiled cockily at Kalona and said, "Fetch."

Zoey

It didn't seem like first hour was ever going to end. I usually liked Thanatos's special class. She wasn't the most entertaining professor at the school (uh, that would be Erik), but she was super smart and she let us ask just about anything—as long as we were respectful to her and to each other. I squirmed in my chair and glanced behind me. Dallas, of course, wasn't in class. As far as I knew Stark and Kalona hadn't returned to campus yet, with or without him. But all the rest of the red fledglings were here. The kids who weren't part of Dallas's group, like Shaylin and Kramisha, Johnny B, Ant, and the rest of Stevie Rae's red fledglings, were sitting up toward the front of class, just behind the first row where my circle and Aphrodite and I sat. Nicole had come in with Shaylin and was sitting beside her. She'd totally ignored her ex-friends, who stared at her like she was road kill when she'd walked past them.

Aurox wasn't sitting all the way over on the side of the room by himself today. When he'd walked in he'd hesitated as he started past us, and Damien had waved at him and told him since Rephaim was in the infirmary with Stevie Rae, the two seats next to him weren't taken. Aurox had only paused long enough to glance at me. I'd kinda half shrugged and half nodded, and then he'd thanked Damien and sat beside him. So, there was only Aphrodite and Damien between him and me. I could see him taking notes as Thanatos opened the lecture by talking about the five major rituals discussed in *The Fledgling Handbook*.

Huh. Maybe Aurox was a good student. That wouldn't be Heath-like at all. The thought almost made me giggle—as in the beginnings of hysteria, not as in a funny giggle—and I coughed to cover it.

"You okay?" Shaunee asked me softly. She was sitting on my left and I could see that I'd worried her.

"Totally fine. Just a tickle in my throat," I assured her quickly.

Thanatos had turned to the Smartboard and was pulling up a picture of a super decorative knife on it. From the back of the room a balled-up sheet of paper was tossed onto my desk. I could see that there was writing on it. Frowning, I smoothed it out and read: TO BAD U DON'T DIE.

Aphrodite snatched up the note and crumpled it up, dropping

it into her purse. "Ignore them," she whispered. "Even I can spell better than they can."

Dallas's red fledglings hadn't been as openly jerk-ish as they tended to be with Dallas leading the way. Instead they were a silently simmering pile of pissed off. They didn't answer any of Thanatos's questions and they never commented during her lecture. They just did mean stuff like throw notes when her back was turned. And I swear I could feel their beady little red eyes staring at me. I glanced over my shoulder.

"Stop looking at them," Aphrodite whispered as Thanatos passed out copies of *The Fledgling Handbook* to all of us. "They want attention. Don't give it to them."

"I wish I knew if Dallas had been caught," I whispered back.

"He will be. He's not smart enough to get away from Kalona," she said.

"I would like to discuss the second of the Major Rituals described in this chapter of your Handbook, Cleopatra's Protective Ritual." Thanatos's commanding voice called our attention to the front of the class. She pointed to the Smartboard and the pictures of the decorative daggers. "Who can tell me what these are called when they are used only for rituals and spellwork?"

Damien's hand shot into the air.

"Damien?"

"Athame," he said.

"I knew that," Aphrodite whispered.

"Correct. Thank you, Damien," Thanatos said. "You will note that in the purest and most ancient form of Protective Ritual, fire is traditionally the element invoked." She bowed her head briefly and smiled at Shaunee, who nodded enthusiastically back at her. "As we are fortunate enough to have a fledgling at this school whose affinity is fire, perhaps she can tell us what it is that is utmost in importance in a traditional Ritual of Protection."

"Oh, that's easy! It's the High Priestess who casts the ritual that's most important. Even though fire is an awesome protection, it's only as strong as the Priestess who sets the spell," Shaunee said.

I was super glad she'd answered because all I could remember about the Protective Ritual was that Cleopatra cast it and then messed up because she got all infatuated with Mark Antony and in the end he died and her element turned into a burning snake and ate her. Eesh.

"Absolutely correct, Shaunee. Thank you. So, students, the lesson we need to learn from the Protective Ritual isn't about protection at all. It is about focus and integrity and purpose," Thanatos said. "Events at this school have had me considering the lesson of the Protective Ritual carefully. As I meditated on this lesson it came to me that in the ancient world, vampyres tended to be more gifted than today's vampyres." Thanatos paused and looked at me. "Though recently the trend toward less gifts and less power in young vampyres seems to be shifting." I didn't know what she was getting at, but she definitely had my interest. "Consider, for a moment, the ramifications of such a shift. In ancient times, highly gifted vampyres, such as Cleopatra, were held accountable for their choices and their actions by the power they wielded. As you can read in the Handbook, and as reported by our historians, Cleopatra misused her Goddess-given gift. She stopped listening to her people. She took her affinity for granted. She thought only of her own needs and desires. Ultimately, her element, fire, consumed her."

I tried not to fidget. Was Thanatos trying to tell me that I was messing up? I mean, I knew I'd been kinda short with people lately—and the whole Aurox/Heath thing was confusing and frustrating—but was she saying that I needed a five-element smackdown?

Hell! I hoped that wasn't it! I'd been doing my best. Yeah, I'd been frustrated and annoyed, but at least I hadn't been whining too much. Lately.

Aphrodite's hand went up, surprising me and shutting off my inner babble.

"Yes, Aphrodite, you have a question?" Thanatos called on her.

"Yeah, I was thinking about what you said—how vampyre gifts were stronger and more frequent in ancient times—and how that looks like it's changing, and I wondered if you have any idea why the power shift is happening."

"That's a good question, Aphrodite. I wish I had a definitive answer for you. I can tell you that I believe the shift has to do with a major change in the balance of Darkness and Light."

"Maybe Nyx is giving us gifts so that we can fight back and balance things again," Shaunee said.

"Perhaps," Thanatos nodded.

"Could it have something to do with Old Magick?" Aurox asked.

We all gawked at him.

"What makes you ask that?" Thanatos said.

He shrugged and looked uncomfortable. "The bulls. Are they not a manifestation of Old Magick?"

"They are," she said.

"Zoey's Seer Stone is Old Magick, too. Isn't it?" Aphrodite said. I frowned at her.

"That is true as well," Thanatos said.

"Okay, but does any of us know what Old Magick really is?" I said, irritated at the whole subject.

"Old Magick has not manifested outside the Isle of Skye for longer than I have been Marked," Thanatos began slowly, as if she were remembering and reasoning aloud at the same time. "From what I know of it, the best description I can give you is that it is energy at its most basic level—raw, powerful, and neutral. Old Magick is creation and destruction at once."

"Which is probably why ancient spells, like Cleopatra's Protection Ritual, were so dependent upon the Priestess who cast the spell," Damien said. "It could be that the five Major Rituals all had roots in Old Magick."

"That does seem logical," Thanatos said.

"It still doesn't explain exactly what it is or why it's become active again," Aphrodite said. "But I'd say it's definitely active again. Wouldn't you, Z?"

Thankfully, the sound of the classroom door banging open and Kalona striding down the center aisle interrupted her.

The winged immortal bowed respectfully to Thanatos. "High Priestess, I have returned with your prisoner."

"You have done well," she said, and then faced the class. "I want you all to assemble at the center of campus near the pyre site immediately. Class is dismissed."

As we filed out of class, I watched Thanatos speaking quietly to Kalona. I saw the immortal's eyes widen, and then he nodded, and bowed to her again—this time unusually low, holding the pose longer than normal. While he was still bowing, Thanatos went to her desk, picked up the phone, and punched a button. Her voice echoed from the school's intercom system. "All students and faculty will assemble at the center of campus at the pyre site! Professors who are members of our Council will report to the Council Chamber immediately. All classes are suspended until after our assembly." Then she clicked off and hurried out through the back door to the classroom, with Kalona on her heels.

I had a bad feeling. "I wonder what the hell's going on?"

"Don't have a clue," Aphrodite said. "But whatever it is, it's going to happen in front of everyone *and* it gets us out of at least one class, so how bad could it be?"

* * *

We went right to the pyre site and formed a big circle around the black burned area that had definitely seen too much use lately. I looked for Stark, but didn't see him or Kalona. Darius met us, taking Aphrodite's hand and saying he didn't know what was going on, either. Just when everyone was starting to get restless and the talking was heading toward the I-have-to-yell-to-be-heard level, the people at the opposite side of the group I was in shifted and then parted.

Thanatos stepped into view first. She'd changed her clothes to a long black velvet dress that was decorated only with the emblem of Nyx in silver thread, hands upraised cupping a crescent moon. Thanatos had let her hair down, and it fell long and dark, in a thick veil around her waist. Within its depths I could see silver glinting, which reminded me of the thread used to embroider Nyx's emblem. Her face was grim. I thought she looked scary but beautiful—ancient yet timeless.

Then my attention was pulled from her as Kalona and Stark came into view. Dallas limped between them. He looked like crap. His hands were tied in front of him. His face was a bloody, scratched-up mess. His clothes were wet and filthy. Buried to its feathers, one of Stark's arrows was stuck through his right thigh. Kalona and Stark looked as serious and powerful as Thanatos as they pulled Dallas into the center of our assembly. They didn't stop until he was standing right in the middle of the blackened pyre site.

Dallas didn't look grim or powerful. He looked pissed. I saw when his eyes found Shaunee. He sneered at her and hacked up a nasty loogie, then spit it into the ashes at his feet.

"Professors of the Tulsa House of Night Council, come forth!" Thanatos commanded.

Lenobia, Penthesilea, Garmy, and Erik stepped from the

crowd to stand to one side of Thanatos. I was thinking that the Council looked sparse with the absence of Dragon and Anastasia Lankford and Professor Nolan, when Thanatos continued, "I also command our two Prophetesses, come forth!"

"Oh, for shit's sake," Aphrodite grumbled, but she let go of Darius's hand and went to join Thanatos. Shaylin took longer to make her way forward, but when she joined Thanatos, the High Priestess nodded and motioned for her to stand beside Aphrodite.

"Our school has been richly gifted with two additional High Priestesses. Sadly, one of them, the first red High Priestess, Stevie Rae, is unable to take her place beside me today because she has been gravely wounded." I was just realizing she'd said *two* when Thanatos's dark gaze found me. "But I do call our second High Priestess to join me. Zoey Redbird, come forth!"

Feeling nervous and unsure, I went to stand beside Aphrodite and Shaylin.

Thanatos faced Dallas. "Are you the red vampyre known as Dallas?"

Dallas curled his lip. "Everybody knows who I am."

"Dallas, at dawn you attacked the red High Priestess, Stevie Rae, with the intent to expose her to sunlight until she died. Do you deny this?"

"No, I ain't denying it."

"Dallas, at dawn you also planned to kill the fledgling Shaunee with the power you have been gifted with by Nyx. Do you deny this?"

"I ain't denying anything!" His voice was mean and his eyes glinted with a rust-colored glow. "Shun me! I'm more than ready to leave this shithole of a school."

Thanatos turned so that she faced the crowd. "I know this vampyre has followers who share his same views. I believe they knew and even may have assisted him in his crimes. They, too, should share his fate. I now call forth the followers of Dallas who wish to stand with him!"

I was super curious about what was going to happen next. There were probably about ten kids who hung around Dallas all the time. Well, nine now that Nicole had come over from the Dark Side. I kinda expected a whole herd of his red fledglings to come forth, swaggering like jerks and throwing notes at people.

Only two actually joined Dallas. One of them was the big kid named Kurtis. I remembered him from the fight in the tunnels. He was a total ass. The other kid was Elliott, the fledgling I'd watched die all those months ago in English class. I knew Elliott was a mean breather (a kid who didn't do much in class but breathe), but I would have figured he was too lazy to stand up with Dallas, especially since it looked like he was going to be kicked out of school with him.

Oh, wait. *That* made sense. The kid didn't like school. Getting expelled with Dallas would seem like a permanent vacation to him.

"Elliott and Kurtis, do the two of you knowingly stand with this vampyre as accomplices to his crimes?" Thanatos asked.

"Hell yes!" Kurtis said. He looked nervously around, but he was trying to sound all tough and sure of himself.

"Yeah, whatever," Elliott said.

"Now I ask my Council—do you acknowledge the guilt of this vampyre and his fledgling followers?"

The instant Thanatos asked that question, my Seer Stone began to radiate heat. I cupped my hand around it, wishing I knew what it was reacting to, and wishing I knew what to do about it.

Each of the Council members answered Thanatos by solemnly saying, "I do."

"Prophetesses of Nyx, these three have been found guilty of plotting to murder a vampyre High Priestess. Look within you.

Use your gifts. Are you in agreement with me that, as in ancient times, their punishment should be swift and public?"

Aphrodite answered first. "I agree with you."

Shaylin took longer. She walked a few steps closer to where Dallas, Kurtis, and Elliott stood and studied them. Her face looked like she smelled something disgusting, but she didn't say anything to them. She returned to her place near Thanatos. She still didn't say anything. She just stared at Thanatos for what seemed like an uncomfortably long time. Finally, Shaylin drew a deep breath and said, "I believe the right thing to do is to agree with you." Then Shaylin bowed her head. I was pretty sure she also closed her eyes, and it looked like she might have been praying, but I didn't have any more time to watch because it was my turn to be called on.

"Zoey Redbird, as the only other High Priestess present, do you stand in agreement with me and my ancient right to condemn these three for the violence they admit to conspiring and committing?"

I felt like I got the easiest question. "Yes, I agree," I answered quickly. The Seer Stone was scorching my hand.

Thanatos raised her arms. Power crackled around her, lifting the hairs on my neck and arms. Her voice was amplified by the power of Nyx and she sounded like Death personified.

"Then I invoke my right as High Priestess of this House of Night. Crimes against a High Priestess under my protection shall be punished as they were in ancient times. I command my Oath Bound Warrior to execute the red vampyre and then to cast his two fledgling followers into the country, far enough away from any vampyre that their bodies will reject the Change and they, too, shall die!"

I didn't even have time to gasp. Kalona moved with lightning speed. He drew the longsword that had been strapped across his back and in one swift stroke beheaded Dallas. Stark stepped away as the body convulsed and blood geysered from the stump that had been his neck. I couldn't stop staring at Dallas's head. His eyes were wide open. He looked stunned. And his mouth kept opening and closing—opening and closing—like a fish on dry ground.

Kurtis and Elliott screamed and started to run. The winged immortal caught them before they'd broken the circle of the shocked crowd. He grabbed them around their waists. The crowd surged away from him and he ran forward, taking mighty strides, his huge wings beat the air once, twice, three times, and then he and the two boys were airborne. The boys kicked and screamed, but it didn't seem to affect Kalona at all, and within moments he'd flown out of sight, to the west, and into the darkness.

"Silence!" Thanatos's command was like an off switch. It was then that I realized that everyone around me, except Stark, Shaylin, and the members of the School Council, had either been crying out in horror or sobbing in shock. "The time for weakness and infighting is finished. Violence against our House will be avenged. Our Goddess is merciful, but she is also just, and all who come against her shall feel her righteous wrath. Let this be your warning and my promise to you—those who stand with the Goddess and me will be protected. Those who come against us will be punished. Tulsa House of Night, make your choice!"

CHAPTER SEVENTEEN

Zoey

Cupped in my palm, the Seer Stone blazed. I knew why I hadn't dissolved into tears or shrieked out in hysteria.

Thanatos was right. It was time to publicly swear allegiance to our House of Night and take a stand for good. We were up against too much to have to fight each other, too. It's what she'd been saying all along. It's what I'd come to believe as well.

I stepped forward, careful to stay out of the circle of Dallas's blood. Holding tight to my Seer Stone I drew a deep breath and prayed, *Old Magick, help me—strengthen me!* Heat exploded from the Seer Stone and power sizzled through my body. When I spoke, the volume of my voice reverberated my words over the crowd.

"My circle and I choose the path of Nyx. We stand united with this House of Night!"

Damien and Shaunee were the first of my circle to join me. They moved up beside me and bowed respectfully to Thanatos, echoing me by saying, "We stand united!" Shaylin and Aphrodite stepped forward so that they were beside them. Darius and Stark and, I saw with a happy jolt, Aurox joined us. Surrounding me, the rest of my circle fisted their hands over their hearts and bowed respectfully, showing our solidarity.

That broke the tide. Kramisha, Erik, Johnny B, Ant, Nicole,

and all the rest of Stevie Rae's red fledglings swarmed forward through the crowd. I could see that some of them had been crying. Others, like Erik and Kramisha, were white-faced with shock, but they all bowed and swore allegiance to our House of Night.

The rest of the school began bowing and speaking their vows to stand together and follow the Goddess's path. I paid special attention to the handful of kids left from Dallas's fledglings. They were easy to pick out. The boys were super scruffy and slouchy, and the girls wore more eyeliner than clothes. They weren't acting all tough and rebellious now, though. They were looking and acting scared. They all bowed to Thanatos. I couldn't help but wonder how sincere their pledges were, because, seriously, what choice did they have? I thought about what I'd do in their place. No way would I take a chance at being killed. I'd totally pretend to join Thanatos. Later, though, my choice might be different.

And just as if it had never been a miniature oven, my Seer Stone cooled down, leaving me dizzy and nauseous, with a pounding headache starting in my right temple.

Old Magick was so creepy!

"And now I command that we return to the business of living. School shall continue," Thanatos was saying. "We will be vigilant as to the Dark forces at work around us, but they should not be at work among us any longer. I ask Zoey and her circle to remain here and meet with me briefly, the rest of you have five minutes before second hour commences. Professors—see to your fledglings, and may you all blessed be."

I felt a little like someone had just thrown cold water all over me. Dallas had been beheaded. Two fledglings were going to be dead very shortly, but don't be tardy for second hour? WTF? How could it be that simple to go on with the day as if nothing had happened?

"Zoey, I need you to cast a circle," Thanatos said, striding over to me as the silent crowd dispersed.

"Here? Now?"

"Here, yes. Around the vampyre's body. But not now. Wait until the fledglings have returned to class."

"Okay," I said slowly. "But I'll need someone to stand in for Stevie Rae."

"I can stand in for Stevie Rae."

Everyone stared at Aurox.

"Why you?" Stark asked before I could say anything, which annoyed the crap out of me. It was *my* circle—not his!

"Why not me? I know where north is. I can hold a green candle and call earth. And I want to help Zoey."

"Sounds good to me," I said, not looking at Stark. "Damien, would you, Aurox, and Shaunee gather the circle candles and matches?"

Aurox bowed respectfully to me before the three of them headed toward Nyx's Temple for the circle supplies.

"What's going on? Why the circle now? Shouldn't someone be cleaning up this mess?" Aphrodite asked, motioning to, but not looking at, Dallas's body.

"That is exactly what Zoey and her circle will be doing," Thanatos said. "A condemned and executed vampyre doesn't deserve a pyre and the traditions of a funeral. He also shouldn't be buried anywhere that could be made a shrine by misguided followers. His remains need to be simply, quietly, and quickly immolated."

"Oh," I said, getting it. "You want me to cast a circle and strengthen Shaunee so that she can, well, uh—" I hesitated, not sure how to put it, and feeling very squeed out at the thought of what we were going to have to do.

"Clean up this mess," Aphrodite finished for me.

"Yes, well put." Thanatos sounded like she was talking about taking out the trash. "And the less attention paid to this cleanup, the better. So, I thank both Prophetesses for fulfilling your role with dignity and wisdom, but now I must insist that Aphrodite go to class, and Shaylin join her directly after she has invoked water in Zoey's circle."

Aphrodite frowned. Class was not her favorite place to be. I frowned at her—not that she noticed—thinking that I'd be happy to change places with her.

"Come, my beauty, let us walk together," Darius said, taking her hand and moving toward the main school building.

"I'll go get my blue candle and tell Damien and those guys to hurry up," Shaylin said. She began walking toward Nyx's Temple, then she paused and turned back to Thanatos. "I read your colors. You were doing what needed to be done. Sometimes the ancient ways are the best," she said.

"That is what I believe as well," Thanatos said.

"That doesn't make what happened here any less horrible," Shaylin continued.

"Not less horrible, no, but necessary," Thanatos said.

"The entire school isn't for you," Shaylin said.

"I am aware of that."

"I think you would be surprised to know who all is having second thoughts about their pledge to you and to this school," Shaylin said.

"I imagine you could tell me that by reading their colors, though. Couldn't you?" Thanatos said.

My stomach rolled. "Okay, hang on," I said. "I'm totally for a united front against Darkness, but I'm not for Shaylin being used to invade people's thoughts."

"What point are you making, Zoey?" Thanatos's gaze seemed to pierce through me.

"That Shaylin shouldn't be used as your spy!" I wasn't sure exactly why the idea pissed me off so badly, but it definitely did.

"If she's working in the service of Nyx—" Thanatos began.

I cut her off. "Nyx has given us all free choice. That means it's not against even the Goddess's rules for any of us to question the choices we've made and are going to make in the future. There's nothing wrong with that. Only an idiot never questions what she's been told to do."

"Shaylin, did Dallas's colors tell you he was dangerous?" Thanatos asked her, without taking her gaze from mine.

"I knew he was angry and violent. I didn't know he was going to try to kill Stevie Rae and Shaunee."

"But had Dallas been stopped because of what you saw within his aura before this morning, Stevie Rae would have been saved great pain," Thanatos said.

"Stopped? Do you mean killed before he actually did anything?" I felt like I was going to explode.

"I don't think that's what Thanatos means," Stark said.

"I'd like to hear Thanatos say that," I said.

"In ancient times only vampyres who actually committed violence against other vampyres were executed," she said.

"This isn't ancient times," I said. "And I don't think it's anyone's business what people *think*. But you know who believed it was her business to listen in to what we all thought? Neferet. I don't like what that did to her."

Thanatos's brows went up. "That is a point well taken, young Priestess."

"Shaylin, go on and see what's taking Damien and those guys so long," I told her. Shaylin hesitated for just a second, then she bowed to me and hurried away.

"You have strong opinions," Thanatos said.

"So do you."

"Will you cast your circle and lead Shaunee in immolating the guilty vampyre?"

"Yes. I don't want him martyred any more than you do," I said.

"Thank you. Then I will leave you to your circle." Her gaze went to Stark. "You did well today, Warrior. I am proud of you. Blessed be." She bowed her head slightly and walked away.

"I swear she acts more and more like Death every day," I said, staring after her.

"Z, I think she's only doing her best to keep us all safe."

My first impulse was to argue with Stark, to ask him why he wasn't taking my side, but when I really looked at him I saw that his clothes were torn and muddy, and he had Dallas's blood spattered all over his shirt and pants. His face was pale and strained, and I understood that even though Kalona had announced he'd brought Dallas back to school, it was Stark's arrow that had made his execution possible.

Then Stark had watched Kalona behead the kid.

I put my arms around him, pressing my face into his shoulder. "I think *you're* doing your best to keep us all safe."

"Are you okay, Z? I wanted to tell you what Thanatos was going to do, but there wasn't any time." He hesitated, then added, "I felt that huge surge of power you had when you spoke up. It wasn't like how you feel when spirit fills you, so I figured it might have something to do with Old Magick. Was I right?"

I fidgeted uncomfortably. "Well, my Seer Stone got hot, and now I feel crappy. So, yeah, I'm thinking it had something to do with Old Magick."

"Guess that makes sense, especially with Thanatos invoking ancient rules and all."

"Yeah, we were just talking about that in class, but I wish I knew whether that meant she's doing the right thing or not," I worried aloud.

"Hey." He lifted my chin. "You're the one with the Seer Stone. All you have to worry about is whether *you're* doing the right thing. Cleaning up the Dallas mess is definitely the right thing to do. Okay?"

"Okay." I kissed him. "How are you?"

"Tired," he said. "And the whole cutting Dallas's head off thing—well—I knew what was going to happen and I thought I was ready for it. But . . ." His words faded and he held me tightly.

"Stark, I don't think there's any way to get ready to see a kid's head cut off." I squeezed him back. "Hey, you should go take a shower and change. How about we meet at lunch?"

"How about we make a date to do nothing but curl up together after school *alone* and Roku a *Big Bang Theory* marathon."

I grinned at him. "No one but me knows what a dork you truly are."

"I need to laugh, and Sheldon makes me laugh."

"Okay, but only if you don't make fun of me when I don't get all his jokes," I said.

"That's part of what makes me laugh," he said.

"Fine. Laugh at me. I'll sacrifice for you," I said kiddingly.

His expression went serious. "I'll always sacrifice for you." He drew a deep breath, then blurted, "I don't want you to start hooking up with Aurox."

I pulled back from him. "What are you talking about?"

"I know I said I'd share you with Heath but I really only said that after the kid was already dead and now he's back and I don't think I can share you and I want you to stay away from him," he said all in one big rush.

"Sorry it took forever! Someone put the ritual matches in the smudge stick drawer. I thought we'd never find them. I hate it when things get out of place," Damien gushed, all out of breath and frazzled-looking as he, Shaylin, Shaunee, and Aurox hurried up to us, their hands filled with candles and matches.

"Shaylin told me what Thanatos wants, and I'm ready," Shaunee said.

"Is something wrong?" Shaylin asked, looking from Stark to me with unsettling concentration.

"No, everything's fine," I said. "Stark was just on his way to take a shower and change. Right, Stark?"

Stark put his arms around me and pulled me to him. Then he kissed me. Right on the lips. Hard and possessive. One of his hands trailed down my back and rested on my butt as he said, "Right, Z. I'll see you tonight. During our date. Alone." He squeezed my butt and then hurried away.

Shaylin handed me the purple spirit candle, and I resisted the urge to throw the thick pillar at him. What the hell was I going to do about Stark? And did he really think acting possessive and telling me what to do was the way to get me to *not* want to be with another guy? Hell, no!

I pushed aside my irritation and forced a cheerful smile on my face.

"So, let's get this circle cast," I said. "Everyone ready?"

As we took our positions I ignored the fact that Shaylin kept watching me, and then I realized that I was going to have to take my position in the center of the circle, which meant I was going to have to stand by Dallas's decapitated body in the middle of blood-soaked ash and burned earth, and I decided I didn't care how close Shaylin was watching me or what an ass Stark was acting like. I just kinda froze at the edge of the blood, hating that the smell of it made my mouth water, but the sight made my stomach clench.

"Don't look at him." Aurox's voice had me lifting my gaze from the horrible headless body. He smiled at me from the northernmost part of the circle. "Go to Damien and call air. By the time you have to move to the center you will be strengthened by the elements. You can do it, Zo."

That last little part of what he said sounded so much like Heath it made my eyes fill with tears. I blinked hard, nodded, and went to Damien.

And Aurox was absolutely right. By the time I moved to the center, lit my purple candle, and called spirit I felt steady and grounded. It wasn't difficult for me to lead Shaunee in forcing a blast of flame at Dallas's body. After it was burned to ashes, it felt natural for me to ask Shaylin to have water wash the pyre site, and Damien to have wind blow away the burning stench. Finally, I used Aurox as the conduit for earth. Together we coaxed the ground to sprout fresh green grass where before there had been only ash and blood.

"That's way better," I said, standing in the middle of soft green grass and breathing deeply of springtime after I'd closed the circle.

Damien pulled his cell phone from his man purse and checked the time. "Oh, good! We've only missed half of third hour. I love lit and Professor Penthesilea."

"Third hour! That's fencing for me," Shaunee said. "I'm outta here. See you guys at lunch."

We waved bye to her and I sighed. "I wish it was sixth hour."

"I thought you liked lit class," Damien said.

"I do, but I don't like Spanish class, which is fifth hour. So if it was sixth hour I would've missed Spanish." I rubbed my forehead, feeling achy and dizzy again.

"Are you okay?" Shaylin asked.

I looked at her. She was staring at me. Again. Irritation bubbled, along with the rumble of my stomach. The Seer Stone started to heat the center of my chest, which only intensified my irritation. "Shaylin, *stop creeping on me!*" I hadn't meant to sound as pissed as my words came out sounding, and I totally hadn't meant to make Shaylin jump like I'd just smacked her, but that was exactly what happened.

"Sorry. I didn't mean anything," she said, almost cringing away from me.

I sighed and my hand found the stone, which had cooled to ordinary rock. "Look, I didn't mean to yell at you. I have a headache and I'm hungry, that's all."

"Well, Z, you just circled. You should ground yourself. Go to the cafeteria and get something to eat," Damien said, patting my arm. "I'll tell Professor P where you are. It'll be fine."

"You're right, Damien. Food would definitely help my head."

"Food or brown pop?" Damien asked, smiling.

"Brown pop is food," I said.

"Zoey, do you mind if I go to the cafeteria with you?" Aurox asked me.

"Don't you have to get to class?" I said.

"No. I only go to first hour. Then I patrol the school grounds."

"Oh, I, uh, didn't know that," I said inanely, not sure whether to be envious of him or feel sorry for him.

"Actually, it's probably a good idea if Aurox ate something, too," Damien said. "It was his first circle." He paused and smiled at Aurox. "And you were excellent. Well done you."

"Hey, thanks Damien." A grin broke over Aurox's face, making his eyes sparkle a little too familiarly.

How the hell could moonstone-colored eyes remind me of Heath's?

"Zo, you don't mind if I go with you, do you?"

I realized I'd been staring at Aurox—while Shaylin and Damien and Aurox had been staring at me—and I blinked. "No, that's fine. You'll have to hurry, though. I should try to make at least the last few minutes of lit class. Just because it's not math doesn't mean I'm great at it." With Aurox following, I practically jogged away, saying a quick bye to Damien and Shaylin.

The cafeteria was deserted, but I could hear pots and pans clattering in the distance from the kitchen, and something smelled delicious. My mouth was watering like crazy when Aurox said, "If you get our drinks I'll go back to the kitchen and see what's ready to eat."

I said okay without thinking about it, and went straight for the brown pop, sucking down a glass before I even left the drink dispenser. My head was a little clearer when I carried two big glasses to the table my group usually sat at. Sipping the cold brown goodness, I thought about how strange it was that some rooms totally changed when they were empty. Like, the cafeteria was usually loud and filled with kids and food, but right now, half an hour before lunch, it seemed unusually big and almost alien, as if it echoed with the ghosts of kids not here, but still, somehow, watching me.

It gave me a seriously creepy feeling.

"I got you grilled cheese sammiches and tomato poop." Aurox smiled happily as he slid in beside me, plopping a tray filled with soup and sandwiches in front of us.

All I could do was stare at him.

His smile faded. He looked at the grilled cheese and soup, and then at me. "I thought you would like this. I can take it back. They have turkey and cheese, too, and the cook said they're almost done making cobb salads."

"It's not that. I love grilled cheese. And the soup."

"Then why do you look like that?"

"Grilled cheese sammiches and tomato poop. Why did you call them that?"

His brow scrunched. "It just came out of my mouth. That's not what you call them?"

"Aurox, it's what I've called them since grade school. It's also what Heath called them. It was our favorite lunch because our school made seriously crappy spaghetti."

"Psaghetti," he said softly.

My mind told me to tell him to shut up and eat, but my mouth said, "We only call it that when it's good. *Psaghetti madness* can't happen with crappy spaghetti." I knew I was babbling, but I couldn't stop myself. "There's a song and a dance that go with *psaghetti madness*, too."

"I know."

"What else do you know?" I felt hot and cold at the same time.

"That I want to touch you so badly that sometimes I think I might die if you don't let me," he said.

My stomach butterflied. "I'm with Stark."

"I know, and I think you should take a chill pill about that."

Chill pill! When he said that he sounded so much like Heath I couldn't breathe.

Neither of us said anything, and then he reached slowly up toward me. One of my hands was resting on the table between us. Gently, he turned it over. With one finger he softly traced the filigree pattern of the tattoo that covered my palm.

"These were gifts from Nyx," he said.

"Yes."

"You have more special tattoos." He moved his finger from my palm to my face, where he stroked the repeated pattern there.

His finger was warm and it brought alive my nerves so that everywhere he touched I tingled. He followed the line of my neck down to the deep vee of my BDG T-shirt, and began to trace the tattoo that stretched over the puckered scar, which ran from one of my shoulders to the other.

"This almost killed you," he whispered.

"Almost." The word came out breathy, like I was trying to talk and jog at the same time.

His fingertips still on my body, his eyes met mine. "You Imprinted with Heath and he saved you. That is why this didn't kill you."

"Yes."

"You drank his blood."

It was too hard to speak, so I just nodded.

"Zo, I want you to drink my blood."

"Heath, uh, Aurox," I stuttered, "I can't. It would hurt Stark and—"

My words broke off when he lifted the knife and pricked the tip of the finger that had been touching my chest. A single drop of scarlet welled. The scent of his blood washed over and through me. It wasn't human. It wasn't fledgling or vampyre. It was magick.

I licked the tip of his finger and he moaned my name, *"Zo!"*

The taste hit my body like a nuclear bomb. My hands covered his, clutching, imprisoning, needing. I closed my eyes and took his finger in my mouth. He leaned forward, his head pressing against mine.

The bell that signaled the end of third hour and the beginning of lunch rang. My eyes opened wide and I realized what I was doing.

"No, this isn't right! No. Aurox." Shaking my head, I let loose his hand.

He was breathing as heavily as I was. "I won't tell anyone. I won't ever betray you like that."

I wanted to cry. "If you really care about me you'll just go. Please."

He nodded, wrapped a napkin around his bleeding finger, and bolted from the cafeteria.

I drank an entire glass of pop in a single gulp. I wiped my mouth. I smoothed my T-shirt. I picked up a triangle of grilled cheese and forced myself to eat it. And when my friends all crowded into the booth I smiled and talked and let Stark put his arm around me possessively.

No one knew I was screaming inside. No one.

CHAPTER EIGHTEEN

Neferet

Neferet's eyes moved under her closed lids as she relived the twentieth century. For a time that ultimately brought her such power, and the beginnings of her immortality, it really had been a terrible bore.

Two things had been the exception: her dreams and the old woman. The first had proven to be lies and the second to be spectacularly more than the truth. It was ironic that her dreams were the more enjoyable to revisit.

Neferet had returned to Tower Grove House of Night and to a school all too willing to shower her with concern and compassion. Too close together had been the untimely deaths of her first familiar, little Chloe, and her Warrior. Everyone understood when Neferet withdrew from social events and spent an unusual amount of time in meditation and prayer.

They had no idea that Neferet actually spent her prayer time in a deep, drugged sleep, yearning for the god that came to her only when she was unconscious.

Kalona had been clever. Though he was spectacularly handsome, he came to her dreams as the Faceless God, who asked only that she reveal her fantasies to him and allow him to worship her.

It hadn't been like dreaming at all. Afterward—after it was far too late—Neferet realized that she had *not* been dreaming—that Kalona had been entering her subconscious mind and manipulating her. Then, all she had known was the desire his immortal touch ignited within her. She continued to open herself to him, and as her subconscious listened to his whispers, Neferet grew stronger. She began to question the modern ways of the vampyres surrounding her. And, ultimately, to believe that it was her destiny to loose a god from his unjust imprisonment so that she and he could rule side-by-side, Nyx and Erebus on earth. Together they would herald a new age where vampyres would no longer exist in an uneasy, pathetic peace with humans. Quietly, Neferet set about events that would irrevocably change the shape of vampyre-human relations. As the immortal had told her in her dreams: *Why do the gods who walk the earth bow to those who should be worshipping them?*

Neferet used the loss of her Warrior as an excuse to travel, to not be tied to the tedious job of being a professor. Seeking, always seeking that which filled her dreams but eluded her in life, Neferet had smiled when they began to call her an ambassador of Nyx, whose visits blessed each House of Night in a special way.

Neferet thought of herself as an ambassador of power.

She used her psychic gift to know which High Priestesses wanted, *needed,* to be flattered or challenged, threatened or praised, adored or ignored, and then she gave them what they wanted: information, a healing touch, insight, excitement . . . the list of High Priestess needs and wants had been endless. While Neferet "served," she gained standing in the vampyre community. She thought of herself as a powerful, alluring chameleon. She learned how to make her people see in her what each of them most trusted, respected, and ultimately, worshipped.

And always, always, Neferet was drawn to the heart of the nation—to Oklahoma, the land the color of old blood, and the young city, Tulsa, where she had buried the record of her human past, and where Kalona's dreams, whispers, and touch kept pulling her.

Seek my release . . . seek my release . . . His whispers had filled her dreams and haunted her life.

It was the twenty-second of April in the year 1927 when the wealthy human couple, Waite and Genevieve Phillips, issued an invitation for vampyre High Priestesses to attend the grand gala they were holding to celebrate the completion of the mansion that was being called Philbrook.

Neferet made quite sure she was among those who accepted the invitation. Philbrook did not interest her, nor did the philanthropic, liberal human couple and their wealthy socialite friends.

The city did interest Neferet. It smelled of oil and alcohol, money and blood and power—always power.

It was the scent of power, like the essence of her dreams, that had her leaving the Phillips party that night and wandering through the city. Newly completed oil mansions dotted the landscape. Neferet drifted past them, unseen. She hardly glanced in their windows—barely noticed the leaded glass and the ice-like sparkling of the new electrical chandeliers. Instead she was pulled away from the glittering mansions, following a melodic little brook that seemed to be whispering a song to her.

The mansion appeared suddenly, as if it had materialized especially for Neferet. It was enormous, set in the middle of immaculately tended grounds dotted by oak trees. Neferet remembered thinking how odd it was that there was only an iron gate at the entrance from the street and not a wall surrounding it.

Then she saw the sign and realized that, though it appeared to have been fashioned after a European villa, or perhaps even a castle, the massive stone building was a private school.

Neferet was drawn to it even before she saw the old woman. She entered the campus, her interest completely aroused. There were two main buildings, both built from a uniquely textured stone. The campus appeared new, so new that it looked dark and uninhabited. It was as she wandered through the slumbering campus that the whispering song she had been hearing all night became reality and Neferet's dream coalesced.

She heard the sonorous beat of the drum first. Neferet had followed it to a far easterly spot at the very edge of the campus grounds. There the scent of sage and sweetgrass led her to an enormous oak, big enough even to shield the light of a campfire. She noticed that birds filled the limbs of the oak. *Ravens,* she remembered identifying them with an afterthought. *Odd, ravens aren't usually seen at night.*

Neferet circled around the tree and saw the campfire.

Then the drumbeat filled the clearing and all of Neferet's attention had focused on the crone. She knelt near the fire with a large drum before her, which she beat with a simple stick wrapped in hide she held in her right hand. In her left hand she held a hatchet. Every few drumbeats she chopped a fist-sized section from a long, thick rope of dried herbs that lay beside her. The fire hissed as it ate the herbs, belching sweetly scented smoke.

The woman's dress, though yellowed with age, had an unexpected beauty to it. Delicate beadwork reflected the firelight, and long fringe swayed gracefully with each drumbeat. Her face was ancient, her thick braid of hair completely silver, but her voice was as clear as a girl's. She began to sing and Neferet had been entranced by her words.

Ancient one sleeping, waiting to arise . . .

Neferet moved silently toward the old woman as the song pounded through her body in time with her heartbeat.

> *When earth's power bleeds sacred red*
> *The mark strikes true; Queen Tsi Sgili will devise*
> *He shall be washed from entombing bed.*

Neferet stepped within the firelight. The crone looked up at her through rheumy eyes that might have once been blue. Her song faltered.

"No," Neferet had insisted. "Keep singing. It is a lovely song." The old woman's expression had tightened, but she'd continued:

> *Through the hand of the dead he is free*
> *Terrible beauty, monstrous sight*
> *Ruled again they shall be*
> *Women shall kneel to his dark might*
>
> *Kalona's song sounds sweet*
> *As we slaughter with cold heat.*

Kalona! The name of the god had pierced Neferet. "Sing it again, old woman," she had commanded.

"I have finished. I go."

The old woman began to rise, but Neferet had moved swiftly to stop her. It had been too easy to take the hatchet from the crone—too easy to press it to her throat.

"Do as I command or I will slit your throat and leave you here for the birds to pick your ancient bones clean."

The old woman had closed her eyes; drawn a deep, shaky breath; and then began to sing, over and over, until Neferet was certain she had the song memorized. Only then did she allow the woman to stop. Only then did she probe within the crone's mind.

"You think of yourself as a Ghigua. What is that?" Neferet had asked.

The old woman's eyes had widened. She hadn't answered Neferet, but her mind had suddenly been washed in panic and strange words: *Ane li sgi, demon, Tsi Sgili, soul-eater, man-killer.* That tide of words had been carried to Neferet on a wave of dread and terror.

"You're very frightened of me." Neferet had smiled and sat closer to the old woman, resting the hatchet in the small space between them.

"You hear what is in my mind," said the woman.

"I hear more than that," Neferet said. "Your song—I believe I understand what it means."

"I sing this song each new moon as a warning."

"Certainly, to some it would be a warning. To me it is a promise." Neferet had probed the old woman's mind further. "You do not fear me because I am vampyre."

"I have no fear of vampyres."

"Yet you fear me," Neferet had said. "And you sing of my lover. Let me see, how did that song go—*The mark strikes true; Queen Tsi Sgili will devise.* Tell me, old woman, who and what is Queen Tsi Sgili?"

You are, demon! Delighter in pain! Feeder from death!

The condemnation echoed from the old woman's mind to Neferet, but the crone said only, "I have spoken enough for one night. Now I will say no more." Then she had pressed her thin, wrinkled lips into a stubborn line.

Neferet had smiled silkily at her. "Ah, but I do not need you to speak in words. Your mind is shouting quite loudly enough. I can glean all I need without you uttering a syllable, old woman."

But Neferet hadn't had time to rape the woman's mind as she had intended. With an ear-piercing war cry, the crone had snatched up the hatchet and sliced it across her own throat, opening her carotid artery.

"No!" Neferet had screamed, pressing her palm against the old woman's flesh, trying to prolong her last minutes as she probed her mind, seeking answers from fading images and half-formed thoughts.

In her den Neferet's body twitched and quivered in response to the memory. The old woman had sacrificed herself for nothing. Her dying mind had held information enough for Neferet to begin two things—her quest to release Kalona, and her transformation from unfulfilled High Priestess to an immortal goddess, Queen Tsi Sgili.

Zoey

I loved sixth hour. Not only was Lenobia the coolest professor ever, but *it was a class where I got to ride a horse!* I have no clue how that could be more perfect. Today it seemed like Lenobia knew we needed to get rid of some stress. When class began we entered the arena to find big black steel barrels set up in a triangle formation.

Lenobia galloped up on Mujaji. The black mare slid to a stop in front of us.

"So, fledglings, does anyone know why those barrels are out there?"

My hand shot up.

"Zoey?"

"They're for barrel racing."

"They are," she said. "Have you raced barrels before, Zoey?"

I smiled, a little nervously. "Well, sorta. My grandma's horse, Mouse, was a retired barrel racer. Grandma used to set up barrels for him. Even when he was really old he'd perk up and race around them like he was a colt again. Basically I just hung on and let him do all the work, but it was fun."

Lenobia smiled. "That's a lovely story, and a special memory, Zoey. Treasure it."

"I will. I do."

"So, has anyone else had experience with barrel racing?"

The other five kids shook their heads and squirmed.

Lenobia frowned, and grumbled, more to herself than to us, "It's always so disheartening to be in the middle of Oklahoma and be surrounded by young people who know nothing of horses." Then she raised her voice and continued, "No matter. I have devised a very large, very simple, very obvious example for you to follow." She clucked at Mujaji and the mare moved aside so that Travis, riding his big Percheron mare, Bonnie, could trot into the arena.

He pulled the mare up in front of Lenobia and tipped his hat to her. "Ma'am, I didn't just hear you call my mare big and simple, did I?"

She caressed Bonnie's muzzle and kissed her softly before answering him. "I would never call this magnificent creature big and simple—I was speaking of you, sir." Her eyes sparkled at the tall, handsome cowboy.

"Well that's fine, ma'am," he said. "Glad to know I'm appreciated."

Lenobia's laughter sounded girlish and I thought I'd never seen her look so beautiful. "Just take Bonnie around the barrels for the kids." She swatted playfully at Travis's boot.

Yep, she was definitely in love.

"All right, my girl, let's show these fledglings you don't have to be a quarter horse to barrel race!" He pulled Bonnie around to a starting position, and then gave her a big kick and smacked her on her very large butt with his hat. The Percheron mare almost sorta took off.

Lenobia explained what Bonnie was doing—how she was following a cloverleaf pattern—in exaggerated time. But still, when the giant mare came charging down the center with Travis whooping, and the arena floor seeming to shake, we all cheered and clapped.

And that was just the beginning of the fun. For almost an hour we took turns running the barrels with our chosen horses. Persephone was "my" mare. I adored every inch of her beautiful roan hide. She could move, too! Persephone totally knew how to run a cloverleaf. As Stevie Rae would've said, all I had to do was to make like a tick and stick tight to her.

For that time—for those fifty-something minutes—I forgot about Neferet and Stark and Aurox and Heath and the Change and Old Magick. For a little while I was a girl again, laughing and riding a horse, and loving life.

It was over too soon. Usually grooming Persephone helped to quiet my mind. Today it had the opposite affect. Maybe it was because I hadn't thought at all while I'd been riding her, but as I swiped her off and worked through her mane with the currycomb, my problems roared.

Worrying about what Neferet was up to should have been my biggest problem, followed by trying to figure out how my Seer Stone and Old Magick were working—or *not* working—but what kept circling around and around in my mind was the Heath/ Aurox/Stark situation.

Holy crap, I'd licked blood from the kid's finger.

What the hell was I going to do?

"Good job today, Zoey."

Lenobia's voice startled me and Persephone tossed her head at my jumpy reaction. I soothed the mare and gave Lenobia an apologetic look. "Sorry, my mind wasn't here."

"I completely understand." She leaned against the stall doorjamb. "Grooming Mujaji is like taking a sleeping pill for me. She's made me so relaxed I've even curled up in her stall and slept afterwards."

I sighed. "Yeah, Persephone usually does that for me, too."

"But not today?"

I shook my head. "Not today."

"Want to talk about it?"

I almost gave her my automatic, *that's okay, I'm fine*, answer, but then I remembered how she'd said she'd waited to find Travis for more than two hundred years. She must know about complicated love—plus, Lenobia was more than just a professor, she was my friend. I changed my auto answer. "Yeah, if you have time, I do want to talk about it."

Lenobia pulled a bale of hay into the stall and sat. "I have time."

I drew a deep breath, not sure where to begin.

"Just groom the mare and talk. The rest will come naturally," Lenobia said.

I grabbed the soft curry brush and followed the sleek pattern of Persephone's coat. And I talked.

"I know it's normal, actually it seems to be kinda expected, for a High Priestess to choose more than one guy, but I just don't get how they do it."

Lenobia laughed.

"What'd I say?"

"Oh, Zoey, I apologize. I'm not really laughing at you. It's just that I forget how very young you are and how many things there are about vampyres that you don't truly understand."

"Like how to juggle more than one guy," I said, nodding.

"Well, perhaps, but it seems to me that the first thing you should understand is that High Priestesses are not *expected* to have more than one lover at a time. They simply have the option to choose more than one partner without being judged, as would a human woman in today's culture." Lenobia crossed her legs and leaned back against the stall wall, as if she were settling in for a long, intimate talk. "Zoey, think about what your life-span will be when you complete the Change."

"If I complete it," I said.

Lenobia smiled. "I have confidence in you, so let's say *when* you complete it. Do you know how old I am?"

"Old," I said before thinking. "Uh, sorry. It's not like you look old or anything."

"I am not offended. I was born in the year 1772."

"That is really old!" I blurted.

Her smile widened. "If fate is good to me, I have probably only lived half of my life-span. Since 1772 I have loved only one man, but that was my choice—my vow. Most vampyres find several loves during their lifetimes. Sometimes they are already involved with another vampyre when they meet a new human love— sometimes it is the other way around."

"So, it's not about being expected to have lots of guys at the same time," I said.

"That's right. It's more about logic and life-span. And choice. Because we are a matriarchal society, we can choose without judgment or condemnation. Does that help you with your problem?"

"Well, yes and no. Thanks for explaining the multiple guy thing to me, but I still don't know what to do about the Heath slash Aurox thing," I said miserably.

"Why do you have to do anything?"

"Because I *have* done something. And ignoring it isn't fair to Aurox or to Stark." I sighed again. "Or, I guess, to Heath."

"So you have taken Aurox as your lover, along with Stark?"

"No!" I squeaked, and peeked over Persephone's shoulder at Lenobia. She gazed steadily back at me, nonjudgmental and serene. "I drank a little of his blood, though," I admitted.

"And because you're not like a normal first-year fledgling, that's very addictive and exciting for you. Correct?"

"Yeah, correct," I admitted.

"Does Stark know?"

"Oh, god, no! He'd totally freak. He's already acting like a possessive jerk whenever Aurox is anywhere near me."

"But he knows you were mated to Heath and that Heath's soul is within Aurox."

"That's why he's acting like a possessive jerk. Apparently it's *not* okay with Stark for me to see Heath, ur, Aurox. And as far as Stark knows we've hardly even talked to each other."

"Aurox is drawn to you."

She didn't phrase it as a question, but I answered. "Yeah, he is. It's because Heath's inside him. It's not like a conscious thing. It's weird—and unsettling. Aurox will just be this kid who is kinda cute, but who I'm not particularly attracted to or anything, and then—*bam!*—I'll blink and he'll say or do something that is so Heath-like that it makes my heart hurt."

"If you weren't bonded with Stark, would you want to be with Aurox?"

I chewed my lip. "I'm not sure. I love Heath. I'll always love Heath. But Aurox isn't *really* my Heath."

"You mean it's like how Kalona was drawn to you because within you is the maiden A-ya's soul, and he recognized her presence?"

That comparison surprised me, but the more I thought about

it, the more it made sense. "I think you're right about that. Wow, that actually makes it easier for me. Kalona did want me because of A-ya, and I have to admit I could feel a deep pull toward him, too. But it wasn't real. I'm *not* A-ya, and *I* didn't choose to love him. Aurox isn't Heath. *He* doesn't need to choose to love me—remnants of Heath love me, that's all."

"I hate to complicate things for you, but to be fair you need to know that Aurox could love you as well. Travis is a reincarnation of my only mate, Martin. He does not have Martin's memories. He is actually very dissimilar to my Martin, and yet he is as eternally devoted to me as I am to him." Lenobia's smile was tender, her eyes filled with tears. "You do get to take love with you, and some of us are lucky enough to find it again."

"Lenobia, I'm super happy for you, but you did just complicate the crap out of this for me," I said.

"Zoey, your situation was already complicated. Do you want my advice on how I would handle it?"

"Hell yes," I said.

"This is going to sound cold, selfish even, but were I in your place, I would decide who I truly wanted to be with without worrying about what either of those boys wanted. The only way you will ever be content with your choice is if you make it for yourself and not for someone else."

I put down the curry brush and stared at her. "Is it really as simple as that?"

"If you can be honest with yourself, and then follow through with that honesty, yes, it is," Lenobia said.

"You've given me a lot to think about, but at least now I have a direction to go," I said.

"You have to love and be true to yourself before anyone else can love and be true to you."

The bell that signaled the end of school rang. I fisted my

hand over my heart and bowed respectfully to her. "Thank you, Lenobia."

Lenobia returned the traditional gesture and said, "I wish you always to blessed be, Zoey Redbird."

"Stark, we need to talk." I hated to say those words probably as much as Stark hated to hear them. I mean, who doesn't? Has anyone's mom or dad, girlfriend or boyfriend, teacher or boss ever started a *good* conversation with them?

"Okay, but I thought we were going to watch *Big Bang Theory* and, you know, spend some alone time together." He gave me a halfhearted attempt at his cocky grin.

"Well, we can still do that. Maybe. If you want to after we talk."

"You're freaking me out," he said.

I held my hand out to him. He took it and sat next to me on the bed. "I have to say some things to you that are gonna probably be hard for you to hear, but you don't need to be freaked."

"Because no matter what I'll always be your Warrior and Guardian?"

He looked super nervous. I threaded my fingers through his. "Yes, that's part of it, but there's also the part about me loving you."

"Oh, good. I like that part."

"Me, too," I said. "But I also have to like you."

"I thought you just said you did."

"No, I just said I loved you. And I do. But you've been doing some things lately that I don't like very much and we have to talk about it."

"What do you mean?"

I decided that if I was going to be honest with myself, I had to be honest with Stark, so I told him the truth—straight out. "I don't like how you treat me when Aurox is around. You act like a possessive jerk, and I want you to stop."

He tried to pull his hand from mine, but I wouldn't let him. "The point is, I don't think you *are* a possessive jerk. I like who you really are, and I want you to go back to being that guy, all the time."

"Fine. Whatever."

"No, Stark. This isn't gonna work if you're not honest with me, and with yourself. You'll always be my Warrior, but if you get all defensive with me and we can't talk about our problems, it'll end up that you'll only be my Warrior and nothing else."

"Is that what you want?"

"Seriously, Stark, think about it. If that was what I wanted, why would you and I be having this conversation?"

"So, you're not breaking up with me?"

"I hope not," I said.

He slowly let out a long breath like he was deflating. His shoulders slumped and he stared at the floor between his feet. "Knowing that you love Aurox is driving me fucking crazy, and I'm sorry it's made me act like a douche. I don't know what to do about it, though, because I can't stand to think about you being with him."

"Okay, first, I don't love Aurox. I love Heath. I'll always love Heath. You know that."

"But Aurox has Heath's soul inside him."

"Yep, and I'm glad he does because that's all that saved Grandma. I'll always appreciate Aurox for that, but I don't love him."

"You don't want to be with him? For real?" Stark pulled his gaze from the floor to look at me.

"I've decided I don't want to be with him. For real," I said.

"Why not?" Then, before I could answer him, Stark cut me off, "No—no, nevermind. I don't care why not. I just care that you don't want to be with him. I don't want to know anything more than that."

Okay, I'd meant to tell Stark about me tasting Aurox's blood, and that it was really hard for me when I caught glimpses of Heath peeking out from inside Aurox, and that I did actually still love Heath *and* him. But even with all of those ands I'd decided that I just couldn't handle having more than one boyfriend at a time. Instead I didn't get to say any of that because Stark pulled me into his arms.

"I'm so damn glad you picked me!" he whispered.

I could feel that he was trembling, so I held him and whispered, "Me, too." Then he was kissing me with a need that burned so hot that I couldn't think about what I'd meant to say. All I could think about was his touch and how much I loved him.

It was later, after the sun had risen and Stark slept soundly beside me, his arm draped across my body, his side pressed intimately against me, that my mind started to work again, and I knew I had to talk to Aurox.

CHAPTER NINETEEN

Zoey

It wasn't hard to slide Stark's arm off me and sneak out of bed. Stark was totally passed out. I didn't think an exploding bomb would wake him up. Still, I meditated on how sparkly my new phone cover was as I got dressed and tiptoed from the room.

A bomb might not wake Stark up, but my emotions going crazy probably would.

Thankfully, no one was around. Even though it was midmorning the sky was the color of a bruise and it smelled like spring thunderstorms. On the way to the field house I noticed the wisteria planted along parts of the school wall was budding up with big purple bunches of blossoms. Then I sneezed. Yep, thunderstorms, flowers, and allergies. Spring had to be coming to Oklahoma.

I went into the field house through the stables and paused in the hall between buildings, breathing deeply of horse and hay and trying to keep my emotions calm.

I'm just going to be honest. It'll hurt his feelings more if I stretch this out and avoid him. Heath would understand.

I snorted a laugh at myself. No, Heath would not understand. Heath would tell me, *"We belong together, babe!"* and ignore the fact that I was breaking up with him. Again.

Kalona was standing by himself in the hallway outside the entrance to the basement.

"Zoey, you're up late," he said as he fisted his hand over his heart and gave me a little bow.

I hadn't seen him since he'd cut Dallas's head off and flown away with two fledglings struggling under his arms. He didn't look any different. I suppose I shouldn't expect him to. Still, I couldn't help being morbidly curious. "Hi," I said. "So, how'd things go with the two fledglings?"

"As they were meant to go."

"Are they, you know, *dead*?"

Kalona shrugged, causing his massive wings to rustle. "I left them in the middle of the Tall Grass Prairie. With the storms covering the sun they might last the day, but they certainly will not last another."

"Are you going to take care of their bodies?"

He shook his head. "Coyotes will do that job for me."

"That's really cold," I said.

"Justice often seems cold. That is not a trait Thanatos and I originated. Judging, condemning, and carrying out justice is not pleasant. Is it not this country whose symbol for justice is a blind maiden holding scales of judgment?"

"Uh, I don't think that's because she's cold. I think that's because justice shouldn't be based on the way a person looks or who he or she is—it should be based on the facts."

"I do not understand the distinction you are making."

"Nevermind." I gave up. "I'm looking for Aurox. Have you seen him?"

"It was his turn to patrol the school perimeter. If you go out the front entrance to the field house, he should be circling back around shortly."

"Okay, great. Uh, I'd appreciate it if you didn't mention to anyone that I was looking for—"

Kalona held up a hand, cutting me off. "I will not tell tales to your Warrior."

I thought about correcting him and saying that wasn't it at all, that I just didn't want fledglings to be gossiping about Aurox and me, but my mouth wouldn't form the lie, so I sighed and said, "Yeah, thanks." And then I scurried away.

No one was out in the front side of the school, either, and I found a bench not far from the field house door. While I sat and waited for Aurox, I watched the thunderclouds get closer and thought about what Kalona had said.

Maybe he was right. Judging others wasn't pleasant. There was a time when I would have also thought judging others was wrong, but I'd agreed with Thanatos in her condemnation. I suppose I even agreed with her penalty. So, did that make me a hypocrite when, afterward, I felt all squeamish and disgusted? Or did that make me humane? *Or* did it make me too damn dense to ever be a decent High Priestess?

"Zoey? Is everything okay?"

I hadn't heard Aurox approach, so it was a shock to look from the thunderclouds to his moonbeam eyes. I blinked and shook myself, trying to refocus and at least do this one thing right.

"Yeah, everything's fine. I just needed to talk to you. Is now a good time?"

"Of course." He gestured toward the bench beside me and nodded, "Oh, yeah, go ahead and sit down."

He sat and I tried not to fidget or pick at my fingernail polish.

"It looks like it's going to rain," I said. "And I think I just heard thunder off in the distance."

"The scent of lightning is in the air," he agreed.

I relaxed a little. That was definitely *not* something Heath would have said. "I never thought about lightning smelling like anything, but you're probably right. Thunder and lightning go together."

"Zo, what's up?"

My eyes went to his. Yep. Heath was definitely in there. "I can't drink your blood again."

"But you want to," he said.

"Aurox, no one gets everything they want."

"But this isn't everything, it's just a small part of everything."

"If I really drank your blood, we'd make love. We'd probably Imprint. That wouldn't be a small thing to me or you or Stark."

"It's Stark, then. He's the reason why you won't be with me," Aurox said.

"No. It's me. I can't be with two guys at the same time."

"And you will not choose me over Stark because I am not Heath."

"I won't choose you over Stark because I'm already committed to Stark," I said firmly.

"It's because I'm not good enough for you—because of how I was made—what I can be."

I put my hand over his. "No, Aurox. Please don't think that. You're not to blame for any of that, and I don't think about that when I'm with you."

"What do you think about?"

I smiled, even though I felt sad, and continued to tell him the truth. "I think about how glad I am that you're here. I also think you and Heath make a really good team."

"You know we love you," he said.

"I know." I spoke softly, and pulled my hand from his. "I'm sorry."

"Where do we go from here?"

"I want to be friends," I said.

"Friends." The word sounded so flat when he repeated it.

"Yeah, and Stark's not going to act crazy around you anymore," I said.

"Zo, that's because he doesn't have any reason to." Aurox leaned over, kissed my cheek, and then sounding completely defeated, said, "Would you let Kalona know I am going to check the perimeter again?"

"Yeah, sure . . ." I said to his back as he sprinted away toward the school's stone wall.

I stood, feeling heavy and super, super tired. *Well I told him the truth, but it definitely sucked.* Trying not to think about anything but sleep, because the last thing I needed was for Stark to be awake and asking where I'd been and what had made me feel so crappy. I retraced my way into the field house and down the hallway that led to the entrance of the basement. Kalona wasn't standing there. I sighed and stuck my head into the field house. He wasn't there, either. Guessing that he was in the basement doing a quick check on the sleeping kids, I padded back toward the stairway.

"Yes, I've been watching Zoey like I said I would."

At first when I heard my name I stopped because I was surprised. The voice drifted from the stable area, coming from the half-opened door that separated the hallway between the field house and the barn.

"And? For shit's sake, do I have to ask you everything?"

Then I realized who was talking about me, and I crept closer, listening in disbelief.

"And her colors got super crazy during the funeral. But I think I know why, and it doesn't have anything to do with her losing control of her temper or her powers."

"Shaylin, you're making my ass hurt. Just tell me what you saw."

There was a long pause. I heard Shaylin blow out a long breath and then my insides went cold as the Prophetess told Aphrodite, "I saw her looking at Aurox. A lot. Her colors were crazy. That made me think—so when she and Aurox went to the cafeteria together after the circle casting, I followed them."

"Shit, Shaylin! You're not a Prophetess, you're a super spy!" Aphrodite said, laughing. "Tell me that Z and Bull Boy did the nasty."

I bit my lip to keep from screaming.

"Almost. The two of them are definitely all into each other. She sucked blood from his finger."

"That's practically doing it for Zoey, and oh crap. That's too fucking close to what I saw. Then, let me guess, her colors went crazy? All confused and frustrated and pissed?"

"Totally. Especially after she—"

I'd heard enough.

"*Shut up!*" I yelled. My chest was burning as hot as my face as I slapped my hand against the door, making it fly open and smack against the wall.

"Uh-oh," Aphrodite said.

"Zoey! This isn't what you think!" Shaylin said, backing away from me as I came into the room.

"Really? How is *this* not what I think it is when I *hear you telling Aphrodite that you've been spying on me*!" I didn't think. I reacted. Fisting my hand around the burning Seer Stone, I lifted my other hand and thought about how badly I wanted to knock Shaylin on her butt.

A ball of blue fire burst from my hand, knocking Shaylin off her feet. She landed on her back, out of breath, gasping and crying.

I didn't care about her bawling. It felt good to put her on her butt. Shaylin deserved it.

"Stop it. Now!" Aphrodite stepped in front of me.

I narrowed my eyes. "You were talking about me behind my back!"

"And I'll tell you why in a second. First, you need to check yourself. Get control of whatever crazy bullshit you've got going on and calm it down, *right now*." She glanced over her shoulder at Shaylin. "You go back to the basement, *right now*."

Still crying, Shaylin scrambled to her feet and ran past me.

"So, what is she, your own little private Prophetess?"

Instead of answering me, Aphrodite watched Shaylin go, and then she planted her hands on her hips and faced me. "Seriously? You're trying to talk shit to me after you used that fucking stone to hurt Shaylin? You have lost your damn mind."

"Stone?" I blinked at her, and then looked down at my chest, realizing I had been holding the Seer Stone so tightly that it had pressed painfully into my palm. As soon as I felt the pain the stone went cold. I dropped it. Feeling disoriented, I tried to keep my focus on what had pissed me off—Shaylin spying on Aurox and me. "I'm not talking about the stone, and I'm not talking shit. I want to know what the hell you think you're doing having me followed around."

"I had a vision. It was from your point of view. You were doing some of what Shaylin saw you doing with Aurox."

"When did you have this vision?"

"A couple of days ago. That doesn't matter. What's important is—"

"It doesn't matter that you kept a vision *about* me *from* me for days?"

"No, what's important is why. Why is because I also saw you losing your fucking temper and not able to control that fucking stone. Which is exactly what just happened."

"No, that's *not* what just happened. I controlled the fucking stone. I wanted to knock Shaylin on her butt, and it did exactly what I wanted."

Aphrodite shook her head back and forth. "Are you even listening to yourself? Yeah, you should be pissed about what you overheard. But Normal Zoey would never have wanted to hurt Shaylin. And, by the way, *Normal* Zoey wouldn't have said 'fucking,' either."

"*Normal* Zoey wouldn't have thought one of her best friends was talking behind her back and having her spied on!"

"I was going to tell you about the vision. I was going to tell you about Shaylin. I just needed to wait until the right time," Aphrodite said.

"You know what, Aphrodite? The right time wasn't *after* you talked about me and spied on me. Oh, to hell with this. I'm out of here." I started to walk away from her, but Aphrodite stepped in front of me again.

"Z, there's more going on here than just you being pissed at me. I think Old Magick is affecting you, and not in a good way. We need to talk about this. You have to let me tell you about the rest of my vision."

"I am so damn sick of hearing about what I *have to do*. Back off, Aphrodite." My chest was blazing when I pushed past her. She stumbled away from me, making a shocked noise. I didn't care. I'd had it with her.

I didn't know where I was going. I just knew I had to *go*. If I'd had the keys to my Bug I would've driven to Grandma's house, but my keys were up in my room and I didn't want to see Stark right now and tell him why I was so upset. Hell, if it hadn't been during the day, I would've already run into Stark, thanks to the stupid bond we shared.

I needed time. I needed space. I felt like anger was crawling under my skin. I couldn't get away from it because I couldn't get away from everyone pissing me off and telling me what to do. I needed to think without being pecked to death by ducks!

I changed direction, walking away from the dorms, until I came to the wall that enclosed the school. The wall Aurox patrolled. Damn! I didn't want to see him, either.

That's when I decided to hell with the cops and their house arrest crap. I hadn't killed the mayor, and if I needed to go for a walk off campus, I was going to go for a walk off campus! I started jogging for the easternmost part of the wall, and the hidden door I knew was not far from there.

Shaylin

Shaylin tried to stop bawling. She wasn't usually a crier. She was used to *not* feeling sorry for herself. But this was different. First there was the horrible thing that had happened with Dallas and the two fledglings. She'd known about it. Shaylin had seen their deaths in Thanatos's colors. And she'd shut her mouth and believed Thanatos was doing the right thing.

Then Shaylin had done the exact opposite—she'd opened her mouth and blabbed Zoey's personal business because she felt like she was doing the right thing. Well, Shaylin had also felt like she was fitting in at the House of Night and doing a good job using her gift.

But that couldn't be true because she'd felt absolutely terrible after Dallas had been killed, *and* the most powerful fledgling in the world had just knocked her on her ass.

She'd totally messed up. Twice.

Shaylin curled up in the dark corner of the basement where she'd made a little pallet for herself. She sat with her legs pulled up and her pillow on her lap. She pressed her face into the soft pillowcase to muffle her sobs. She shouldn't have bothered, though. Most red fledglings slept during the day like they were dead.

That's what I should have been doing, too, she chided herself. *I should have been sleeping and not talking to Aphrodite about Zoey. Now they're mad at each other, and at me! I'm never going to figure out this Prophetess thing.*

Shaylin didn't think about the fact that Aphrodite had, apparently, been right about Zoey's anger and control problem. At that moment Aphrodite being right didn't matter to her. At that moment all that mattered was that it felt like her world—and her friends—were falling apart.

"Hey, Shaylin, what's wrong?"

Stifling a sob, Shaylin looked up to see Nicole standing above her, rubbing her eyes and looking tousled, like she was sleep-walking.

"N-nothing. I—I'm f-fine," she whispered, then wiped her face on the pillowcase and forced herself to stop crying.

Nicole sat beside her. "No, you're not. You're bawling your eyes out."

"Shhh," Shaylin hushed her, looking around to be sure everyone else was still sleeping. "I'm f-fine.

Nicole scooted over closer to her, so that their shoulders were touching, and whispered. "It's okay. They won't hear. Tell me what's wrong."

Shaylin wiped her eyes again, and then spoke softly. "I think I messed up using my Sight."

"Hey, you're good at using your Sight. You saw that I'd changed." Nicole smiled at her. "You should have more confidence in yourself."

"I should learn when to open my stupid mouth, and when to keep my stupid mouth shut," Shaylin said. She fished around inside her purse and found a wadded-up tissue, and blew her nose.

"You're not stupid."

"If you had known Thanatos was going to tell Kalona to cut off Dallas's head, would you have said something?"

Nicole grimaced. "You can't ask me that. I'm not objective about Dallas."

"Are you still in love with him?"

Nicole shook her head quickly. "No, that's the point. I never really loved him, and I knew how dangerous he was. So I can't be objective about his death."

Listening to her, Shaylin hiccupped a little sob. Nicole put her arm around her.

"If you're upset because of what happened to Dallas, don't be."

"It's not just him, even though that was bad. I talked to Aphrodite about someone else's colors, and I should have stayed out of it."

"But Aphrodite's a Prophetess, too. She's kinda mean and crazy, but still, a Prophetess. I'm thinking it's okay for one Prophetess to talk to another about stuff like your True Sight."

"That's what I thought, too. Now I'm not so sure. I wish I knew the exact right thing to do."

"I think there are a lot of times when there isn't one exact right thing to do in a situation."

Shaylin looked up at Nicole. "You're really smart."

"Nah, I've just made a ton of mistakes." Nicole smiled at her. "But I'm not making one right now. I got you to quit crying."

Shaylin's smile was tentative. "I guess you did. Thank you. And, by the way, your colors have really turned pretty."

"See, if you think my colors are pretty that proves what a great Prophetess you are."

Shaylin was grinning up at Nicole when the fledgling bent and slowly, gently, kissed her on the lips. When Shaylin froze, eyes wide in shock, Nicole leaned away from her and quickly took her arm from around her shoulder. "I'm sorry," Nicole whispered. Even in the darkness of the basement, Shaylin could see Nicole's cheeks had turned red. "I don't know why I did that. I'm really sorry," she repeated.

Shaylin kept staring at her, seeing the soft beauty of her colors and feeling the soft, lingering warmth of her lips.

"Don't be sorry. I'm not." Then she put her arms around Nicole's slender waist, rested her head on her shoulder, and said, "Would you stay with me and hold me?"

Nicole's arm slid back around her shoulder. "Shaylin, sweetie, I'll stay with you forever if you want me to."

CHAPTER TWENTY

Kalona

TEN MINUTES EARLIER

Kalona was standing by the basement entrance waiting for Aurox to return, and thinking the boy might be a while since Zoey had gone to look for him, when a familiar hot, itchy feeling lodged under his skin.

"Erebus . . ." he grumbled.

"Did you say something?"

Kalona's gaze darted down the hallway. "Aphrodite, what may I do for you?" He didn't fist his hand over his heart or bow. Yes, this girl was a Prophetess of Nyx, but she was also the most annoying human he'd ever known. And Kalona had known *many* humans.

"I need to talk to Shaylin. She's in the basement, right?"

"All of the red fledglings are," he said.

"Except the two you dropped off in the wilderness to die."

"Is there a point you wish to make?"

"Nope, just stating the obvious. I'm gonna go wake up Shaylin. I'd appreciate it if you'd give us some privacy to talk."

"As you wish, Prophetess. Is your Warrior within screaming distance in case trouble breaks out below?"

"I don't need Darius to deal with red fledglings. I have this."
She patted her purse.

"You think to break up a fight with a handbag?" She almost
made him laugh.

"No, I think to break up a fight with *this*." Aphrodite flipped
open her leather bag. Kalona peered within to see a small black
cylinder.

"You're going to throw your perfume container at someone?"

"Oh, please, get with this century. It's pepper spray, not perfume. I've been living under a basement in tunnels downtown.
The Brady district and Greenwood and such are undergoing
a lovely renovation, but I've learned it pays to be protected and
prepared."

"Then I will give you your privacy." He did bow to her then.
Aphrodite was so annoying that he tended to forget how amusing she could be as well. She made a shooing gesture at him with
her pink painted fingertips before she ducked down into the basement.

He considered calling after her and telling her Zoey was just
outside with Aurox, and then he reconsidered. It really would be
amusing to see what would happen if Aphrodite discovered Zoey
in Aurox's arms.

Kalona was chuckling as he left the field house, exiting through
the stables. He stood outside, collecting himself, and tried to as-
certain from which direction his bastard of a brother would be
arriving. It did not take him long to figure it out. Dreading the
encounter, but resigned to its inevitability, Kalona headed for Nyx's
Temple.

He didn't attempt to enter. Truthfully, he averted his eyes as he
passed the wide wooden doorway and followed the stone building around to the rear of the temple, hoping that when his brother

manifested, in his typically garish fashion, he'd do so wherever Kalona stood and the building would block enough of his light to keep from bringing the entire faculty down upon them.

Kalona did not have to wait long. The ball of sunlight that materialized above the ground was, indeed, garish, but Kalona did not give in to the urge to shield his eyes. Erebus stepped from the blinding rays, nodding and smiling wryly.

"Excellent job coming when I summoned you, brother," Erebus said.

"It baffles me how you pretend that I want anything to do with you. *You* have been coming to me. I have existed for centuries without, as they would say in the modern world, giving you a call—or a thought."

"Or a thought? Really? I believe your thoughts have often turned to the Otherworld since your Fall."

"You are not Nyx, brother. It also baffles me how you mistake interest in the Goddess for interest in yourself."

Erebus smiled. "I can end your bafflement with that. Nyx and I are inseparable. Her interests are mine, just as mine are hers."

"Inseparable? Truly?" Kalona made a big show of searching around his brother. "Is the Goddess hiding in your sun ball? Oh, no. She wouldn't be. I seem to recall the Goddess prefers the cool, soft touch of moonlight to the vulgar light of the sun."

"Nyx sent me here!"

Kalona's smile was slow and satisfied. "Then I welcome you, brother, as the Goddess's errand boy."

Erebus unfurled his wings. They spread around him and shimmered like sunlight on gold bullion.

"I come not as a boy, but as an immortal, Consort to the Goddess of Night, and I come with her warning!"

"Impressive," Kalona said dryly. "But if you don't stop sparkling and shouting, your warning will be witnessed by all of midtown Tulsa."

Erebus's wings folded along his back. His voice lost its Otherworldly volume, but his expression lost none of its immortal self-importance.

"Have you captured Neferet yet?"

"Surely you watch me enough to already know the answer to that question."

"So, you have ignored Nyx's edict."

"I have not ignored anything. I've been busy fulfilling my oath bound duties to this House of Night's High Priestess," Kalona said.

"You're out of practice if executing three children can distract you so much that you ignore Nyx's command *and* fail to notice that Old Magick is manifesting in the modern world."

Kalona refused to rise to Erebus's bait. He didn't address his remark about Nyx, and only said blandly, "Sgiach has been wielding Old Magick for centuries."

"Yes, Kalona, but Sgiach is an ancient queen who has been wielding Old Magick for all those centuries on the Isle of Skye, a place that has long been devoted to preserving Old Magick. Tulsa, Oklahoma, is *not* the Isle of Skye, and there is no ancient vampyre queen here experienced in the use of Old Magick." Erebus spoke in a patronizing tone as if he lectured the empty-headed village idiot.

"I know exactly where I am and who is with me. My facts are correct, unlike yours. I beheaded a *vampyre* who had been condemned for attempted murder by my High Priestess. She did not wield Old Magick. She simply invoked ancient law. And the vampyre I executed was not a child," Kalona added, as usual not appreciating his brother's tone.

"The boy was barely eighteen."

"If you wish to take issue with the execution of a confessed murderer, then take issue with Thanatos, the school's Council, two Prophetesses of Nyx, *and* Zoey Redbird."

"Yet none of them lifted the sword that severed the vampyre's head, just as none of them left two fledglings to certain death," Erebus said.

"I am sworn Warrior to Thanatos. If she commands something of me I am bound to obey."

"It is sad, for you, that you did not show Nyx that type of blind loyalty while you were *her* sworn Warrior," Erebus said.

Kalona met his brother's amber gaze steadily. "I have learned from the mistakes in my past. Have you?"

Erebus looked away.

"Pass along the warning you were sent here to deliver and be-gone. You bore me," Kalona said.

"Very well, you are warned that by invoking ancient laws Old Magick has been awakened. Nyx cautions that you are playing with forces you may not be able to control."

"Shouldn't Nyx be telling this to Thanatos? It is her High Priestess who has begun trafficking with those forces."

"And yet it is you who can tip the scales in a battle between Light and Darkness. The Goddess has seen it happen before near you. Raven Mockers were fashioned from Old Magick."

Kalona felt a terrible stab of guilt, but still he said, "My sons were fashioned from rape and rage."

Erebus nodded solemnly. "Yes. Old Magick."

"Nyx wields Old Magick!" Kalona said.

"Have you become so delusional, so arrogant, that you believe you can wield the same power as the Goddess?"

"I harbor no delusions! My mind has not been so clear since I Fell." Kalona advanced on Erebus. "And my arrogance is nothing compared to yours, little brother. Without me to provide balance, it is *you* who believes he is as mighty as Nyx."

"Balance is exactly my point, brother. The bulls are Old Magick, and should be eternally locked in combat," Erebus said.

"I have naught to do with the white and black bulls."

"Do you truly believe that? You were by her side long enough to know that Old Magick is as tricky as it is powerful. Be wise! Be thoughtful! Have a care for the powers you are awakening before it is too late. That is the Goddess's warning!"

Kalona squinted and looked away as the ball of sunlight engulfed Erebus and then disappeared, leaving annoying gold glitter that the immortal had to brush from his own wings.

"Nyx!" Kalona spoke to the sky. "He calls me arrogant, and yet he disappears in a sunburst of golden glitter. I do not understand how you continue to bear his foppish presence!"

Familiar laughter that had always reminded the immortal of a full harvest moon echoed around Kalona. He closed his eyes against the pain of her absence, even as hope increased his heartbeat.

"You watch me. I know you do," Kalona whispered.

The laughter faded. Kalona opened his eyes. Feeling as if he carried a great weight, he started walking. He needed to get back to watch over the fledglings. That one thing he could do, and do well.

"No other fledgling will be allowed to do anything stupid enough to be condemned for—not as long as I watch over them," he spoke his thoughts aloud. What Kalona didn't say, didn't even like to admit silently to himself, was how he could not get the two fledglings' cries for mercy from his mind. Beheading the vampyre hadn't been difficult. Dallas had attempted to murder a vampyre and had been justly condemned. It was the two fledglings who haunted him. *They had been boys who had simply chosen unwisely and followed the wrong leader,* he thought.

"*Compassion.*"

The whispered word halted Kalona's. "Nyx?"

"Compassion."

The word was repeated. It was spoken too softly for Kalona to be certain, but the warmth, the infinite love in it, had to be Nyx. And then Kalona realized where he had stopped. He was standing before the wooden door to Nyx's Temple.

The door that turned from wood to stone under his touch as his Goddess denied him entrance.

Slowly, as if moving up through the centuries of longing for her, Kalona lifted his hand. He pressed his palm against the door and waited for it to turn to unyielding stone.

It remained wood.

Kalona's hand trembled when it touched the door handle. He turned it and pushed, and with the sound of a woman's sigh, the wooden door opened.

Kalona stepped into the foyer of Nyx's Temple. He heard running water, though he hardly glanced at the glistening amethyst fountain that was recessed into the niche in the thick stone wall. He passed beneath an arched doorway and entered the heart of the Goddess's temple.

Vanilla and lavender scented candles filled the room with sweet, heady fragrance. They were suspended from the ceiling in iron chandeliers. Freestanding tree-shaped chandeliers along the wall held more scented candles. Sconces shaped like a woman's graceful hand were lit in the corners of the room. An open flame burned from a recess in the stone floor. Kalona barely noticed any of that. His sole focus was on the ancient wooden table in the center of the temple. It held an exquisite marble statue of Nyx. Kalona stumbled forward and knelt before the statue. He stared up at her. She seemed to glisten, and Kalona realized his eyes had filled with tears.

In a voice choked with those tears, he spoke to her. "Thank you. I know I do not deserve to kneel at your feet yet. I may never deserve it. Not after what I have done to us both. But thank you for allowing me entrance to your temple." Then Kalona bowed his head and, for a very long time, knelt before his Goddess and wept.

Neferet

Neferet curled in upon herself, hugging the threads of Darkness that still covered her, and she relived the end of her journey.

Cascia Hall was what the humans had called the preparatory school that had been built in the heart of midtown Tulsa on the land that so called to Neferet. All male, of course, the human school had been newly founded by an Augustinian branch of the People of Faith. In the year 1927 it was not for sale. That fact had not troubled Neferet. The High Council was not ready to purchase another school in America—at least not in the Tulsa, Oklahoma, that existed in 1927.

Neferet had known that time was in her favor. In the seventy-five years it took for her to manipulate, intimidate, guide, and bribe the High Council into making the Augustine monks an offer they could not refuse, *and* appointing her High Priestess of the newly acquired House of Night in Tulsa, Oklahoma, Neferet discovered her true nature.

She was Tsi Sgili. No, she was more than a simple Native American ghost story. She was a powerful High Priestess whose gifts were so much more than they had seemed. Neferet was Queen Tsi Sgili.

Little wonder she had been so drawn to Oklahoma. It was through the Cherokee people who had settled there that Neferet discovered a hidden aspect of her intuitive gift. Not only could she read people's minds—she could also absorb their energy. But only at the moment of their deaths.

The old woman had taught her that. Neferet had done more than steal her thoughts as she'd died. She had absorbed the old woman's power.

Death became a drug, and Neferet had not been able to get enough of it.

She'd followed the echoes in the crone's mind and begun to ask questions about the Tsi Sgili.

What Neferet learned was her own story. A Tsi Sgili lived apart from her tribe. They were powerful and delighted in death. They fed on death. They could kill with their minds. That was the *ane li sgi* the old woman had thought of just before her death—death caused by the mind of a powerful being.

The old woman's Cherokee husband had inadvertently taught Neferet how to use her gift more fully. He had been less brave than his wife. Thinking to save himself he had opened himself to Neferet. Through the memories he willingly shared with her, Neferet learned much more about the Tsi Sgili. She fed from the tribal stories he had in his memory and discovered it was possible to slide into a mind and stop the beating of a heart while she fed on her victim's thoughts, energy, power until he was drained dry. Draining the body of energy was so much more satisfying than simply draining it of blood. And so much more effective.

As Neferet had grown in power, so too had her dreams of the winged immortal, Kalona. He made love to her as she slept. Not as her inadequate human or vampyre lovers had attempted. Kalona had taken possession of her body and used pain for pleasure, and pleasure for pain.

All the while his whispers painted pictures of a future where they ruled as gods on earth and ushered in a new age of vampyre enlightenment. Where she was his Goddess and he her adoring, powerful, seductive Consort.

"But first you must free me," he had said as his cold fire had deliciously scorched her body. *"Follow the song to Tulsa, and there you will complete the prophecy and find the means to free me!"*

Neferet had listened to him. Oh, but she had found so much more than the means to free him. She had discovered the means to free herself!

She did not fully understand until she had taken possession of her own House of Night in Tulsa. There was power in that land that had resonated within her. It was there in 1927, and it had remained there after the turn of the twenty-first century.

The red earth had drawn her with its ancient power, but it was the death of her first fledgling that had truly set her fate.

Neferet had, of course, witnessed the death of many fledglings before she became High Priestess of Tulsa's House of Night. She had often been summoned to soothe a dying fledgling's passage with the gift of her touch. Neferet was revered for her ability to calm a fledgling who was rejecting the Change. Not one vampyre ever guessed that she took as much as she gave. The fledglings knew it, though. In their last moments, as Neferet held them in her arms, they knew she fed from their energy. Of course by that time they were beyond the ability to share that knowledge with anyone else.

So when the young fourth former who had named herself Crystal began to cough out her life's blood in the middle of Lenobia's first equestrian class at the new Tulsa House of Night, Neferet was immediately called for—not just because she was their High Priestess, but because she had been known far and wide to be able to soothe the pain of the dying.

"Move aside! Make room! Lenobia, take the fledglings to the

field house and have Dragon Lankford bring Warriors and a gurney for the child," Neferet had commanded as she'd rushed into the stables. Then she had turned her attention to Crystal. The fledgling had crumpled to the sand and dirt floor of the arena, convulsing and bleeding from her eyes, nose, mouth, and ears.

Neferet paid no heed to the blood and mud. She'd pulled the fledgling into her arms, soothing with her magickal touch as she began to slide into Crystal's mind and to absorb her waning life energy. Neferet had been prepared for the surge of power that came with the absorption of life force. She had not been prepared for the pure and delightful gift that came with the death of *her* first fledgling.

In her den Neferet's body trembled in the pleasure of reliving that powerful moment.

Crystal had stared up at her through blood-soaked eyes. "No!" she'd coughed and gasped and managed to cry, "I'm not ready to die!"

"Of course you are, my dear. It is time. I am here."

"Won't leave me?" the child had sobbed.

"*You* won't leave *me*," Neferet had whispered as she took Crystal's mind.

The fledgling's life force cascaded into Neferet. So pure, so strong, so sweet, that it was as if the fledgling hadn't been dying at all, but had instead been transformed into a being of light and power that would now live within Neferet.

Neferet had bowed over the dying girl's body reverently, accepting this new gift that came to her with the Tulsa House of Night.

The Warriors had believed that Neferet had been overcome by emotion at the death of the first fledgling at her own House of Night, and that is why she had been found bowing over Crystal's body, sobbing hysterically.

They hadn't understood Neferet's tears had been of joy—that her sobs were because she'd finally recognized her destiny. Queen Tsi Sgili was a modest title. She should truly be called *Goddess* Tsi Sgili, for she had become immortal and would one day take her place among the gods and be worshipped as such!

Her gift had not been finished there, though. Even before Neferet had fulfilled the Cherokee prophecy and freed Kalona, the fledglings in her House of Night had begun a metamorphosis along with her.

Neferet's body twitched. Her breathing quickened as she moved up through the layers of unconsciousness and the realms of time.

Fledglings who died at her House of Night were reborn anew, bound to her through Darkness and blood. Neferet believed she had birthed a new kind of army, along with a new breed of vampyre. These new creatures would protect and serve her when she and her Consort ruled the new age of vampyres.

Then Zoey Redbird had been Marked, and what followed was one misstep after another—one irritation atop another—one defeat after another. Neferet hated that fledgling and her mutinous friends with a passion that overshadowed all of her other passions.

Zoey Redbird was the reason Neferet hid in a den, clothed only in Darkness and blood.

A goddess should not be plagued with such an annoyance! A goddess should not be hindered in her divine destiny!

As if in response to her tumultuous emotions, the sky outside her den growled with thunder and lightning struck, cracking the earth with a force that rippled through Neferet's skin.

Neferet, Queen Tsi Sgili, opened her eyes.

"I have been such a fool! I am an immortal. No one can dim

my majesty unless I allow it. I shall no longer allow it! World, prepare to worship me!"

Thunder and lightning applauded Neferet and rain caressed her as she prepared to step from her den of hiding out into a future, newborn, ready to embrace her destiny.

CHAPTER TWENTY-ONE

Zoey

At first I didn't know where I was going. I just needed to get the hell out. I slipped through the hidden door in the wall and cut around the south side of the school until I ran into Utica Street. I glanced to my right, considering. Utica Square was just down the street. It was Sunday morning, but Starbucks would probably be open. I could get one of those fudge cappa-frappa-whatevers that had a bazillion calories in it and sit outside and try to figure out what had happened to my life.

No. I didn't want to see people. I didn't want to talk to people. I didn't want to have to deal with the *looks* my tattoos would get from people.

I didn't want to deal with *anything or anyone.*

Thunder rumbled in the distance and I glanced up at the darkening sky.

"Go ahead. Rain on me. I don't care. My day can't get much crappier." I was talking to myself as I crossed the street.

Yeah, I was pissed.

I could not believe what Aphrodite and Shaylin had pulled. They were supposed to be my friends! Well, at least Aphrodite was supposed to be my friend. I'd thought Shaylin and I were becoming friends. I mean, we'd had that talk in the kitchen at the tunnels. She'd opened up to me about using her True Sight. We'd even talked about how invasive her gift could be. We'd had a plan, for god's sake! And no part of that plan involved her spying on me and tattling to Aphrodite like a damn middle schooler.

My face felt hot just thinking about her watching Aurox and me in the cafeteria. Hell, my whole body felt hot! No wonder I knocked her on her butt. Aphrodite had been so shocked by what I'd done, but Aphrodite had also been the one who'd set up the whole spying thing.

Was Aphrodite really my friend? She'd definitely been a hag from hell when I'd met her. Had she changed, or had I just made myself forget who she really was and become blind, not seeing what I didn't want to see? Had I just been believing what I wanted to believe about her?

Hell! Was Aphrodite still all about power and popularity? Was spying on me just part of her plan to undermine me and take my place?

The sky rumbled, seeming to echo my emotions.

My chest burned as I crossed another street and paused, noticing I'd come to the edge of the neatly maintained houses. Holy crap, I'd walked all the way to Woodward Park. I almost turned away. It was Sunday, which was when people would usually be flocking there to take pictures with the flowers and trees and such, but as I looked around the park it seemed empty. Obviously the thunderstorm that was coming had canceled the picture takers. I noticed the daffodils had started to bloom. I'd always loved it when the daffodils pushed up through the grass and lifted their yellow heads. Grandma and I used to talk about how magickal it felt when the spring bulbs appeared so quickly and unexpectedly.

I definitely needed a little spring magick today. Woodward Park it would be!

Feeling relieved at finding a destination, I headed into the park, making my way through the tufts of daffodils and meandering toward the area that was bordered by Twenty-first Street. On top of that ridge was where the azaleas were thickest. I liked the craggy, ridge-like area with stone paths winding between the bushes. I could find a bench tucked beneath the azaleas at the bottom of the ridge, and try to wrap my head around my problems. If it rained on me, so what? At least it would keep the gawkers away.

I walked the flagstone path, curving through azalea bushes as tall as me. I could see that their buds had started to form, but I couldn't tell what color they'd be yet.

The stupid thunderstorm would probably beat them to death and they'd never bloom anyway.

I kicked at a rock.

Aphrodite had had me spied on! I just couldn't let that betrayal go. I wondered what Stevie Rae would say when I told her. Then I realized if I told her I'd also have to tell her about Aurox and me in the cafeteria and I sure as hell didn't want to tell Stevie Rae or anybody about that—

I stopped. "Ah, hell! I'm not going to have a choice about telling people. No way are Shaylin *and* Aphrodite going to keep their mouths shut." I'd come to the stone stairs that led from the top part of the park down to the rocky, grotto-like areas and the shallow pool that wrapped around the western part of the park.

I considered hurling myself off the side of the ridge, but decided it wasn't high enough so it probably wouldn't kill me. And I really didn't want to kill myself. Now, had Aphrodite been there, I might have considered shoving her off the ridge!

The thought was disturbingly satisfying.

I took the stairs down to street level. There was a stone bench not far from where the steps opened to the grass. Thunder sounded again. I sat and frowned at the sky. Yeah, it was definitely going to rain on me. Soon. I sighed and looked around. Maybe it was the impending rain, but this little section of Woodward Park suddenly reminded me of the Isle of Skye. An unexpected feeling of homesickness washed over me. *I should go back there. I was happy there. No one spied on me. No one tried to kill me. And I could ask Sgiach what the hell was up with my stupid Seer Stone. Stark would go with me. I wouldn't have to see Aurox every day and wish . . .*

No! I derailed that train of thought. I didn't wish anything. I'd made my decision. It was just this crap with Aphrodite and Shaylin that was messing with my head—messing with my heart.

And I couldn't run away to Scotland. Or at least not right now I couldn't. I had to stay here and face my friends—and ex-friends—and clean up the mess that the House of Night had turned into.

God, it was depressing. And annoying. And exhausting.

Thunder rumbled, this time closer. It wasn't fixing anything to run away or to hide. I should go back to school. Maybe I'd get lucky and Stark had actually slept through my emotional explosion and I could crawl into bed and still get some sleep before I had to face the poo storm that would be waiting for me when the sun set.

I'd stood and turned to climb back up the stone stairs when I saw the two men. They'd just stepped out of the azalea bushes and were pausing at the top of the stairs. They were scruffy looking, dirty even. Their clothes didn't fit right. One of them carried a plastic garbage bag slung over his shoulder, making him look like an anorexic Santa. That one saw me first. He nudged his friend with his elbow and jerked his chin in my direction, grinning with a rot-toothed smile. His friend nodded and they started down the stairs.

Ah, hell.

I should have hurried toward Twenty-first Street. That was the smart thing to do—the safe thing to do. I almost did, but then I remembered who I was and I got pissed. I wasn't some weak little kid who people could scare and push around. I had an affinity for all five elements. I was a High Priestess in training. Hell, I was almost a vampyre! Why shouldn't I be able to be in the park on a Sunday morning and *not* be hassled by anyone?

Instead of running away I sat back down on the bench. Maybe they'd just walk past, say "morning," and that would be that. Maybe.

"Hey, girl, you, uh, got any extra money?" the first guy said as they got to the bottom of the stairs.

"Yeah, we could use some cash for food," said the second guy.

I'd had my face turned away, hoping that they'd walk on by. Now I lifted my chin and looked straight at them. Their eyes widened as they saw my tattoos.

"Really? In what universe do you think it's okay for two men to ask a girl, who's all by herself in a deserted park, for money?" As I spoke I felt my anger heat up again.

"Hey, what's it to you?" the guy with the garbage bag said. "You're a vampyre. It's not like *we* scare *you.*"

I knew they thought I was a full vampyre. I knew that made them afraid of me.

I was glad.

"So, you're used to scaring human girls into giving you some cash?" What total jerks!

The second guy shrugged. "If a girl don't want to be scared, she shouldn't be out here alone."

"Oh, it's the *girl's* fault?" I'd meant the question hypothetically, but the garbage bag guy didn't get that.

"Yeah, it's the girl's fault!"

"But we won't scare nobody if they just give us some cash."

"We don't take no credit cards, though." Garbage bag guy laughed and smacked his friend on the arm.

"You're jerks. You're both jerks. How about you get jobs instead of messing with little girls?"

"Messing with little girls pays better," said the garbage bag guy.

"I was sitting here, minding my own business. You two need to remember that. You brought this on yourselves." I stood. My whole body felt hot. I was really pissed. "Guess what? You should've picked another little girl to mess with today."

"Hey, we wasn't messing with you. We was just passin' by," said the second guy. He grabbed his friend's arm and started pulling him away.

"Relax, girlie. No harm, no foul," said the garbage bag guy, sending me a sarcastic grin and flashing his black, broken teeth.

So they thought they were going to slither off and find a real girl, a normal girl, to scare?

I felt like my heart was going to blaze out of my chest.

"No! Not today you're not!" I threw my anger at them. It was a glowing blue ball of light. It slammed into the two guys, lifting them off their feet and hurling them against the stone wall of the ridge.

I was breathing hard and feeling good about what I'd done. They'd think twice before they messed with any other girl! Assholes!

Thunder cracked above me and a fork of lightning stabbed into the center of the park, making the hair on my forearms lift. It was then I realized I had my fist wrapped around the Seer Stone.

I blinked and shook my head. Wait, what had just happened?

I stared at the men. They were still there, lying in the shadow of the stony ridge. They weren't yelling back at me or brushing themselves off and getting up, or even taking off because I'd scared the crap out of them.

I couldn't see that they were moving at all.

Holy crap! I'd used Old Magick to attack the two men. It had been just like when I'd knocked Shaylin off her feet. I'd done it automatically after the burn of my anger had become unbearable. But the burn hadn't been *my* anger, it had been the Seer Stone heating up, penetrating my body, feeding from my emotions and then striking out.

I let loose the stone and looked at my palm. A perfect circle had been burned into it.

Dazed, I looked up, seeing smoke coming from the heart of the park above me. The air smelled of electricity and fire and I realized lightning must have struck a tree, or maybe even one of the park buildings. Woodward Park was on fire.

Firemen would be coming soon. So would the police.

My knees were wobbly and my head hurt as I stumbled forward, getting closer to the men, staring at the two shapes that were crumpled at the base of the ridge. One of them moaned. The other's arm twitched.

The sky opened and ropes of rain began falling, so that I couldn't tell if the wetness was water or blood or my tears.

I didn't think. I just ran.

I didn't need to call mist and shadow to me. The thunderstorm cloaked me. No one noticed a lone girl, running through the rain, away from the burning park, especially since emergency vehicles and the police were swarming in the opposite direction.

I ran around the school wall, entering back through the hidden door. And I kept running until I was inside the stables, gasping and shivering. I went to the tack room and got a clean towel. Wrapping it around myself, I walked down the long line of stalls until I found Persephone. I slid the door open and entered the warm, dark stall. Persephone was sleeping the way horses do, standing with one leg cocked and her head low, eyes half-lidded. She barely moved when I went to her and wrapped my arms around her neck and sobbed into her thick, soft mane.

What was happening to me?

The guys in the park had been jerks, but they couldn't have hurt me. Sure, they preyed on girls, scaring them into throwing cash their way, but they couldn't have hurt me. I could've walked away and made an anonymous call to the police, given a description of them, and told the cops that they were loitering in the park, threatening girls. The cops would've run them off.

Instead I exploded on them.

I hadn't even thought it through. I hadn't done it on purpose. It had just happened. My anger had literally exploded through the Seer Stone at them.

What was it Aphrodite had been trying to tell me? Something about her vision and Old Magick and me losing control of my anger. I hadn't listened to her. I'd cut her off and believed she'd betrayed me. I'd let anger control me.

"Oh, Goddess, that was wrong—so wrong of me," I cried.

Then, through my sobs and the thunderstorm that roiled in the sky, I heard a siren. It wasn't a fire truck. It wasn't an ambulance. It was a police car. And it wasn't speeding past the school toward Woodward Park. Its siren was getting closer and closer. It had to have entered our gate and pulled up to the school.

As if I were walking through a dream, I unwrapped myself from Persephone's consoling neck. I dropped the towel. I left the stable and made my way outside to the sidewalk that led to the entrance foyer of the school.

Rain pelted me, but I didn't pay any attention to it.

"Z! There you are! Shit, you're soaking wet." Stark ran up behind me, holding a big coat over himself.

"You shouldn't be out here," I told him woodenly. "The sun's up. You'll burn."

He gave me a weird look. "I'm tired and it's not real comfortable, but the clouds are covering enough of the sun that I can be out here. Well, at least for a little while. Z, get under my coat with me and let's go back to our room. I know something's wrong with you, but I don't know what it is."

I shook my head. "No. I have to go to them." I kept walking toward the front of the school. There were two police cars, lights still on, parked there.

"Them who?" Stark asked, trying to hold his coat over my head and his.

"Stark, go back to bed. You can't help me out of this."

"Zoey, what are you talking about? What's going on?"

I put my hand on the front door. "Go back," I repeated. "You can't save me anymore."

He looked scared. Really scared.

I didn't let myself feel anything. I turned my back on him and opened the door.

Thanatos was there. Darius was, too. As well as Aphrodite. For an instant I was surprised to see them, then I realized that Aphrodite must have gone to Thanatos after I'd taken off. It was the right thing for her to do. I would have done it if I'd been in her place. If I'd been thinking like myself, like Normal Zoey.

Detective Marx was there with two officers in uniforms.

"Z, did you get done walking the perimeter with Aurox?" Aphrodite spoke quickly, walking up to me. "I was telling Thanatos that I was worried about you out there in the thunderstorm. There're even tornado warnings for Tulsa County."

"Don't," I told her. "I don't ever want you to lie for me." I looked from her to Darius. "I don't ever want any of you to lie for me." Then I met Detective Marx's gaze. "Why are you here?"

"Two men were just murdered in Woodward Park. Someone with supernatural power killed them—power no human has. That's why the officers and I came directly here." His face was grim. His voice lacked any emotion.

"And I was reminding the detective that our school is under lockdown. No fledgling or vampyre has left the campus since the night the mayor was killed," Thanatos said.

"I left campus. I went to Woodward Park. I slammed those two guys against the stone wall at the bottom of the ridge. I killed them." My voice sounded as dead as the men, as dead as I felt.

"Zoey! Why the hell would you say something like that?" Stark grabbed me and gave my shoulders a shake. "Snap out of it!"

I stared at him, hardening my heart, freezing my feelings. "You need to stay here. I don't want to see you again. I don't want to see anyone. I did this. I deserve this." I moved out of his grasp. As I walked toward Detective Marx I reached up, grasped the Seer Stone, and pulled, breaking the silver chain that held it. I handed it to Aphrodite. "Don't let anyone except you or Sgiach touch this thing. You were right. It's awake, and it's bad."

Then I faced Detective Marx. "I'm ready to go with you."

He glanced from me to Thanatos. "I'll wait for you to contact the High Council and abrogate their legal claim to responsibility for this fledgling so that I can take her into custody."

"No," I said. "Before this happened I had broken from the High Council. I don't recognize their jurisdiction over me. I don't recognize Thanatos's jurisdiction over me. Treat me the same way you would anyone else who has confessed to being a murderer."

He sighed deeply and then pulled the handcuffs from his

back pocket. "Zoey Redbird, you are under arrest for the murders of Richard Williams and David Brown." He closed the cold cuffs around my wrists. "You have the right to remain silent. Should you give up that right, anything you say can and will be used against you. You have the right to have an attorney present at your questioning. Should you not be able to afford one, an attorney will be appointed for you. Do you understand your rights?"

"Yes. I don't need an attorney. I confess that I killed those two men. I deserve to go to jail," I said as *I deserve this . . . I deserve this . . .* echoed through my mind.

CHAPTER TWENTY-TWO

Neferet

When she was finally ready to emerge from the den, rain bathed Neferet, cleansing her of the blood and dirt in which she had been clothed. The area was in utter chaos. Despite the rain, a fire raged in the park above her.

Neferet thought it was a delightful greeting.

She fed off the death and destruction around her, and used the energy she gleaned to conceal herself.

Her auburn hair was slick against her body, like a living cloak. Neferet's faithful threads, sated and pulsing with power, lifted her. As if she had commanded a thundercloud to do her bidding, Neferet floated from the park within a veil of thunder and lightning, mist and madness.

She threw her head back, loving the caress of the rain as it slid down her bare skin, cleansing her. Her arms lifted, and tendrils of Darkness wrapped around them. She laughed at their cold, wicked touch.

"Let us go home. We have so very much to do!" Moving through Midtown, the storm that was Neferet drifted toward downtown Tulsa and the penthouse she had made her own at the Mayo.

"Ah, but not so quickly," she purred to the Darkness that cradled her. "Shall we not go to dinner? I find that I am simply starving!"

The threads of Darkness quivered with excitement, impatiently awaiting her command.

Neferet reached out with her mind. Seeking . . . seeking . . . perverting the gift she had been given so many decades ago.

She followed Fifteenth Street to the west, still seeking. It was at Boston Avenue that she felt the pull to the north.

"True north! And all of those delicious souls pretending to be so very, very good!" Neferet shivered in pleasure. "All gathered together so very, very conveniently for me. It is as if they already knew to worship me." She made a sweeping gesture to her right. "Take me there!"

When she reached the cathedral Neferet commanded the threads to pause—to allow her to take in the perfection of her choice. The building was truly magnificent. It glistened in the rain. The upward spires of the main tower looked like teeth. The smaller spires appeared to be upraised hands, sharp with talons, their metal surface slick and wet and ready for her to ravage.

"Release me! Allow me to be seen!"

The cloud of magick dissipated. Neferet settled silently to the pavement. "Come with me, my darlings," she told her threads. "Our fast is over. Let us gorge ourselves as I deserve!"

Neferet climbed the many limestone stairs as Darkness, like the train of a queen's coronation mantle, flowed behind her. She glanced up. Statues jutting from the outer wall were golden gods astride rain-washed chargers. They seemed to bid her welcome.

Below them, carved over the three-peaked doorways, were men bowing.

"To me." She spoke to the silent statues. "You bow to me." Staring up, Neferet read the words written beneath each of the three groups of worshipping statues: THE FRUIT OF THE SPIRIT IS LOVE,

JOY; PEACE, LONG-SUFFERING, KINDNESS, GOODNESS; FAITHFUL-
NESS, MEEKNESS, SELF-CONTROL.

Neferet laughed. "This is going to be easier than I imagined."

Naked, Neferet entered the church, choosing the door that held the word LONG-SUFFERING. Within, the walls were painted a muted pink that reminded her of blood diluted by a wash of tears. She thought it a perfect color. Turning to her left, she followed a curving hall until she came to the main entrance of the sanctuary. The doors were closed. Neferet smiled fondly at her threads of Darkness. "Yes, do please open them."

The threads obeyed her.

Neferet stepped within the large, oval room. A hymn was just in its last few notes, and as they drew out the *aaaamen,* Neferet took the opportunity to appreciate the setting before she was noticed. It really was a lovely sanctuary. Though with the pale violet velvet cushioned seats and the art deco stylized stained glass windows decorated in colors of blush and lilac, she thought that it looked more like one of the ornate theaters that so proliferated in America at the turn of the last century than a church. Its round, tiered seating tapering down to a central stage was obviously created more for drama than worship.

Neferet smiled, enjoying the irony.

"Psst!" A whisper came from the shadows at the back of the room as the pastor began to lead the congregation in a tediously repetitive prayer. "Excuse me. Do you need help?" A thick, middle-aged woman approached Neferet. She was so entranced by Neferet's naked body, that she hadn't even glanced at her tattoos.

Neferet turned to her. "Yes, I do." Neferet held open her arms, as if she wanted the woman to embrace her. Blinking in confusion, the woman stepped closer to her. Neferet struck with blinding speed, ripping her talon-like fingernails across her throat, and catching the woman as she collapsed forward. Neferet did embrace her then, but the kiss she shared with the woman was pressed to the bleeding gash of her throat. Neferet drained her body as she fed from her energy.

Someone in the rear of the congregation screamed.

Neferet looked up as the people turned to her. She released the woman. Her body fell to the floor with a satisfyingly final thud.

Lifting her chin, Neferet swept her hair back and strode forward to stand within the sanctuary.

"Oh my god! It's a vampyre!"

"She's naked!"

"She just killed Mrs. Peterson!"

People began screaming. Some even started to flee their pews.

Neferet lifted her arms. "Seal the doors! And reveal yourselves to them!"

The shadows around Neferet rippled as the thick snake-like tendrils took a form humans could see. The congregation paused, staring in horror, as they slithered to each of the doors and, web-like, sealed them from within.

"What is it you want?" A white haired man wearing a black robe trimmed in scarlet velvet strode from the pulpit toward her.

"I am Neferet," she said cordially. "And you are?"

"I am Dr. Andrew Mullins, pastor of Boston Avenue Church. What is the meaning of this violation?"

"Violation?" Neferet smiled. "Oh, I have barely begun violating. This"—she waved her blood-soaked fingers at the woman's body—"was not even an appropriate appetizer."

"With the power invested in me through our Lord and Savior, I demand you leave this holy place and harm no one else!"

"Pastor Mullins, even though I don't look it, I am quite a bit older than you, so let me share with you a little something I've learned over my many years: *real* power trumps *invested* power every time. So, I do believe I'll use my *real* power and choose not to leave."

"Very well. If you will not leave, then we shall!" the pastor said. As if he were gathering hens around him, the man gestured for the people to come to him while he backed down away from Neferet.

"I'm afraid I cannot allow you to leave. Any of you." Neferet pointed at the pastor. "Bring him to me!"

A thread, thick as a man's forearm, unwrapped from around Neferet's ankle and sped toward the pastor. When it reached him, the tendril whipped around his waist, slicing into him. Darkness dragged the screaming pastor toward Neferet.

"Oh, cease that ridiculous noise!" Neferet gestured, and a smaller tendril wrapped itself around the pastor's face, over his mouth, gagging him.

"That's better, isn't it?" She glared around her at the panicking congregation. "Unless you want me to gag you all, stop screaming!"

Except for muffled sobs, the people went silent.

Neferet approached the pastor. "I do like your robes. I especially appreciate the scarlet color. Take them off!"

With trembling hands the man complied, and dropped the robe at her feet.

Cocking her head, Neferet studied him. He was wearing a white dress shirt and slacks underneath. "You were so much grander in your robe. Now you remind me of a denuded mouse." Neferet slid into his mind. "Oooh, no wonder you're not staring at my body. Chastity is so tedious, isn't it? Here, allow me to put you out of your misery." She slashed his throat. His eyes bulged huge as she told the two threads, "Yes, you may have this one." Darkness pierced his mouth and his waist, drinking deeply from him as he convulsed in agony.

"Neferet! Why are you doing this?"

Neferet's attention turned from the dying pastor to a man standing toward the front of the sanctuary. Recognizing him, she smiled.

"Councilman Meyers! How lovely to see you," she said.

"H-hello, Neferet," he stuttered, grasping tightly to the hand of the well-dressed woman beside him. "I was there during your press conference. You—you said you were allied with humans and against violence."

"I lied." Her smile widened at his horrified expression. The woman beside him sobbed, her hand pressed against her mouth trying to staunch her cries. "Are you Mrs. Meyers?"

Trembling and crying, the woman nodded.

"How tastefully you are dressed. Do I recognize Armani?"

Again, the sobbing woman nodded.

"And you must be about a size six, correct?"

"Y-yes. Take my clothes! Just let us go, please," she pleaded.

"Ah, how nicely you asked! Take off your dress and bring it to me, and I shall consider your request."

"Neferet, please don't hurt—" her husband began.

Neferet slid into his mind and told his heart to stop beating. Councilman Meyers gasped, and slumped to the floor.

His wife screamed.

Neferet sighed. "Mrs. Meyers, I find it so disheartening how no one today seems to be able to follow simple commands. Don't you?"

"Do you intend to kill us all?"

Neferet's gaze went from the hysterical Mrs. Meyers to an attractive, middle-aged woman who had stepped into the aisle. She lifted her chin and faced Neferet, showing no outward sign of fear.

Neferet was intrigued. "And who are you?"

"Karen Keith, one of Tulsa's County Commissioners. I was also there the day you gave your press conference and pledged your allegiance to our city."

"Oooh, another politician. How delicious!"

"You didn't answer my question. Are you going to kill us all?"

"Forgive me, Karen. May I call you Karen?"

"I'd rather you didn't."

Neferet's brow raised in surprise. "You have a lovely energy about you, Ms. Keith. You will serve as my main course."

Tendrils of Darkness began to slither toward the Commissioner.

Karen Keith did not flinch as they wrapped around her. She met Neferet's gaze and said, "After this, everyone will know you for the monster you are."

"No, Ms. Keith, everyone will know me for the *goddess* I am."

The Commissioner did not scream as she died, but the people around her shrieked and began surging, in reckless panic, toward the sealed exits.

"Well, I suppose it is too much to expect dinner conversation," Neferet said. She lifted her arms. "Have care with the Armani dress, but kill them all!"

Neferet, and her servants of Darkness, descended upon the congregation. They fed and fed, gorging on blood and stolen energy, until the sanctuary was a graveyard.

Neferet bathed herself from the holy water basins, and used the pastor's scarlet trimmed robe to dry herself. Then, dressed in Armani and pulsing with glorious power, she left the Boston Avenue Church.

It had stopped raining. The sky was newly washed blue. The air smelled of springtime. Neferet wiped a last drop of blood from the corner of her full lips. Smiling, radiant, Neferet pointed toward the Mayo.

"Take me home. I have so missed my penthouse."

Throbbing and fully sated, her threads came to her, lifting her gently. Wrapped in Darkness Neferet drifted, invisible, through downtown Tulsa as *I deserve this ... I deserve this ...* echoed through her mind.

The center golden limestone statue above the entrance to the church quivered, shifted, and in a fetid burst of freezing air, the white bull materialized. As he emerged from the skin of the church, his hooves sparked, causing the ground to shake. He snorted, staring after where Neferet had disappeared.

"Now that, my heartless one, surprised me ..."

THE END
For now ...